Banished to Brighton

Banished to Brighton

RAKES ON THE RUN

SYDNEY JANE BAILY

cat whisker press
Massachusetts

Second Paperback Edition
ISBN 978-1-957421-30-8

Published by Cat Whisker Press

Cover: Victoria Cooper Art
Book Design: Cat Whisker Studio
Editor: Chloe Bearuski

DEDICATION

To Chef Jeff
For seamlessly joining our family
With your love and generosity

Keep on cooking!

ACKNOWLEDGMENTS

I'm so grateful to this book's beta readers for their help and suggestions: Philip Ré, Toni Young, Lana Birky, and Heather Brinkley. And, as always, thanks to my beloved mom, Beryl Baily, for all her love and support.

PROLOGUE

1815, London

"Despite the edge of the divan digging into her back, Glynnis Talbot clasped her hands behind Lord Hargrove's neck where his brown hair rested on his collar, and she ardently returned his kiss. Finally, something was going in her favor. Thrice earlier in the Season, she'd attempted the very same plan—being compromised by a nobleman in a passionate embrace. Each time, something had gone amiss, but still, she could think of no other way to quickly secure a wealthy husband.

Of all the men she'd kissed, she hoped this one would be forced to offer her his name. Hargrove made her skin prickle and her heart skip a beat whenever she saw him. And his first kiss, mere hours after they'd met at Wellington's Apsley House two days earlier, had nearly dropped her to her wobbly knees.

Tonight, her body liquified once again at the touch of his firm lips against her mouth.

"Show me the library," she had whispered a few minutes earlier in the deserted hallway. By unspoken mutual agreement—with a raised eyebrow on his part and a nod of the head on hers—they'd exited the ballroom about half a

1

minute apart. At her suggestion, his deep blue eyes glittered and darkened with desire and a grin spread over his handsome face. She let him take her gloved hand, knowing a group of women were heading to the same room momentarily.

And in two shakes of a maid's mop, she found herself pressed against a pink and silver tufted divan. His hands roamed her body, tracing the curves of her breasts, making her nipples pearl, before he tucked his palms under her rear end as he leaned over her.

Capturing her mouth, sucking on her lower lip, his breath was ragged and hers caught in her lungs while her core began to throb. Seeing as how she hoped to marry the man, she might let him compromise her farther than a mere kiss. Easily, her thoughts imagined him drawing up her sheer silk evening gown and petticoat, and stroking her where she was becoming desperate to be touched.

His tongue sought entrance to her mouth, and she parted her lips with a sigh of delight.

"Yes?" he asked on a husky note without halting the kiss.

"Yes," she answered, not knowing exactly the question but hopeful it meant he would continue his sensual ministrations.

She wanted so much more. As if he knew, he drew one hand out from under her and palmed her breast, his thumb caressing her nipple through the layers of fabric.

Heat pulsed low between her hips. *Dear God!*

Suddenly, he rose to crouch over her, one of his jacket buttons practically stabbing her in her eye. He wrapped his arms around her head to shield her while mucking up her coiffure.

Only then did she realize the library door had opened, and her plan was reaching fruition. Their evening's hostess must even then be standing in the doorway. However, Hargrove was hiding her from prying eyes and keeping her reputation safe.

The devil take him and his chivalry!

Before Glynnis could struggle out from under him and show her face, the footsteps receded and the door closed.

"I cannot breathe," she mumbled against his fine wool jacket, and Hargrove climbed off of her.

His visage displayed his fury. "How did you know they were coming in here?"

The question was, *how did he know she knew?*

She felt her cheeks warm causing his eyes to narrow, but she remained silent.

"I heard you'd played this game before, but I didn't believe it," he said. "Why would a pretty viscount's daughter need to trap a husband in such an underhanded way?"

Mortified, she denied everything, feeling a twinge of sadness because she really liked Hargrove, and her desire for him was entirely genuine.

Glynnis sighed at the collapse of her perfectly good plot for her own ruin and left the seething viscount alone in the library. He was not about to ask for her hand in marriage. Moreover, he wasn't even going to finish the delightful compromising of her person.

Dash it all!

CHAPTER ONE

Late July, 1815, Brighton

Brighton! thou loveliest neighbour of the wave,
Whose stately cliffs the rolling surges lave,
Where roseate health, amid the breezes play,
Whose gentle breathings cool the fervid ray
Of scorching summer.

– *Brighton. A Poem* by Mary Lloyd, 1809

With a sharp snap, Glynnis Talbot closed the book she'd borrowed from Miss Widgett's circulating library and set it upon the table before her. While the long poem about Brighton painted an accurate picture of what she'd seen so far, it didn't bring her any closer to her true aim, nor for that matter had the costly expense of coach fare and a sunny hotel room.

Glynnis was ready to tear her hair out, which would be a shame as she considered her dark and glossy locks to be one of her more stunning features. London had been a disaster when it came to snagging a husband, Bath had been woefully barren of eligible bachelors, and now Brighton was giving her a fit of the blue devils. Moreover, she was nearly out of blunt. To put it plainly, she was a hairsbreadth away from being entirely dished up, mucked out, and penniless.

A viscount's only daughter ought to have a generous allowance and a substantial dowry. She had neither. Unlike her ne'er-do-well brother, she hadn't gambled her money away, nor spent it on lady-birds and lightskirts. She had used every penny to keep their London home running as best she could. However, Rhys had the saving grace of a face that could charm the skirts off a woman while sharing her coin purse, too! He was considered by one and all as a bang-up dashing cove! Moreover, his impending title kept him a valuable commodity on the marriage market for those females wishing to one day become a viscountess.

Glynnis had the family good looks to be sure, sable-colored hair and even darker brown eyes. However, no title and no money made her less desirable than any number of marriageable young ladies who had one or both, even if they were dowdy or tart-tongued shrews.

During the past London Season, without a wealthy patron to sponsor her and with her parents remaining steadfastly in Wales, she'd been shoved aside like three-day old haddock instead of valued as a young lady with good humor and a tad more than a feather-brain.

Why, all she wanted was a halfway attractive buck— naturally plump in the pocket—someone with whom she could get leg-shackled. *Why was that so hard?*

After her brother spent a month's allowance from their parents by the end of a single week, Glynnis had given up trying to keep their London home and gone uninvited to Bath, hoping to find a single man who would appreciate a woman of sense and style. While residing with a spinster great aunt who enjoyed eating slip-slops for every meal, she'd discovered the resort to be populated by elderly couples and widows, mostly staying there for health reasons.

The foreshadowing of her own future—frighteningly embodied by her fussy, gray-haired Aunt Mimsella with too many cats roaming her small home—caused Glynnis to take flight after a week and a half. While her aunt believed she'd gone home to Llandeilo, just north of the Swansea Bay in Wales, Glynnis had decided to try the seaside town where the Prince Regent was known to bring an abundance of noblemen in August for his birthday. Thus, Brighton was her last hope to find a suitable mate before another year had passed.

Unable to come up with the rent for one of the nicer homes on the Marine Parade, or even the noisier but popular location of the Steyne, she had taken a room at the gracious Old Ship Hotel, sharing it with many of the London gentry. With most of its public rooms designed by that much admired Scottish architect Robert Adam, Glynnis was in the lap of luxury, which she could ill afford.

Everything was meticulous—the ornamentation was small and light, even whimsical, in a classical style that conjured up the ancients while feeling fresh and beautiful. Her third-floor room, although modest in size, was tastefully furnished, and the only disadvantage was its view of Ship Street instead of the sparkling ocean.

With merely a handful of the hotel's bedrooms facing the sea, and those being reserved by the wealthier guests, she hadn't the means to look out a window with eight pretty panes of glass directly to the sea. Yet even with an inferior view, the weekly rate of her lodging was draining her funds too quickly. By the time she got word to her parents in the south of Wales and hopefully was sent some small gingerbread in return, she would be begging for farthings on a street corner like Mad Tom!

Besides, her parents thought her still in London. If they knew she'd left the safety of her brother's so-called protection, they would be furious. For his part, Rhys thought her still in Bath. And thus, she'd firmly reprimanded herself over the past fortnight for not being patient and staying with Aunt Mimsella an extra two weeks. Instead, to avoid a dreadful fate of cats and watery porridge, she'd arrived too early for the nobs she sought.

In the past few days, however, traveling carriages had started filling the boulevards of Brighton, and she could see quite a cross-section of its population below her street-side window, including the newest arrivals from London. Moreover, the coach that stopped regularly at the Old Ship was depositing ever more guests, from dandy prats to purse-proud goldfinches.

Finally, she could concentrate upon her latest ambition—to meet and fall in love with one of the single nobs booked into an ocean-facing room or, although less likely, a member of the *bon ton* in one of the rentals along the wide Marine Parade that ran beside the sea, down to the Royal Crescent at its end.

At last, after nearly two weeks' wait, there would be someone at whom she could set her cap!

An hour earlier, she'd heard rather than seen the Prince Regent arrive. A large fuss was made and folks started to cheer along the Grand Parade a few streets away, leading to the prince's strangely exotic Pavilion. People all over Brighton had picked up the merriment and joined in with *huzzahs* and *hoorahs*.

Naturally, Prince George had come by way of the north road through Cuckfield, directly from London, with no need to travel along the waterfront. Thus, she had yet to see his royal carriage. But that very night, there would be a welcoming ball. And God-willing, a party, a dinner, or a ball every night after, as well as bathing parties on the beach, picnics, riding parties, horse-races, and whatnot. Glynnis was determined to attend every event, whether invited or not.

And from the very first night, she would do her best to secure a husband. One never knew how long the prince would grace his favorite seaside town with his corpulent presence. Sometimes for a month around his birthday.

Sometimes longer. All she knew was Brighton was suddenly exploding with wealthy Londoners, but when the Regent left, those either in power or seeking power would leave as well. She had scant time to act.

Hello! Glynnis leaned forward. From where she was seated in the bowed front window of the tea-room attached to the hotel, she watched a man, obviously a nobleman by the manner of his dress, amble along the pavement. To her delight, he entered the door to the Old Ship.

Touching her bright yellow hat to make sure it was still pinned straight, she gave each cheek a pinch and then looked expectantly at the doorway connecting the hotel's lobby to the quaint dining area. Every chance was an opportunity, or every opportunity was a chance. She couldn't recall quite how the saying went, but every rum neddy and well-breeched fellow was potential husband material.

Her *opportunity* strolled into the dining room, glanced around for an empty table, noticed her and grimaced.

Blast it all! It was that wretch of a man, Hargrove. He'd made London a nightmare, and now he was in Brighton.

Glynnis turned away, feeling defeated, not caring if her shoulders slumped as she went back to gazing at passers-by. She had hoped to marry for love when she was a foolish girl being presented to the queen at seventeen. At age twenty, after experiencing much disappointment, she'd met the quick-witted, handsome Lord Hargrove. He had sparked some warm feelings of tenderness she'd imagined might have turned into long-lasting love.

Unfortunately, he'd become skittish and said all sorts of nasty, accusatory things. At that moment, she could only hope to marry without hatred and resentment.

Thinking of which, the vicious viscount presented himself beside her table, looking down at her from his great height, past his perfect nose.

"Why are you here?" he asked without preamble.

Lord Hargrove was as handsome as ever, thick brown hair, a strong jaw, and those shoulders! Her insides did a familiar flip at seeing him. His kiss had been everything she'd ever wished for, giving her all sorts of pleasant, fluttery feelings.

She sighed. If only she had let nature take its natural course instead of pushing her advantage with him. All she'd done was push him away.

"Greetings to you, too. Why is everyone who is anyone here?" she countered, flashing him a smile because she'd become so used to doing so with every male of a certain age.

But Hargrove didn't melt. He wore an irritated expression.

"I have no doubt I am the only one in all of Brighton here for the particular reason of paying penance to the Regent," Hargrove said.

"I believe you *do* penance, not *pay* it."

"Believe me, Miss Talbot, I find my penance to be costly, indeed."

Suddenly, she didn't care about his previous harsh words of condemnation at a ball in Mayfair, nor his accusation of her as a lying jade setting her cap at anyone in velvet breeches. After all, it was true.

Right then, however, she was tired of being alone and desperate. At the least, he could provide a few minutes of companionable diversion.

"Won't you take tea or coffee with me?" she invited.

He hesitated, which made her sad. Before she'd tried to trick him into compromising her, they had been on a good footing. He was amusing and clever, not to mention extraordinarily easy on the eyes. And after some easy banter and light flirtation, he'd kissed her behind a potted plant at Apsley House. She'd never experienced anything like it— the rush of pure pleasure, how her heart had raced, and how her body had warmed from top to toe.

Then, she'd started plotting for their next encounter. It had gone very wrong.

He most certainly hadn't liked being manipulated.

"Come now," Glynnis urged, "don't tell me you're afraid to sit at the same table. It's not like I'll let you kiss me again, at least not here, in public." She teased him because she could. She had nothing to lose in this case. She'd already forfeited any chance with him by her actions at a ball in Grosvenor Square. If he walked away, so be it.

Instead, surprisingly he smiled, drew out the spare chair, and sat.

"True enough. Your claws are long and sharp, but I don't think you can sink them into me in a café. At least, I hope not."

Long and sharp! He thought her a real vixen. Nothing could be further from the truth. She only wanted a home of her own, a husband and some children, a nice house in London, the latest fashions of course, perhaps a trip to the Continent now that the war was over, a country estate that wasn't in Wales as her family's was, perhaps a dog and a cat, a traveling carriage, a . . .

"Miss Talbot," she heard him, realizing her mind had wandered. "Did I lose your attention so quickly?" he asked.

"I'm sorry, my lord. Something about Brighton causes me the most acute wool-gathering. It must be the sun and the heat."

She waited while he ordered coffee and, to her delight, a plate of assorted sandwiches. Glynnis hoped he would pay for her tea, too, and that she could snatch a few of the sandwiches when they came. She was starting to lose weight on her dwindling budget that included lessening her intake of food along with every other pleasure.

If her gowns started gaping and appeared ill-fitting, she would be in dire straits indeed. Eventually, thin and desperate, she would have to remain in her viewless room, eventually to slip the burden of this earth alone at the Old Ship. She exhaled with a despondent moan.

"Miss Talbot," he broke into her thoughts.

"Again, my apologies. Tell me about this penance to the Prince Regent. Mayhap I can help."

Naturally, he gave her a disbelieving look. Quite right, too. *What could she offer?* And yet, she rather preferred to be useful than not.

"Have you ever met His Royal Highness?" Lord Hargrove asked.

"As a matter of fact, yes. Once at a ball, not this Season but the last, he singled me out for a compliment on my gown. I was wearing Pomona green and white. It was a lovely evening." She remembered for a moment being the object of the other ladies' envy and gaining a little interest from some of the gentlemen when the prince seemed to favor her.

"Did you try to get Prinny to compromise you, too?" Hargrove had to go and ruin the memory. "It would have got you nowhere, you know, except the wrath of his mistress. One of them, at least."

Glynnis made a face, but then the sandwiches were placed in the center of the little table along with a plate for each of them. Being insulted, even ridiculed, was a small price to pay for a tasty morsel. She glanced at the food, then at him.

With graciousness, he gestured for her to help herself.

Using a silver spatula, she took two of the small triangles of thinly sliced bread, arranging them neatly on her plate. Then she picked one up and, as a ploughman at his noon meal, she dug in. She'd eaten the sliced beef and mustard sandwich and was starting on the second one of cold tongue and watercress when she realized the viscount was watching her. He'd taken only a single mouthful.

Swallowing, she cleared her throat, sipped her tea, and smiled weakly.

"I skipped a meal," she explained.

"It seems you skipped a few by your wolfish appetite."

How rude of him to remark upon it!

11

"And you have a piece of watercress stuck between your teeth," he added.

She gasped. *Even ruder, although she appreciated his warning.* If she happened to encounter the perfect gentleman after the nuncheon, she would hate to do so with a bit of greenery in her ivories.

Raising her napkin to her lips, she used the tip of her fingernail as discreetly and daintily as she could to remove the offending vegetable. Or tried to.

After a few seconds, she lowered the napkin, abandoned all sense of decency and decorum and asked, "Is it gone?"

Then she bared her teeth.

"Mostly," he said before looking away. "Try sipping the tea and swilling it about in your mouth. That should dislodge the last of it."

Instead of utter mortification, it struck her as humorous. While she did as Hargrove directed, swishing the milky brown brew in her cheeks, she nearly giggled which would have sprayed the white tablecloth. It might have been worth it to see his expression.

Eventually she swallowed, ran her tongue over her teeth and turned to him. She smiled again.

"Perfect," he said, and his gaze lingered upon her mouth. Maybe he was remembering the intense kisses they'd shared.

After his first one at Wellington's Apsley House, Lord Hargrove had approached her at Lady Sullivan's home on Grosvenor Square. Again, she'd allowed his exciting advances. Such wondrous sparks had sizzled throughout her body, she vowed she would never forget.

"Thank you," she said. And quick as a whip, she finished her second sandwich, fearing an efficient server might clear the plate away prematurely.

In companionable silence, she waited while he ate his first. Then he brushed the crumbs from his fingers onto the plate.

"In answer to your question, I'm here at the pleasure of Prince George for a couple of reasons, the main one being

I failed to procure a particular work of art he desired, and therefore, I am in the dog's house."

"Brighton is the dog's house?"

"It's not London," he pointed out.

"Agreed," she said, "but I like the smell of the sea. It's preferable to most of the smells of London, don't you think?"

He shrugged, and she almost sighed at the breadth of his shoulders.

"If you enjoy the aroma of drying seaweed and the pungent fishing boats that seem to be always dragged onto the sand," he said testily. Then he smiled crookedly, and she caught her breath at how fiercely attractive she found him.

"I apologize for being in a tweague," he said. "In truth, if my visit to Brighton were merely for a week's holiday, I would probably enjoy it immensely. Yet being forced to an indeterminate stay at the beck and call of a somewhat capricious prince makes this little seaside resort seem like Newgate jail."

Placing another small triangle on her plate, Glynnis considered a moment.

"This isn't the Middle Ages. Surely, you don't have to sing a tune for him whenever he asks. He's not going to behead you."

He frowned. "It's more complicated than that, but I don't think you would understand."

She stopped mid-chew, despite thinking the cheese and cucumber sandwich superior to the first two, and glared at him.

"Why don't you put to the test my minimal understanding of the important manly things of this world?"

"Very well," he said, ignoring her tone. "Influence and favor are the issues. Or worse, the lack thereof. Fall out of favor with Prinny and I may suddenly find myself adrift without important connections. For fear of my disfavor rubbing off, certain men will cease speaking to me, either in Parliament or at my club."

"Mr. Brummell survived the cut direct from the Prince Regent." She reminded him, recalling the scorching accounts in the newspapers after Beau Brummell pretended not to know the prince and called him "fat" within His Highness's hearing. "Everyone thought Mr. Brummell would plummet from the pinnacle of popularity. Instead, he remains firmly at the top, at least by those who wish to be banged up to the knocker."

"True enough," Hargrove conceded. "However, Brummell runs in different circles than I do. I neither seek nor need approval from those who care about fashion. Whereas he flourishes without the patronage of the prince, it's only because foolish fops still want to see how Brummell turns out, day or evening. Can his cravat be any whiter? And all that sort of figgery!"

She thought Hargrove always looked very well turned out, and couldn't imagine Mr. Brummell doing any better. She almost said so, but the viscount would take it as another play for him.

"Moreover," her companion continued, "Brummell is sorely in debt with no foreseeable way out, and I don't think he would be in such a sorry state if Prinny weren't set firmly against him."

That made her a little sad. Poor Beau, falling from such heights like Icarus. But her own sorry state was nothing to sneeze at. Mayhap she should try to get *into* the good graces of the Prince Regent before worrying about those who'd already lost it. Perhaps into his breeches and his bed, too. Despite what Hargrove said, she could do worse than become a mistress to the Regent who would someday be king. She wouldn't hurt for coin, then!

Shaking her head at her own outrageous thoughts, she surmised, "Regardless of your feelings about Brighton, it will be nearly like London for a short while."

"Hardly that," he said. "Although this year, the queen will attend her boy's birthday, so the polish is on the pig for sure, and had best be on every person as well."

"The shopkeepers have already raised their prices," she couldn't help grumbling.

The year-long inhabitants knew enough to steer clear of anything but their regular purchases of food and wine for the duration of the royal visit. For every milliner and modiste, every cobbler and tailor, and especially every store selling knick-knacks and *à bric et à brac*, as well as furnishings had already raised their prices, raking in what they could off the backs of the visiting nobility and their staff.

She'd seen stores she thought permanently closed when she'd first arrived, suddenly open their doors. London tradesmen kept them shuttered until they could come down and sell to the prince and his entourage.

"Prices are exceedingly dear at the moment," the viscount agreed. "But they are the only thing that makes Brighton like London in my opinion. Which brings me back to my question, why are you here? Although I suspect I know the answer."

If he hadn't added that last bit, she might have told him the honest truth, that she was looking for a life's mate and a father to her future children. But he'd said that smug and knowing line, and she desperately wanted to surprise him.

"I'm here to meet my fiancé," she blurted. That was the truth. She desperately hoped to *meet* a man who would ask for her hand.

And then as she hoped he would, Hargrove misinterpreted her words.

"I say!" he exclaimed. "You managed to bag yourself a wild boar." He feigned astonishment, even waggling his perfectly devilish eyebrows while making an insinuation she didn't particularly care for.

What a brute! After all, she had her looks and her personality.

Tell him he has misunderstood, Glynnis pleaded with her better self. *Tell him the truth!*

CHAPTER TWO

G lynnis couldn't seem to stop herself from digging her hole a little deeper.

"My fiancé will soon be joining me."

Say you were only teasing, she ordered herself, but she said nothing of the sort.

Besides, if she were believed to be engaged, not only by Hargrove but by all the eligible bucks, she wouldn't appear so desperate. The well-heeled gentlemen around her would relax, safely misinformed that she was soon to be yoked and then someone else's baggage.

Glynnis was forming a plan. Being engaged would give her almost as much freedom and desirability as being a tempting widow. Any number of men might try to compromise her merely for sport, knowing her fiancé would be the one to deal with the repercussions after the marital knot was tied.

And she intended to let herself be thoroughly compromised if there was any chance of being discovered while doing so—a shocking, humiliating, ruinous discovery and then a demand for honor to be satisfied.

She could see no other way to obtain the coveted marriage proposal. And as she used to hope for love and then lowered her expectations to someone she didn't despise, now she wished only for any wealthy man to marry her even if she had to cut a desperate sham.

Elsewise the future showed only bleakness, a return to Llandeilo in Wales with nothing to look forward to but the St. Teilo's Fair and a life of spinsterhood, slipping irrevocably into poverty because of her brother's carelessness and her parents doting leniency toward him.

Thus, she looked Hargrove directly in his dark eyes and lied again.

"My fiancé and I knew it would be easier to meet here than in London. With the Prince Regent will come an atmosphere of *laissez-faire*, or so I've heard."

"With the prince comes also the *bon vivants*, to be sure, and with them a goodly number of unsavory people."

She hoped Hargrove didn't count her in such a group. When the Prince Regent traveled, the *demi-reputables* went along, hanging on the outskirts, ready when needed.

"What's his name, this lucky fiancé?" came his quick question.

Glynnis froze, then coughed, then sipped her now-cold tea, and then it came to her.

"Lord Aberavon. I doubt you've heard of him. The baron favors his Welsh home on the Swansea Bay. For me, however, he said he would travel all the way down here to Brighton." That was perfect. Aberavon was merely a man her father had invited to dinner once or thrice. She would recognize him if she saw the man, but they had barely spoken two words. And by the time the baron ought to arrive, she would have put the parson's noose around some other eligible nob.

Or she would have run out of money and departed on the coach that brought her there.

"I confess, I had heard nothing of this," Hargrove said.

"Our engagement was very recent," she said. "I'm sure the banns have been read in Swansea and Llandeilo. But why would you, in London, know anything about it?"

"I suppose you're right." He fixed her with a lengthy stare. "I look forward to meeting the lucky man."

"Me, too," she murmured, staring at her now-empty plate. Then she coughed. "I mean, I look forward to introducing you should we run into each other again."

Lord Hargrove stood. "I must be off. It was a pleasure. I thank you for inviting me to join you."

With a polite nod, he departed, leaving her with her mouth open. He hadn't paid. The blasted bolter had left her with the bill. But also with the last small sandwich. Wrapping this in her napkin, she put the nuncheon on her hotel account and left. At this rate, she would need a husband even sooner.

JAMES LAMBERT, VISCOUNT HARGROVE, knew he should have paid for the food, but Miss Talbot deserved to be taken for a small amount of blunt. After all, she'd been outrageously devious in London and nearly cost him his freedom. However, since the fiery female had also kissed like an experienced Athena *before* she'd wickedly tried to trap him and since she couldn't play any tricks in the café, he'd seen no reason not to sit with her.

The news of a fiancé came as a shock. *Poor bastard!* Someone with more money than sense had encountered the treacherous female. As long as Lord Aberavon didn't mind being a purse with a cock, that was his business.

Besides she was a pleasure simply to look at. All curvy in the right places, with a full mouth and sparkling eyes. The first time he'd seen her, she'd been standing alone by the tall windows in Apsley House during a party after Wellington's triumph at Waterloo. The duke hadn't yet returned from France, but had authorized the celebration in his splendid home overlooking Hyde Park.

Although it was months ago, James could still recall her summer blue gown, the swell of her bosom, and her thick, glossy brown hair. Quick as a whip, he'd had her in his arms for an intimate waltz, and her enticing floral scent had enveloped him. His entire body had recognized her as woman to be reckoned with. And she'd displayed humor and wit to boot!

He might have been happy eventually offering for her if she hadn't spoiled it. Finding out he was no more important to her plan than any jackanape, it had put him off her entirely. When the time was right, he would ask a woman who desperately yearned for him and him alone. And that was plainly not Miss Talbot.

Thus, despite a visceral rush of pleasure upon seeing her in Brighton, James forcefully pushed her from his thoughts.

He had enough on his mind. Tonight, he would see Prinny for the first time since the man had shouted like a child thwarted from getting his favorite toy. Then the Prince Regent had ordered him from his private chamber at Carlton House with the command to meet in Brighton.

Brighton! All wet and sandy!

Brighton, which was definitely not London.

The only cheerful spot so far was how James could see the beach from the upper level of his rented house, not too many yards away from the Old Ship. He could stand in his bedchamber and watch the ladies strip off a few layers and take the salt waters for their health or even to cool off. He'd arrived the night before and hadn't seen Miss Talbot yet on the beach, but now he knew she was in town, he hoped she would treat him to a display of her fine figure.

It was a small benefit. That and knowing Prinny had brought with him the delightful *demimonde*, a little bit of voluptuous and blowsy London ripe for enjoyment at the seaside.

Meanwhile, knowing the Regent's fondness for late, long parties, James had hours to kill and found his university friend, Lord Rufus Payton at home.

After they slapped each other on the shoulder a few times, James said, "I'll allow you the honor of buying me a drink or two."

Payton enjoyed a complimentary house on the Royal Crescent in return for service to Prinny nearly year-round in the seaside town.

"I didn't expect to see you here," Payton said once they had drinks in hand and had asked after each other's families.

"It all started with a dog," James grumbled, having told Miss Talbot only half the story of why he was in Brighton.

Payton laughed, causing James to set down his bumper, already only half full of bitter beer.

"No, truly. A little mutt, the size of a rat."

"Are you sure you weren't foiled by a rat?" Payton asked.

James sent him a withering look. "If the lady in question hadn't had a blasted cur beside the bed, everything would have been smooth as silk. Instead, despite sleeping soundly, the beast started to break wind, wholly ruining the amorous atmosphere I'd spent all evening creating."

James tapped the table irritably and glanced around the dim interior of the St. James's corner tavern. He had a feeling he would spend an inordinate amount of time in his namesake while enduring his banishment. A smattering of coals was glowing in the hearth, but since it was a warm night, he and Payton sat across the room from it, next to a window looking out at German Place.

"I'd already been forced to ignore the strangely loud snores."

"Your paramour's?" Payton interrupted.

"The dog's!" James retorted. "I swear the first time it started up, I jumped. I thought another man was in the room."

"I imagine you ought to put a little blame for your downfall on the fact you were cuckolding one of the Crown's favored captains," Payton reminded him. "And a friend of the Prince Regent's younger brother, to boot."

Shrugging, James gestured to the serving wench for another beer.

"Honestly?" he asked with a grimace.

"Yes, we're friends," Payton replied before taking a healthy swallow from his glass tankard.

"I didn't realize she was married."

Payton winced. "Hard to credit that, old chum, given your reputation."

James drew himself up, then slumped again as he couldn't summon any righteous indignity.

"Raffish, yes," he agreed. "But prone to adultery? No! Why would I get into the suds with other men's wives when there are lonely widows aplenty, especially since the war?"

"And then there's your mistress."

"Exactly. Usually I don't even bother looking elsewhere, but this captain's wife was all over me like a vixen on a mouse."

"You're the mouse, I take it."

"She lied and she enticed," James fumed. "As a rule, I leave married women alone. I wouldn't want to be cuckolded so I don't do it to others. What's wrong with these knavish females?"

"More than one?" his friend prompted.

"If you combine her wretched actions with that of another conniving wench I met two months ago."

He thought about the dark-haired and deceitful Miss Talbot. His pride had been pricked, thinking she truly fancied him. Moreover, he had really enjoyed her company and her kisses until she'd shown her true colors. He wouldn't name her. That would be most ungentlemanly.

"A young lady tried to trick me into compromising her. She was intent on setting the perfect parson's mousetrap. It nearly worked, too."

"Poor Hargrove, always the victim in the affairs of the bedchamber." Payton's grin filled his whole face.

"I tell you this time it was the dog," James grumbled. "He had it in for me. After the room filled with his noxious vapors, the captain's lady jumped up, drew back the curtains, and raised the sash, intent on providing us both a little air. She was bare as Eve!" He ran a hand through his hair. "She didn't know her husband had put a watch on the house to keep her safe."

"Safe?" Payton echoed, then chuckled.

"You know what I mean. To keep her from sharing her apple dumplings and woman's wares, which are quite fabulous, I tell you." He tried to think back to the married beauty, but instead Miss Talbot's luscious figure came to mind. She was a fine bit of muslin and no mistaking that. He had hoped to do more than merely kiss her and fill his hand with her soft, full breast.

At least with the captain's wife, he'd got around to stripping her bare and stroking her smooth skin. He ought to be relieved he hadn't tupped her since he could've found himself in even worse trouble. On the other hand, he'd been royally taken to task by a hypocritical prince who was enjoying a well-known affair with the lovely and very married Marchioness of Hertford. Thus, all things considered, seeing how he'd ended up exiled from London, James might as well have enjoyed the lady thoroughly.

Payton nodded with understanding. "I suppose any good husband would hire a watchman while across the Channel fighting Boney."

"You would take his side, wouldn't you? Damn dog!" James had wasted the better part of an evening cozying up to the woman who'd caught his eye at Vauxhall.

"And so, upon the evidence of her showing her pretty cat's heads to the street, the watchman told her husband you were there having a slice," Payton summed it up succinctly.

James shook his head. "The dog was my downfall. Suddenly, it jumped up and went to the open window, paws on the sill—"

"The tiny dog reached the sill?" Payton wasn't even trying to hide his laughter any more.

James shrugged. "Maybe it was a wee bit bigger than a rat. It started baying at the moon or scenting a bitch for all I know. Raised a holy ruckus. The lady asked me to get up and drag him back, which I stupidly did. There we were, my bare chest *and* hers, the bright moonlight on us both."

"If only it had been a regular cloudy, sooty London eve." His friend shook his head in mock sympathy.

"True," James griped. "What are the odds? Anyway, I heard a man yell and knew the jig was up. I got out of there in a hurry, tripped over the damn dog, nearly shattering my skull, but he confronted me at the door. By mid-morning, I was summoned to Carlton House, given a reprimand on account of the captain's closeness with Prinny's brother, and banished to this godforsaken place."

Payton grimaced, and James spread his hands.

"My apologies. I know for you Brighton is home most of the year. But I'm a Londoner through and through. I've been sent into exile as surely as Bonaparte to St. Helena, and with as little hope of returning to the mainland, or in my case to the civilization that is Mayfair."

"Don't worry," Payton promised. "London's worst toadies have arrived to keep you company. This place will be packed for two weeks before Prinny's birthday, a week at least of birthday celebrations, and probably a week after."

"Then what?" James tipped his glass and drained the strong beer.

"Then it goes back to being a godforsaken place." Payton declared. "But it's an easier task, overseeing the Prince Regent's holdings, when he's away."

"I'm not a caretaker!" James pointed out.

"Nor am I," Payton shot back, his tone sharp for the first time. "I'm not a bloody clerk of the kitchen. May I remind you I am a valued member of the prince's council, dealing with a budget of over £200,000 for all of his residences and holdings."

"Sorry, old chum," James said immediately. His friend was smart and sensible. Every man-Jack who knew him and knew Prinny appreciated Payton hovering somewhere nearby to whisper words of wisdom into the prince's tin ear. For all the good it would do!

Payton shrugged and James knew he was forgiven.

"Anyway," his friend said, "if you'd brought back the art from the Louvre as you'd been asked, you would have been so high in Prinny's good graces you could have swived with the queen herself without recrimination."

"Again, not my fault." James thought back to his wasted trip to Paris.

"Not a dog's fault either. Not that time," Payton reminded him.

James fixed his university chum with a hard stare. "No, it was the damned Prussians that time, swarming into Paris and taking everything that wasn't nailed down before the British could get their share of the art."

"You mean before Prinny could. After all, Wellington was there, wasn't he, helping every nation?"

James rolled his eyes. "Everyone except me. While his troops made sure the Flemish and the Dutch got their paintings, Wellie gave me the cold shoulder regarding what Prinny wanted."

"Did you get anything?" Payton asked.

"I managed a few small sculptures, a vase, and some old Spanish masters that even Ferdinand VII didn't want back. *Ha!* They are rather dark, mind you. The opposite of our Prinny's taste. He wanted some of those Prussian paintings from the Kassel Museum, but so did old Friedrich Wilhelm III."

"Not that old. The Prussian king is only in his thirties, I believe."

"You have a way of missing the point." James was prepared to drink heavily over his recent bout of bad luck. "Most of all, our regent wanted the Apollo Belvedere, as he fancies there's a likeness, but of course, that got sent back to the Vatican."

"A likeness! Between Apollo and Prinny!" Payton had to take a few moments to laugh until he nearly cried. Finally, he said, "So your banishment is the Pope's fault."

"No," James disagreed, and this time he couldn't help cracking a smile. "Again, the Prussians! They accompanied crates of art all over the Continent, not only the Apollo I was after, but also the Medici Venus."

Payton nodded, "For Prinny's bedchamber, no doubt."

His mock-serious tone was all it took to finally restore James's humor. "I can just imagine our prince ogling that perfect representation of womanhood every evening before he retires to bed. His mistresses would be jealous of Greek marble, would they not?"

For an instant, his mind went to Miss Talbot, another perfect representation of womanhood, except for trying to trick him into marriage.

"Never mind, old chap," Payton said. "We shall do our duty here, two men under the thumb of His Royal Highness, and then we'll move on. Or at least you will. I shall stay put at least until next spring."

Thinking of his comfortable life in London, his home on Hanover Square, his experienced and welcoming mistress, James sighed.

"It was the dog's fault," he muttered again before signaling the serving wench for another pint.

CHAPTER THREE

Around the beauteous lawn, gay buildings rise,
There the Pavilion wooes admiring eyes.
Within, the lovely edifice is grac'd
With every beauty of inventive taste.

— Brighton. A Poem by Mary Lloyd, 1809

That night, James strolled along the Steyne where fishermen had recently been told to stop drying their nets as it wasn't the view the Prince Regent wished to see when he looked out of his Pavilion's eastern windows. Prinny's other guests were also mostly on foot. James liked how people went around Brighton by foot since it was so compact. Carriages were hardly necessary. He certainly wouldn't bother until he was climbing in his own to head north to London.

The exterior of the Marine Pavilion's cream-glazed Hampshire tiles were glowing delicately in the light of lanterns. From a simple classical exterior of stately columns and symmetry, it was well-known the entire structure was going to be made over with a Far East influence to match the exotic stables built seven years earlier in the northwest corner of the property.

The famed architect John Nash had begun the project early in the year, and from what James heard the new Chinese-inspired gallery where the west corridor used to be was already completed and would be the highlight of the evening's open house. Naturally gainsayers were already declaring the entire plan—using the Orient, India, and Arabia as the main influences—to be a "mad-house" and in extremely poor taste before it was even built.

And then there was the dreadful cost!

James walked past the south wing where Prinny's private apartments were and along the narrow-edged portico of columns, to enter through the salon's grand dome. He was greeted by vases of fresh flowers, the heady aroma filling his head and lifting his mood. The cheerful chinoiserie style of decoration that the Prince Regent so admired was in evidence everywhere, and thus, the predominant colors were rich red and glittering gold.

James could only hope the pieces of art he'd brought with him, packed in straw and carefully crated, would tickle Prinny's fancy enough to soothe his prickly royal temper. Then he would be released from this infernal banishment. Even if Payton thought Brighton was all the crack and more, James wanted to go home.

As usual at any princely party, it was overly crowded and loud. Servants were milling about carrying trays of glasses filled to the brim. James took one, wondering how long it would be before Prinny started telling his infamous off-color jokes. Scanning the room, he noted the usual flatterers who offered an abundance of palaver and flummery to the eldest royal son, awaiting the day he became their king.

And then he saw *her*. Not Prinny's former mistress *and* former wife, Mrs. Fitzherbert. Nor was it his latest mistress, Lady Hertford, who may or may not be bold enough to come to Brighton and risk Mrs. Fitzherbert's considerable wrath. No, neither of them. It was Miss Talbot who caught his eye.

Her appearance stopped him in his tracks and checked the breath in his lungs. Perfectly coiffed and downright desirable, she was a jewel clad in shimmering ruby satin with cream-colored gloves and a matching feathery thing in her hair. Her breasts were magnificent, and he knew if he got close enough, she would have a distinctly floral scent he recalled from London.

If she wasn't so dangerously willing to be compromised, he would consider her a welcome diversion until he could return to his London mistress.

Then he recalled she was engaged and smiled to himself. With someone else on the hook for her future security, she was far safer to play with. He couldn't stop staring.

The feathers in her hair moved as people came and went in the main salon. When a single cream quill disobediently flopped in front of her face, she made an adorable moue with her lips and blew the feather upward. Dutifully, it returned to its place. Meanwhile, his shaft had stiffened at the sight of her puckered mouth, and he found himself walking toward her, helplessly drawn.

"We meet again, Miss Talbot. And you look positively ravishing."

Her cheeks pinkened under his compliment. She, too, held a glass of wine and raised it toward him. "Thank you, Lord Hargrove. And you have quite the dash-fire about you tonight."

Sincere or not, her words cheered him. "May I have a dance?"

"Certainly, my lord. Let's hope the sea air hasn't put all the instruments out of tune."

He frowned. "Is that a possibility?"

"Very much so," she said, looking serious. Then she smiled. "I have no idea, but it sounded plausible, didn't it?"

His mouth opened before he snapped it closed. "You made that up for amusement?"

"Gracious, don't look so nettled. I was teasing. I'm sure the musicians and their violins and whatnot will be as good as when they play in the smoky air of London."

She was an odd fish. "I shall find you for the first dance." He bowed and too took his leave of her.

Strange chit! Then his glance landed on Prinny, glass in hand, a questionable female on either side of him, hanging on his every word. One laughed wholeheartedly at something he said until her low décolletage nearly slipped and delivered a show. If not his famed vulgar jokes, then Prince George was amusing them with stories of leading battalions of soldiers despite having never gone to war. It was a strange game he played, fooling no one but himself.

James would have to make his dutiful presence known, but he might as well wait until the Prince Regent was fully in his cups and in the most joyful of moods.

First, however, he would see who else was at the party. Meandering around the room, over-furnished and crowded as all the prince's residences, he sipped the claret. Superior wine, to be sure. The food would also be of the highest quality, making these tedious royal parties at least bearable. He nodded to Payton who had just arrived, nodded to two others he knew from Town, and then found himself looking for Miss Talbot again.

She stood by a gilded mirror, and thus, James was able to see her from the front and the back. The reflection of her fine dark curls and long neck and the way her ruby-colored gown dipped low at the back to display her straight back and creamy shoulders aroused him out of all proportion to what he was seeing.

Presently, she chatted with Lord Leilton, who was always on the shadier side of Sunday. At that moment, the man was sending surreptitious glances down the neckline of Miss Talbot's bodice and grinning like a fiend.

James sighed. Leilton was a dissolute philanderer, careless and stupid. He'd left behind a bevy of illegitimate children, supporting none of them, despite being well able to afford their care and upbringing.

Feeling a little ill seeing the man leaning close to Miss Talbot, with her impeccably clean gloves and silly, romantic feathers, he couldn't take his gaze away. *Did she have any idea what a libertine Leilton was?*

Although it was none of his business, James was of half a mind to break up the two, and then the musicians started to play. Dancing would go on at various periods throughout the evening as Prinny liked his parties to drag out and be varied. The prince might even play and sing a song later.

For now, their giddy regent was letting the trained musicians handle the music, and they were excellent, too. Not out of tune as Miss Talbot had hinted. Setting down his glass and moving swiftly, he noticed Leilton lift his dullard head, cocking an ear and realizing an opportunity to hold the beauty before him, if only for a wicked waltz.

James quickened his step. "I believe you promised this dance to me," he said, offering her his hand. He thought she looked relieved, but he might be imagining it. In any case, while he whirled her around the small dance floor, he would take the opportunity to warn her away from Leilton.

"Starting the evening with a waltz," Miss Talbot said as they joined hands before he put his other to the small of her back while she settled her hand lightly upon his shoulder. "How exciting!"

James wasn't a coddled innocent, but he had to admit he agreed with her sentiment. One minute, they were behaving in a civilized manner, talking, drinking, smiling, and the next men and women were holding each other, touching one another and not even exchanging partners. That didn't happen in the natural course of every day. And it was absolutely fun.

The dance was long, and by the end of it, they were both breathing heavily.

"I would say we have earned a refreshment, unless you're going directly back onto the dance floor." A quadrille was starting up next.

Looking at him, with her eyes bright, her cheeks flushed, and her lips even appearing redder, James felt the now-familiar surge of desire. When she licked her lips, he bit back a groan.

"I think I would like some lemonade or barley water if it's being served," she said, "and then a walk outside."

"The closest thing to lemonade might be champagne," James told her wryly.

They both laughed at the Prince Regent's excess.

"Then I shall have to suffer with champagne," she teased, and they located a server.

"How can it be cold?" Miss Talbot wondered.

"Everyone is drinking so swiftly, it hasn't had time to sit around and warm up," he mused.

"I realize that, but where is it coming from?"

"Just because we are not in London, as you pointed out earlier, it doesn't mean we don't have all the comforts of Town," James reminded her. "Prinny has a massive ice house on the property. Have you had a tour yet?"

"No, I haven't. Are you offering?" She batted her eyelashes over her dark brown eyes.

He glanced at her sharply, recalling her trap in London. After they'd got on so well at Apsley House, he'd sought her out at the following ball on Grosvenor Square, and she'd asked him if he wished to show her around, particularly the library. Naturally he'd imagined she intended they find a private spot and swive like randy dogs, for she certainly had that effect on him.

Instead, in a well-lit library, which should have been his first clue something wasn't right, while he'd pressed her onto the tufted divan, his passion soaring, suddenly, the door opened to his right. Their hostess, Lady Sullivan entered with what sounded like a gaggle of female guests behind her.

Their esteemed hostess took one look at his appalled face, as he lunged over Miss Talbot to hide her identity, and then Lady Sullivan backed out, closing the door with a bang. She must have trod on a few toes behind her, but he heard her firmly shepherding the party away from the library.

"I cannot breathe," Miss Talbot had complained, and he'd climbed off of her with all due haste, his ardor not only cooled but absolutely frozen.

"How did you know they were coming in here?" he'd raged for she'd shown not the least bit of surprise nor worry. Worse, at his club he'd heard her name from the lips of another single man who'd said she'd tried to get him to kiss her in the garden just as a group of guests were approaching. He'd dismissed the words as a bitter tale due to unwanted advances.

But her cheeks had grown rosy with a blush of guilt.

"I heard you'd played this game before, but I didn't believe it," he said. "Why would a pretty viscount's daughter need to trap a husband in such an underhanded way?"

"What on earth are you talking about?" she'd asked, arranging her features into one of confusion.

"Don't play coy!" James had fumed at how closely her reputation had been ruined, and he would have had to marry her or be deemed the worst scapegrace and hell hound in London. "You specifically asked me to show you the library."

"How could I know Lady Sullivan was going to pick this moment to come in?"

He had almost cracked his teeth for clenching his jaw so tightly.

"How do you know it was Lady Sullivan when I had you covered?"

"I . . . I . . . ," she'd stammered, her cheeks growing redder as she tried to come up with a lie. "By her voice, of course."

"Lady Sullivan said not a word until *after* she closed the door. It could have been anyone. Admit it. You knew our hostess was coming in here and wanted us to be found *in flagrante delicto*."

With her face set stubbornly, Miss Talbot had marched past him, her scheme to trap him thwarted. Only later did he learn from Lady Sullivan—whom he'd actually had a short affair with two years earlier *before* she'd married—that a poetry reading had been scheduled for the library. Solely the female guests had been invited, while the men were to play billiards. Arriving late, James had missed the announcement, but Miss Talbot knew of it.

Fortunately, Lady Sullivan thought she was doing him and his lover a favor by covering for them. Any other female, a vindictive lover or an appalled hostess, could have sent him into the parson's noose that night.

James had sent Lady Sullivan and her husband a barrel of wine in gratitude.

Now, here was the minx casually referring to her despicable scheme. He might have been flattered she'd chosen him if over a cigar at the end of the evening, he hadn't heard from another chap about a *gumptious and brazen hoyden* who'd asked him to show her the library that very night. Smarter than James, the other man had turned her down in favor of billiards and the safety of the herd.

Blast her!

James decided to ignore her pretty eyes and soft lips, or at least try to. "I am sure Prinny will offer a grand tour as the evening progresses."

He bowed, realizing he had to get away from her then or risk giving in to the unmistakable attraction between them.

Then he recalled Leilton just as a dandified buck approached, obviously seeking the next dance.

"Hold a minute," James said to the man, taking her a few steps away for he would not be accused of gossiping, no matter how true and with what good intentions he did so.

Miss Talbot stared up at him with undisguised curiosity.

"You were speaking with Lord Leilton earlier," he said, and she nodded. "In case you are unaware, he is considered to be rather a dastardly damber."

Her eyes widened, but she said nothing, so James continued.

"Reputedly, he leaves a trail of bachelor by-blows if you take my meaning."

She opened her mouth and released a small "oh" of sound.

"Yes, I understand and thank you for the information." Then she glanced away and back at him. "However, it is not my concern as I am already engaged."

"Yes, of course." He looked past her. "I believe your next dance partner grows restless."

She nodded, sent him a smile, and turned away.

Damn him if her mere smile didn't set desire coursing through his blood again. If he wasn't careful, *he* would be the dastardly damber.

To stave off such inappropriate and ill-advised longing, he found himself a cockish wench who had come to Brighton to service the noblemen with no strings attached, although she might empty his purse by morning.

When the dance ended, and he'd all but decided to meet up with the game chit later and take her back to his rented home, James decided it was time to offer a formal greeting to Prinny. The prince had barely left his prime position by the windows, always a drink in hand, musicians close by, candles showing him at his flickering best, and one of the frowsy females still on either side of him.

To his amazement, as James traversed the room, Miss Talbot, bold as a bull, got there ahead of him. *Oddsbodkins!*

James watched as Miss Talbot curtsied low, offering the Prince Regent a fulsome view of the shadowy valley between her exquisite breasts. Outrageously, she introduced herself, as she had no escort nor chaperone, nor anyone close to the prince to stand up for her. If James had got there a moment ahead, he would have performed the introduction, instead, he was hanging behind her as if in line for bread.

Moreover, he couldn't help but listen as she and Prinny immediately engaged in a discourse of utter whipped syllabub—frothy and silly and without substance. They made each other laugh, and then Prince George actually gestured for her to stand beside him, pushing one of the blowsabellas out of the way.

Watching Prinny procure a glass of wine and press it into her hand, James felt a little shudder of apprehension. If she wasn't careful, Miss Talbot would finish the night with her heels up and *everyone* the wiser, ruining her engagement and shredding any good reputation she might value.

Shaking his head, he reminded himself it was none of his business. Then he took a step forward.

"Good evening, Your Royal Highness. You look well tonight."

Prinny stared at him, a hard, unforgiving stare, and James swallowed.

Egad! If he only had fluttery eyelashes and big breasts he wouldn't be in this mess.

"I *always* look well," the Prince Regent told him. "You, on the other hand, look like a man who failed in his duty."

Ouch! "It's true I was unable to bring home the Apollo Belvedere, but I did bring back some paintings and a sculpture never before seen in Britain, sir."

"Are they here?" A spark of interest shone in Prinny's eyes.

"Indeed, yes. I brought them with me from London. However, if you would rather place them on display at Carlton House, I would be only too happy to speed them back up to Town at your earliest request."

The prince flared his nostrils. "We'll see." Then he looked at Miss Talbot. "Hargrove, do you know this delightful creature?"

Know her? He'd kissed her thoroughly, and every part of his body had become inflamed with yearning for her. Catching her eye, he imagined she could read his thoughts.

"Yes, Your Highness. Miss Talbot and I danced at Apsley House."

"Good, then you may keep her company this evening. She's in Brighton without a friend in the world. Except for me," Prinny added, sparing her a warm glance.

She returned him a generous smile, and James rolled his eyes.

"And now, she has you, too," Prince George continued. "Between the two of us, we can make sure she has plenty of amusement while being kept out of the clutches of any rascals, rakes, or niffy-naffy fellows."

James nearly spit his teeth out. *So now he was to babysit the incorrigible wench until her wretched fiancé arrived?*

His expression must have shown his disrelish, for Prinny gave him another cold look. "In fact, for the duration of her stay here, I ask that you keep an eye on this delicate creature with hair like the most beautiful horse's mane."

Again, James caught the sable glance of Miss Talbot, who merely raised an eyebrow. She wasn't in the least ashamed of her treatment of him in London.

"There are rods in brine for you if you don't," the Prince Regent promised, then spread his lips into a meager smile as if he were joking, although James knew he wasn't. Any more slip ups and he would probably lose his viscountcy. He would actually prefer those salted rods to his back.

Still, he laughed as if the notion of being punished was ridiculous.

"I'm sure I can keep her out of the suds, sir."

How hard could it be?

CHAPTER FOUR

"What are you doing?" came a stern voice, making Glynnis jump.

It was Lord Hargrove, who'd become practically her shadow ever since the encounter with the Prince Regent. That meeting had gone better than expected. His Royal Highness had already imbibed enough to be happy and welcoming, but not so much that he later wouldn't recall how well they'd fallen in with one another.

She sensed having his favor for the remainder of her stay in Brighton would be essential. Any friend of the prince's would always be surrounded by the highest level of society. Surely one of the men would want her as his wife.

Thus, she had continued to amuse him until he truly couldn't ignore his courtiers any longer. Finally, Glynnis had curtsied, hopefully leaving him wanting more of her company. As for the Regent ordering Hargrove to look after her, Glynnis hadn't decided yet if that was good or bad. Until that moment . . .

"I am going to join the other party-goers outside."

"Most are indoors, either in the music room or strolling Nash's new gallery."

She frowned. "Do I have to go where everyone else is?"

"It's safer," he pointed out.

Glynnis couldn't help rolling her eyes. "We are in the middle of a royal assembly. It is not yet midnight. The entire town is like a safe version of London."

"Not that safe," James insisted. "The Prince Regent doesn't only bring the—" he coughed once "—the wagtails." She raised her eyebrows, and he hurried to add, "The disreputable females, if you take my meaning."

She nodded, wondering where he was going with this awkward speech.

"Inadvertently, his entourage brings from London the scapegraces and nappers, the light-fingered budges, the bully-cocks, silk-snatchers, and common pickpockets."

She knew she wore an astounded expression.

"You cannot seriously be trying to frighten me into thinking charming seaside Brighton is anything like the streets of London, particularly east of St. Paul's."

They stared at one another in silence, until finally, Hargrove expelled a breath and confessed, "No, I suppose not."

"Then I will head outside, my lord. In all probability, I shall return in time for the next piece. I believe the prince said it would be Beethoven."

"Not without me, you're not."

And then it hit her like an iron spade. If Hargrove wouldn't compromise her, then he would be the perfect witness to some other man doing so. She only need dodge him long enough to get a baron, a viscount, or if she were extremely lucky, an earl to take her behind the hedgerow. She would let him place his hands on her waist and kiss her, and then Hargrove would happen upon them like a dog at the hunt.

He seemed like the type of man who would demand instant satisfaction—and she would find herself engaged before sunrise.

"Very well, but don't hover," she said. "If you do, then people will think we're a couple. What will that do to my reputation?"

He looked at her, narrowing his attractive eyes.

"I shall introduce you to a lady or two, and then you can stay in a group with them, unless you know some from Town."

She hadn't attended a Season or three to make female friends, nor had any of the other ladies. And if one didn't have sisters or cousins or even a mother who had Mayfair friends, then each ballroom was nothing more than a chamber full of vicious competitors.

"I don't need to meet any ladies," she said too quickly.

"You can't meet any more men. You're engaged and that would affect your reputation far more quickly than walking around with me."

"I disagree. Because I am engaged, I should have the freedom to keep company with anyone I choose in the public areas."

He gritted his teeth, and she assumed he was fuming.

As her finger was already on the door handle, Glynnis pushed her way outside. A long expanse of grass met her gaze until it was stopped by another large building across the lawn, a building with whimsical minarets and a massive dome. The prince's famed stables! She strode onto the path winding around the property, although there were people standing around lanterns and under tents.

"What about you? Don't you have a lady-friend here who needs your attention?" she asked over her shoulder, knowing Hargrove was still close. "Don't say you have no intention of maintaining your raffish reputation in Brighton. You'll break all the single ladies' hearts. And some of the married ones, too, I'll warrant."

Glynnis hoped he took it as a challenge and would go off to do something befitting a rum buck. She'd seen him dancing with a woman who, by her dress and manner, was a courtesan. It had given her a small pang of jealousy, knowing Hargrove was free to engage in the mysterious two-backed beast with the harlot, while she had to bait a man and then await her wedding night.

Into the silence, Glynnis turned to observe him. Hargrove cocked his head, gave a single sniff, and then sighed.

"Perhaps I am sticking a little too closely. Nothing can happen here in the garden in sight of the Pavilion's many windows, not with so many others around. But what will you do if I walk away, for I do see a lady of my acquaintance with whom I would like to share a word? Will you simply stand by yourself like a stick in the mud?"

"I shall take a short stroll, and if it makes you feel better, I will even speak with some of the other *female* guests. All right?"

He hesitated, but only a moment. "Very well. I will see you anon." Bowing slightly, he wandered away toward two fair-haired women. Glynnis wrinkled her nose. Maybe he preferred blondes and that had set him against her in London. If she'd been so fair as those girls, maybe he would have allowed himself to be trapped.

No matter. There were plenty of noblemen who liked a chestnut-haired lady. Hesitating, wondering if she should walk right up to a group that had more men than women, suddenly, another solitary individual exited the Pavilion and came sauntering toward her.

To her good fortune, he was vaguely handsome, taller than she was, and not more than a decade older. Thus, as soon as he crossed the paving stones and onto the grass, which was currently yellowing due to the daily hot sun, she was upon him.

"Good evening, my lord, can it be *you*?"

He bowed graciously while wearing a bewattled expression.

"I am not sure who you think I am, dear lady, but to my dismay, I do not believe we are acquainted."

"Goodness! Please excuse my forwardness. I thought you were someone else. I don't know anyone here, and thus must admit to pouncing too quickly upon what I thought was a familiar face."

Then she offered him her saddest pout.

"Never mind," he said. "Why don't we introduce ourselves? Somewhat irregular, wot-wot, but we can always say someone put us up to it."

Perfect, Glynnis thought. He didn't mind a little dissembling.

"That sounds like a grand idea. I am Miss Talbot. My father is the viscount, Lord Dynevor of Llandeilo, Wales." She always tossed that in as soon as politely possible, since being a viscount's daughter was something, as long as word of her penniless state wasn't widely known.

"I am enchanted to meet you, Miss Talbot. I am Lord Cumberry. My family home is in Kent."

She wracked her brain, but didn't recall the name. Without asking, she had no way of knowing his rank. But his cravat was whiter than new snow, his boots were perfectly polished, and his dark jacket and indigo waistcoat had not a thread out of place. He must, therefore, have a valet, and they were expensive to keep.

So far, so good.

"Have you only just arrived in Brighton?" she asked him.

"Indeed, I have. I've taken a house on the Steyne. I like to be in the thick of things."

Or maybe he couldn't afford the first-quality homes on the seafront. But noticeably, he didn't say "we." She could only ascertain he had no wife.

"And you?" he returned, seemingly interested.

"I, too, have recently arrived. I've taken lodgings on the Marine Parade." Or at least, a room in a hotel, but he needn't know that. Not yet.

He nodded. "The sea air and all that, wot-wot."

"I'm sure the air is as fresh and cleansing on the Steyne as where I reside," she consoled him.

"Indeed. Shall we take a turn around the prince's fine yard?"

He offered his arm, and she placed her hand upon it before they started to walk. Occasionally her shoulder brushed against his arm. She had a feeling he was game.

Continuing their promenade, chatting lightly about nothing, they finally approached the large white building in the corner of the property.

"The stables," her escort said as they drew closer.

"Yes, I'd heard of their unusual design, but they are beyond imagining. She took another look at the impressive edifice of minarets and massive windows with its majestic dome towering over everything around it, and she had two thoughts—firstly, there didn't seem to be any lamps lit or party guests near the stables, and thus she intended to steer him back to where someone might see them. Secondly, *gracious!* These horses had a finer home than her parents' house.

As they drew closer, the hair on the back of Glynnis neck seemed to prickle, perhaps because Lord Cumberry's footsteps had sped up. Easily tugging her arm free, she spun upon her heel to start up another path along the lawn and back toward the Pavilion.

"Miss Talbot," came Lord Cumberry's voice behind her. "Wouldn't you like to see the prince's fine horses? I believe you shall find a magnificent stallion inside."

Raising a gloved hand, she kept walking. *Did he think her an absolute ninny?*

"Most assuredly," she declared, "I shall not."

His hurried footsteps caught up to her, and they continued in silence until they reached a yew hedgerow growing at an angle to the house. Suddenly, they were in the shadows, close to the other revelers yet still shielded. Moreover, they were slowing down until they came to a standstill.

"Have you been to Brighton before?" he asked, glancing around him in a manner familiar to her. He was looking for privacy.

She'd already answered this banal question when he'd asked her many minutes prior. She, too, looked around, but she was looking for a witness.

"No, my lord. This is my first time." That made her sound like a debutante at her first ball, a good impression. She blinked up at him a few times as if life in society was entirely new to her.

"I quite like it," Glynnis added in her best breathy tone. "Moreover, I find everything and everyone are of interest to me."

"How refreshing," Lord Cumberry said. "Look up and see how clearly the stars appear."

She did as he suggested, and felt him move closer until suddenly, his lips were upon her arched neck. She shivered, continuing to observe the night sky, and then he drew her against him. This was all very good except she was unsure how to get someone to see their inappropriate behavior. *Should she scream?*

Hating to do that, for she would rather not directly be the cause of their discovery as it could cause resentment in her future husband, she bided her time and let him nibble her neck. Where was Hargrove? She'd hoped he would have discovered her by then.

Instead, Glynnis would have to let Lord Cumberry take a few liberties now in order to ensure he took some later when she had maneuvered them into a more favorable position for being found.

When she felt his hands on her back, she shifted her gaze to his.

"I did see the stars," she remarked, then added coyly, "They gave me the most curiously warm feeling."

He chuckled softly before lowering his head. She closed her eyes and waited. Instead of a pleasant kiss, she heard loud, off-tune whistling.

In a flash, Lord Cumberry darted away from her.

"Cumberry, is that you?" came a familiar voice. *Hargrove!*

"WHAT ON EARTH ARE you about, ol' boy?" James asked. *As if he didn't know!* There they were at the first of Prinny's parties and already *Kissing Cumberry* was up to his usual tricks. He'd been caught kissing more women than just about any man. Not that many a man didn't enjoy stealing a kiss, but the fellow showed no sense about where and when.

Poor Miss Talbot to have foolishly taken a walk with him. He couldn't credit the idea she'd had a hand in enticing Cumberry, not now she was safely engaged. James had kept an eye upon her, ready to run if she so much as set foot in the stables, and was glad she'd shown good sense in turning back toward the party. Then he'd lost them momentarily behind the shrubbery.

"Good evening, Hargrove," Cumberry returned, grinning like an idiot and looking unbothered, while Miss Talbot appeared flustered.

Apparently she hadn't realized her predicament until too late, and luckily James had shown up in time. If he hadn't whistled a warning, he would have been forced to demand Cumberry do the honorable thing and buy the marriage contract from Miss Talbot's fiancé. Probably Aberavon would still have demanded satisfaction by way of a duel.

"Prinny's about to play the cello," James told them, "and everyone has been commanded to enjoy it."

"Don't want to miss such a performance, eh, wot-wot," the man said, practically salivating. Cumberry was a confirmed royal bum-kisser, too.

"We must take another walk soon, Miss Talbot," he added before dashing back toward the terrace doors of the Pavilion.

"I guess we should go inside," Miss Talbot said.

"No rush," James told her. "Undoubtedly, the prince's cello will be brought out, but not yet, not until we're all desperate to leave and Prinny is equally desperate to hold us captive."

She cocked her head. "You lied to Lord Cumberry?"

"Indeed, I did. And now that he's gone, I must warn you not to walk alone with him again. He will attempt to take liberties with your person. Moreover, he is the worst type of petticoat pensioner."

The annoying woman showed no alarm, but simply blinked up at him.

"I beg your pardon."

"Cumberry is a scroof, if you take my meaning. He's a sponge who lives off the women he escorts around Town."

"Ah," she said. "If he's the worst, is there a *better* type of petticoat pensioner?" She offered an amused smile.

"I suppose not. I don't approve of anyone using another person for their own gain."

Her cheeks went a little pink, and it had been harsh of him to say, but he was still smarting over her deceptive behavior on the divan.

"I thank you for your concern once again," Miss Talbot said, albeit a little stiffly. "First Leilton and now Cumberry. Is there anyone at this party who isn't a scoundrel? Anyone safe for an honest woman to chat with or take a turn about the garden?" Then she glanced around.

James realized they were secluded behind a hedgerow. Undoubtedly, she was noticing the same thing.

Looking back at him, her lovely eyebrows rose.

"If there is no cello performance yet," she asked, "what shall we do to occupy ourselves?"

And the chit offered him a wry smile. She was so frank with her stares, he felt a stirring he absolutely didn't wish to feel, the same draw he'd perceived in London.

"We must rejoin the other guests at once, Miss Talbot."

Damn him if he didn't sound like a prude! The sooner her fiancé arrived and took her off his hands, the better.

She insisted on him taking her arm, so they strolled out from behind the hedge, linked together. A few people glanced their way. The only thing saving them was that Prinny's parties often ended in scandalous behavior and an unchaperoned stroll around the grounds didn't seem terribly egregious in comparison, even if a few imagined they had been up to no good.

Still, James would insist she behave better. He almost laughed at himself. *How on earth could he do that?* Moreover, he couldn't imagine how she had become his responsibility.

"I shall leave you here," he said, abruptly disentangling her from the crook of his arm. Her hand gripped his coat sleeve tightly for a moment, then released him. She wandered toward one of the smaller groups of guests which included a few lords and ladies whom he knew, and he felt a little sorry for Miss Talbot.

Shaking it off, having done his duty, he went back inside. But a few minutes later, out of the corner of his eye, he observed her reenter the music room. Suddenly, the pleasant distraction of a well-known Cyprian who'd come down from her infamous perch in London to offer her services to the Prince Regent's friends faded into the background. She was still talking, but her voice faded.

Miss Talbot glanced at him, then looked away, taking in the room, and quick as a whip, she traversed it and left.

"If you'll excuse me," James said to the rouge-cheeked beauty with her feminine assets on display in the sheerest of gowns. He might have a go at those *assets* later if no one else claimed her first.

Following in Miss Talbot's footsteps, leaving the music room behind, he realized she'd already passed through the gorgeous new Nash gallery and was somewhere else in the Pavilion. Unable to tamp down his curiosity, he went after her.

Where was the minx? And why in hell was she strolling alone?

CHAPTER FIVE

To his relief, he spotted her standing quite innocently in the domed salon, apparently doing nothing more than admiring the room, especially the impressive ceiling.

Good, he thought, turning heel before Miss Talbot spotted him spying on her. He didn't want her to think he had designs upon her personally. Returning the way he'd come, this time he took a few moments to admire the exotic grandeur of the Chinese gallery as many were already calling it.

Natural light flooded in through clerestory windows and skylights. Thus, even at that time of evening, the last rays of the sun were augmenting the bright, oriental-style lanterns hanging from fierce red and black metal stands lining the pinkish-hued walls and towering overhead.

Setting one knee upon a bamboo chair, or so he supposed it to be, James leaned closer to the wall to examine the detail of painted trees, rocks, and birds, which he at first took to be wallpaper.

"Hm!" *That must have taken some time.*

Glancing back, still no Miss Talbot reemerged from the far room, so he continued past the cast iron "bamboo" and carefully placed mirrors to rejoin the party. If he had to guess what Nash and Prinny were aiming for, James would say the effect reminded him of a bamboo grove. Frankly, odd though it was at the English seaside, it made him smile.

But would an entire palace decorated thusly be a good idea? It wasn't for him to say. And then his smile died. He couldn't imagine the items he'd brought from Paris being welcome, at least not if the entire Pavilion was to resemble the Chinese gallery.

Spying an acquaintance, Lord Staunton emerging from the music room, they nodded at one another.

"You look fierce," the man said. "Is Nash's gallery so very ugly?"

"No, it's not that. See for yourself," James invited the man, gesturing behind him while not bothering to stay and chat. They weren't friends, and Staunton notoriously voted in Parliament for his own interests over the good of anyone, either the country or even his own county.

James hoped he could still claim the exquisite Cyprian's attention. She had a witty remark for nearly every topic and every person he mentioned. In fact, he had started to gain the impression she'd actually been tupped by everyone they were discussing, too, but that only indicated an extremely proficient level of skill.

Alas, the woman in question had already entranced someone else, no doubt with the intent of making a tidy profit that night, so James approached a group of men over whom Payton was holding court. Since Napoleon boarded the *HMS Bellerophon* off the southern French coastal port of Rochefort earlier in the month, the topic of war had given way to that of grain tariffs.

For a few minutes, he listened while men spouted off irrespective of how ill-informed they seemed about Lord Liverpool's Corn Laws. Payton appeared to take each one's opinion seriously before disabusing them of their belief with his good-natured mild manner. His friend ought to be a foreign diplomat instead of one of the prince's councilors, buried in Brighton.

"We need Staunton's voice on this," one of the others said. "After all, his estate in Norfolk was practically under siege last time Parliament brought up the issue, so angry were the farmers."

Staunton? At once, it occurred to James how the man had brushed past him minutes ago. And then he thought of Miss Talbot, touring the Pavilion. Staunton was married but had a wandering eye, not to mention hands.

With a sinking sensation that he'd allowed a baby duck to swim into the deepest lake, he excused himself and dashed back the way he'd come. When he reached the domed salon where he'd last seen her, there was no one there. The house was one long structure with a wing at either end sticking out to the west, so she could not have circled through rooms and come past him. Although, they could have gone outside. He pressed on in his quest.

The sight that met his eyes in the dining room made his blood boil instantly. Staunton's back was to him blocking the female, but he recognized Miss Talbot's gown and the feathers rising above Staunton's bowed head. The cad had her backed against the gold and red wall and was kissing her mercilessly. If she'd already screamed for help, no one had heard her.

"Hoy!" James called out, as this situation was beyond the polite interruption of mere whistling. "Let her alone."

Not as fast as James would have liked, Staunton turned around wearing a sappy pleased expression that needed to be wiped off his face. Realizing he'd clenched his fists to do exactly that with a punch to the man's nose, James slowed his steps. And then he saw Miss Talbot's face.

She peeked around from behind her assaulter, looking flushed. But she didn't appear upset or as if she had been taken off-guard.

What was she playing at?

"We're a little busy, Hargrove," Staunton said.

"I can see that, but Payton mentioned you in passing and others are starting to wonder where you are."

"I won't be long," the man said, sounding profoundly smug not to mention entirely insensitive to the fact that Miss Talbot's reputation was at stake.

"You've discovered us!" she proclaimed loudly, and James noticed Staunton's head whirl around to gape at her rather swiftly.

"Discovered us?" he echoed. "It's only Hargrove. He won't say anything." Staunton turned back to him. "Will you?"

James ignored him. "Will you come with me, Miss Talbot?"

She hesitated, glancing uncertainly between him and Staunton.

"Is Lord Staunton correct?" she demanded. "You won't say anything, not even to defend my honor?"

Defend her honor? What on earth did she mean? She sounded as if she wanted him to make a hullaballoo over this blatant indiscretion.

"Surely you don't wish anyone to know you allowed a married man to kiss you."

"Married?" she exclaimed, and then her eyes narrowed at Staunton. "Where is your wife? Is she here?"

"Of course not. I always leave her in London."

She pushed way from the wall and skirted her lascivious admirer, striding toward James, her expression furious.

"Are you *all* scoundrels?" she muttered, gliding past him.

She must be a lunatic! She seemed angry to have been taken in by a married man, yet her own fiancé was on his way to claim her.

Turning, he caught up with her. "You are a puzzle, Miss Talbot."

Shaking her head, she wouldn't look at him. "You all stick together, don't you? Even if he had been tumbling me upon the carpet, you would have hushed it up, probably helped him to his feet and dusted him off, rather than call him out to do his duty."

"His duty?" James considered her words. "Whatever can you mean? He's married and his only duty is to his wife, poor sap of a woman."

"But if he hadn't been married, which I didn't know, by the way—"

"Did you ask him?" he interrupted her.

"Not exactly, but he was very ready with the 'I' do this and 'I' do that, and not a single 'we,' just like Lord Cumberry."

"Lord Cumberry is *not* married."

She turned an interested look upon him, and James felt his stomach plummet. *Was she still husband hunting despite having a man on the hook?* It was beyond the pale.

"Cumberry is practically impoverished," he told her in case she hadn't understood his earlier message. "Mostly from hanging around with the Prince Regent and trying to keep up with his royal excesses. I suggest you keep Cumberry at a distance unless you wish to be parted from your own inheritance."

She looked away before he could read what was behind her deep brown eyes.

"I ask again," she began, "if Lord Staunton hadn't been married, then would you have decried his behavior and told him to do the honorable thing?"

James halted his steps and laid a hand on her arm to stop her, too.

"Tell me truthfully, are you trying to free yourself from an untenable situation? Were you forced into an engagement? Is your fiancé a brute?"

She hesitated, and in that moment, he doubted she was going to tell him the whole story.

"I was not forced," she admitted, "and he is not a brute."

And with that, she turned away.

He considered how she'd left the party and went off alone. Again.

"Had you arranged with Staunton to meet? Or was it by chance?"

He heard her sigh before she said, "I am certain that is none of your business."

She'd probably made the arrangement while out in the garden. James wanted to grab her and shake sense into her. Moreover, he didn't like the unfamiliar proprietary sensations he was experiencing. If he were honest, it was jealousy that had coursed through him while seeing Staunton kissing her. Moreover, he would gladly kiss her again himself, if he didn't think her more than half mad.

"Is the cello music starting soon?" she asked.

If she was truly eager to hear Prinny play the cello, then she was entirely light in the noodle indeed.

THE EVENING WAS INTERMINABLE, but Glynnis realized it was the price she must pay while husband hunting. She had chosen poorly twice that night—thrice if she counted talking with the lecherous Leilton who purportedly left bastard children in his wake. Then there was the profligate pauper, Cumberry, who was barking up the wrong tree if he thought *she* had money. And worse, she'd arranged while in the garden to meet a married man who'd done all but lie about his status before kissing her. Not that it had been a bad kiss, simply a pointless one.

Hargrove had come along, which she'd hoped, but instead of declaiming what he saw, he'd shrugged it off and agreed to say nothing. Since Staunton was married, she was relieved there would be no gossip. However, if he hadn't been, she would have wanted Hargrove to scream it from the rooftop, not hide the indiscretion.

It was clear she was going to need a better witness to her reputation-shredding recklessness when she did finally find a suitable bachelor of means and got him to compromise her.

And she had no doubt she would succeed. After all, she'd already had three interested men on the first night, and she'd hardly tried.

Since Hargrove was now chatting with a rouged female and she had grown weary of speaking with strangers, Glynnis decided to spend a little more time with the prince. After all, it wasn't every day one was in the company of the man who would someday rule over a nation.

The party continued with a sumptuous meal, smaller than the actual birthday feast coming up in a few days, or at least that's what the Prince Regent promised. Still, it included an astounding fifty courses. Glynnis hadn't had to keep track because an update on the number was announced by one of the servants every time more courses were brought in from the nearby kitchen. This was occasionally repeated with undisguised glee by Prince George himself.

She had learned in London to take only a mouthful of each dish offered if she didn't want to be ill before the dinner was over, and those Mayfair meals had usually been a paltry twelve or so dishes. Yet with the Prince Regent, the dinner was the main attraction of the evening, and thus, he fully intended them to remain around his table for hours upon hours.

Over the course of the evening, the Regent became louder and began to pick out individuals near him for ribald jests or less-than gentle teasing. Glynnis feared by the third dessert she would still be seated there for dinner the following evening. Hargrove, who was seated across from her and farther up the table closer to the Prince Regent, looked as wary of such an outcome by the way he was openly drumming his fingers upon the tablecloth.

The dining room's door opened and in swept Mrs. Fitzherbert.

Prince George jumped up. "You missed dinner," he said by way of greeting.

"And gladly," his former wife declared, as all the other men rose quickly to their feet. She surveyed the packed room, basking in the frank stares of the guests.

Glynnis had never seen her before, but the woman lived up to her description of fair hair, hazel eyes, a very straight, almost sharp nose, and a good complexion although wrinkled with age. She and the prince had shared a ten-year marriage before he'd been forced to give her up.

"I came to hear you play the cello."

By then, Prince George had taken her hand in his and kissed it. "And I shall do so now. The weather is fine this evening. Did you walk?"

"Perish the thought," she said. "My carriage brought me through the south gate."

The prince laughed at such indulgence. Everyone knew she lived a stone's throw to the south—about one thousand feet, if that far. And since arriving in Brighton, Glynnis had heard there might be a secret tunnel under their very feet linking Mrs. Fitzherbert's year-round home to the Pavilion.

She sighed, thinking of the romantic relationship of the pair, even though they were reportedly not currently a couple. Moreover, she was glad the woman had chosen that moment to come and release them from their gustatory prison. Joining the rest of the guests as they strolled back to the music room, some waddling with discomfort, Glynnis could only hope the cello-playing was a good deal shorter in duration than the meal.

Hargrove was escorting the woman with whom he'd dined, someone without enough money apparently to pay for decent quality fabric, for her gown seemed made of scandalously sheer tissue. Glynnis tilted her chin and looked away. If that was the type of woman the viscount enjoyed, no wonder he was still a single man.

For her part, her dining companions had been old men on either side of her. Notwithstanding, they'd flirted and looked down the neckline of her gown, and she'd tried to enjoy the conversation despite finding it all an utter waste of time.

In fact, any minute when she wasn't actively engaged in appropriating a husband was a nuisance. And while one of her dining companions might have been willing, she wasn't so desperate yet that she would give herself to a man who would need to go through an ox house on his way to bed, as the saying regarding older husbands went—and maybe bring the ox with him.

She shuddered. Glynnis wanted a real marriage with at least a chance at companionship and children. Her gaze drifted again to Hargrove as they all found places to stand in the cramped room, most of them unwilling to sit again until they'd had a chance to stretch their legs. The Prince Regent, however, seemed perfectly happy to take a seat and when his cello was brought to him, a gift from the King of Spain, he tucked it between his legs and began to play.

To Glynnis's surprise, he was exceedingly good. She'd feared he would play the way some debutantes savaged a song or attacked the piano when pressed by eager mothers to perform at a private ball hosted in their homes. Usually, it made one's ears throb. However, she found herself entranced by Prince George's earnest and skilled style. He closed his eyes and appeared lost in the music by Haydn, of whom the Regent was a significant patron.

When he finished the piece, his eyelids popped open, his face split into a smile, and his gaze darted around the room, eagerly awaiting the praise that came from every corner.

Glynnis clapped along with the rest, genuinely impressed.

And then the Prince Regent wondered aloud if he should play another or perhaps move to the pianoforte. She thought she heard a collective sigh. After all, even though he was good, the evening had already been a long one. Luckily, Mrs. Fitzherbert took control where no one else would dare to gainsay the eldest royal son.

"Let your friends go to their beds," she advised. "Tomorrow, you shall see them all again in the daylight for a picnic and a delightful bath in the sea."

"True enough," he agreed. "The party is over."

And just like that, they were released to grab their wraps and coats, top hats and canes, and disappear into the night.

As Glynnis passed under the arch of the south gate, a man was suddenly at her side. Smiling to herself, she turned to see . . . Lord Cumberry.

Why had she expected and even hoped for Hargrove?

"May I escort you back to your house?" he asked.

Pausing her steps as others flowed around them, she supposed walking with him wouldn't cause any harm, seeing as how there were so many people out on the street. But she no longer had any interest in kissing him, knowing he needed money as much as she did.

"Yes, thank you." She would let him accompany her to the Old Ship and then leave him in the lobby. It was probably safer and more acceptable than strolling along by herself, perhaps even being mistaken for a lightskirt.

They walked down the Steyne toward the water, passing by Mrs. Fitzherbert's grand house.

"The Prince Regent used his own architect to design his wife's house," Cumberry offered.

Glynnis startled. No one called Maria Fitzherbert his *wife* out loud since their marriage in her drawing room in London had never been considered legitimate by the king nor the church. Moreover, Prince George was now most *unhappily* yet officially married to his cousin, Princess Caroline.

She wondered if Lord Cumberry was trying to be inflammatory by styling Mrs. Fitzherbert thusly.

"Come, don't look surprised," he said. "Prinny only agreed to give up his precious Mrs. Fitzherbert and marry our Prussian queen-in-waiting so Parliament would pay his debts. Some say they were as great as £650,000."

"Gracious!" Glynnis couldn't even conceive of so much money.

"Who would not happily let a woman go for that type of coin?" Cumberry asked, chuckling to himself, and Glynnis knew Hargrove had spoken the truth about him being a petticoat pensioner. He would undoubtedly give up a woman or take up with one for a great deal less than the prince's debt.

Regardless, this odious man might be correct. She would have to scour her own feelings deeply to come up with the answer.

Would she give up the person she loved for such an enormous sum, especially if it were a debt taken off her shoulders?

Would she take up with a man for the same reason?

It made her sad to think money was worth more than love. And then Lord Cumberry asked, "Where is your oceanside residence, dear lady?"

She squared her shoulders and chose honesty for she couldn't brook his company a moment longer.

"I have a room at the Old Ship, and it doesn't even face the sea."

He stopped so quickly the soles of his leather shoes made a screeching noise upon the modern pavement the prince had ordered Brighton officials to install to keep "his favorite place" up to snuff.

Glynnis turned.

"Is something wrong?" *As if she didn't know.*

"I just remembered a prior engagement," he said.

"At this hour?" She nearly smiled, wondering if Lord Cumberry would have the graciousness to at least look apologetic or ashamed of being such a base mercenary.

He appeared to be neither. He offered her a smile and a wink.

"Good evening, Miss Talbot." He headed in the other direction without even the courteousness to finish escorting her to the hotel door.

With a shrug, Glynnis clutched her lightweight shawl around her and resumed her stroll. She was only minutes from the Old Ship anyway, although the streets had become noticeably emptier as most of those from the party were in lodgings there on the Steyne and had reached their doors or had taken carriages along the Marine Parade to the eastern most part of Brighton, the Royal Crescent.

She hesitated, wondering whether to turn right and weave her way across Great East Street to Black Lion Street, as it would surely be shorter, when the unthinkable happened. Someone slammed into her from behind and tugged hard upon her reticule, as she flailed—and failed—to stay on her feet.

CHAPTER SIX

Screaming, Glynnis pitched forward. First her knees and then her gloved palms hit the pavement. With her feathered aigrette falling over her face, she wasn't even able to catch a glimpse of the culprit.

Shocked and mortified, she remained on all fours a moment, hoping her gown wasn't torn. And before she could climb to her feet, she heard footsteps running to her. Once again, hands were upon her. She let out another shriek.

"'Tis I, Hargrove," came his voice, and she relaxed, letting him draw her to standing, and then she leaned against his firm, safe figure.

"Are you injured?" he asked.

Glynnis kept her eyes closed a moment, catching her breath, feeling his warmth, and taking her own measure. Her heart beat fast from the shock of being shoved, and perhaps also from suddenly being in his arms. Then she opened her eyes and pushed away from him, knowing her knees might be bruised, but that was the worst of it. Glancing down, her dress was dirty but not in need of repair.

"Yes, I believe I am unharmed. Thank you for your assistance." She spoke the words lightly, as if he'd merely retrieved a package or book from the pavement and not her.

When their gazes caught, however, she saw concern. Moreover, angry words spilled from his mouth.

"A cutpurse!" he fumed. "Probably came from London, knowing townsfolk are off their guard when in Brighton."

She looked at the reticule ribbon still around her wrist and held it up for his inspection.

"Fortunately, there was nothing of value in my purse."

"Nothing?"

"Merely a handkerchief," she assured him. "I carried the reticule because I thought it was . . . pretty." Embarrassed at how her voice caught on the last word, Glynnis realized she needed to get to her room and maybe shed a few tears, for the incident had shaken her despite the mild outcome.

Then someone nearby coughed, and she looked past Hargrove to see the woman from the party.

"You will catch your death," she uttered without thinking, but the gossamer gown left nothing to the imagination. And by the pert breasts with pearled tips, Glynnis would say the woman was feeling chilled despite the warm climate.

Hargrove looked at the Cyprian, too—for Glynnis knew what she was.

"Where do you live?" he asked the rouged doxy.

Glynnis started to draw away. This was no longer her business, and he had more important things to do than deal with her.

"Wait," Hargrove commanded her. "I will see you home."

Only because she felt a little dazed, Glynnis did as he said and waited.

The courtesan sighed, realizing she'd lost her customer.

"I'm lodging right there." And she pointed to a private residence a few doors down from Mrs. Fitzherbert's.

"A group of us *ladies*," the courtesan emphasized the word, "have rented the entire house. You'll know where to find me next time, right, love?" she added, then boldly strode forward and ran a hand down his cheek before sending Glynnis a scathing glare. Within moments, the woman had disappeared indoors.

They stared after her in silence. It was his lordship's turn to be mortified, and she felt the awkward pain of having witnessed this brazen encounter regarding the commerce of sexual relations. She supposed it was an everyday occurrence for a rake, but one not usually witnessed by a genteel member of society. And Glynnis liked to think she was that and more, especially in comparison to such a desperate creature who would sell her body on a nightly basis.

Hargrove cleared his throat. "Well." And then without looking her in the eyes, he took her hand and tucked it in the crook of his arm.

"You really don't have to—"

"Yes," he interrupted. "I really do. What happened to Cumberry? I saw the fool playing a gentleman and, as I thought, escorting you home."

"He had other plans when he realized I could not provide his next pension."

She felt him startle under her glove at her quip.

"You're feeling better," he remarked, "if you can jest, but he was the wrong man to choose."

"You misunderstand," she said. "I was walking home alone, and he chose me."

"Even worse!" Hargrove bit out. "First of all, it is absolutely absurd that you are lodging in a hotel entirely alone without a companion or a brother or a chaperone. You've practically marked yourself as a woman of ill-repute."

"I have not," she protested hotly, thinking of the creature who'd just left them, joining the other wanton jades in their seaside house of scandal. Moreover, Glynnis was prepared with her lies. "My companion fell ill, and my brother is occupied in London, but a chaperone is on her way."

"Coming with your fiancé, I suppose," Hargrove sounding like he was annoyed again.

"Yes, precisely. I couldn't ask a stranger, and my family is all the way up in Llandeilo."

He shook his head. "Absurd!" he proclaimed again.

While he was in such a tweague, Glynnis decided to press her advantage, as she didn't want a repeat of tonight's frightening occurrence.

"In the meantime, you will have to do. You may escort me to any and every event, and then I shall seem perfectly respectable. Precisely as I am," she hurriedly added.

"People will think we are a couple," he groused.

"Nonsense, I have a fiancé." She sighed. "Such a lovely word, don't you think? It rolls off the tongue, very prettily."

DROPPING HER ARM AS if it were burning his, James stalked four yards away along the boulevard, took a deep breath, and then returned to the wily Miss Talbot.

"Very well. It seems I have no choice. We both heard what Prinny said. If I cock up this duty, he will send me somewhere even worse."

She laughed, but fell silent when she realized he wasn't in the least bit jolly. Then she asked, "Where do you think that might be?"

"John O'Groats most likely." James considered the single-building outpost at the top of Scotland, practically falling into the cold North Sea.

"You're grimacing," she told him.

His dark blue eyes stared into hers. "You had best behave while under my supervision, or I vow—"

"What?" Miss Talbot asked, looking genuinely interested, her brown eyes sparkling. "Tell me. What will you do?" And the chick-a-biddy grabbed hold of his arm again so they could continue along the promenade.

The deuce! There was nothing he could do except keep her safe until her fiancé arrived. They turned right when they reached the sea, and he could see the sign for the Old Ship.

"If you're naughty, I'll do what any chaperone would do. I'll lock you in your room."

He felt her falter slightly beside him, but she rallied her good humor.

"If you're locked in my room with me, Hargrove, that will be acceptable."

She was baiting him, for it took less than a second to imagine them naked together upon her bed, her mouth puffy and red from his kisses, her thighs falling open, her body ready for him as he pushed inside her.

"Did you just groan?" she asked.

"Don't be ridiculous!" But they both knew he had. The urge to tup her had hit him the instant he'd seen her at Apsley House in London and hadn't waned even a little, despite how she'd hoped Lady Sullivan and a gaggle of gossipy geese would force his hand.

Only by the sheer luck of his Irish grandmother and by the grace of God had he walked away without being bound to the chit. In fact, he could thank the fact he'd parted on good terms with his ex-lover, Lady Sullivan, for the kindness of her discretion.

"I'm sorry you had to say goodnight to your lady-friend," Miss Talbot said, bringing his thoughts back to the Cyprian he'd intended to enjoy in the privacy of his home for the last few hours before daybreak.

He nodded, having nothing to say to that. It was beyond the pale for Miss Talbot even to bring it up. Moreover, as soon as he'd heard Miss Talbot scream and seen her sprawled upon the pavement, all thoughts of another woman fled. Now, when reminded of the light-heeled wench, James wished Miss Talbot hadn't seen them together.

While in the midst of the festive atmosphere at the Pavilion, he hadn't given a fig if the other guests saw him chatting up the pretty whore. For some reason, it now seemed sordid. Paying a woman for her services—be it to do his laundry, cook his food, or provide sexual congress—was as natural as breathing for men of his class. And doing so in London surrounded by the like-minded gave him no pause at all.

But here, with Miss Talbot and her big brown eyes, he wondered if it wasn't a rather sad thing at his age nearing thirty when he ought to be leaving off his Corinthian ways. Instead of a whore, he ought to be enjoying the company of a wife and focusing on begetting a few brats to carry on the family name.

"Here we are," she said. "I hope it's not too far out of your way."

He didn't tell her how close his own accommodations were. If they'd taken a left instead of a right and gone a mere few houses down, they could have easily gone to his lodging. He couldn't deny he wanted to do precisely that with Miss Talbot because the attraction between them was undeniable. But she was engaged, and he wouldn't ruin her for a night's pleasure when willing doxies were easily had.

Even a rake had a conscience!

Instead, he accompanied her all the way inside the lobby, nodding to the night manager. As far as hotels went, it was on the respectable side, not like some of the coaching inns where one might be forced to share a room or a bed if one didn't have the blunt to pay for the luxury of privacy. There was none of that nonsense here. And as a viscount's daughter, he knew Miss Talbot made up in coin what she lacked in sense.

"Are you going to escort me all the way to my room?" she asked, teasing him again. "What if there are robbers in the hallway upstairs or who've already gained access to my room? Maybe you should come check under my bed."

She was outrageous, but James was sorely tempted to claim a goodnight kiss outside her door.

"What!" exclaimed the manager loudly, breaking the spell that they were the only two people in the world. "There are no robbers, miss. And the owner wouldn't like anyone saying such a thing."

"There you have it," James said, knowing he should take his leave quickly. But he was standing too close and drinking in the sight of her, from her twinkling eyes framed by dark lashes to the upper swell of her breasts on display above the ruby bodice of her gown. Despite the opaque fabric, she was far more enticing than the obvious and vulgar Cyprian. If the concierge hadn't been staring at them . . .

Still, nothing would have happened, he reminded himself. *She had a fiancé!*

Clearing his throat, giving the man a look to mind his business, James took her hand and bowed over it.

"I bid you good evening, Miss Talbot."

But she grimaced, pulled her hand from his, and began to peel off her glove.

The small intimate gesture made his loins tighten. *What on earth!*

"I fear my palms and my knees took the brunt of the assault," she explained before holding out her bare hand for him to see.

The fleshy part at the base of her thumb was red and scraped since her thin evening gloves had given scant protection. He had the insane urge to raise her hand to his lips and kiss the area that looked painful.

Instead, he quipped, "I ask you *not* to raise your skirts and show me your knees, although I'm sure they pain you as well."

She responded with a serene smile. "I will behave with all due decorum and keep my abraded knees to myself. And tomorrow, or rather later today, I shall obtain some witch hazel."

They stared at one another a long moment, and again James felt the overwhelming impulse to kiss her, not her hand either, but her full, exquisite lips. She knew it, too, for her nostrils flared, and her gaze went to his mouth, which suddenly felt dry as Brighton sand.

Why, if he were as raffish as people believed, he would accompany her upstairs after all, strip off her other glove and the rest of her clothing as well. But he wasn't. He didn't destroy nice young ladies for sport, especially not newly engaged ones, no matter how appealing.

"Will you come," she began, and his cock stiffened, "to fetch me for the picnic tomorrow? Since you've agreed to become my escort, I mean."

Had he agreed? Yes, he supposed he had. This was going to be torture he decided right then and there. On the other hand, it was a rather enjoyable torment—to be tempted by a beautiful woman.

"Yes, I will collect you mid-afternoon."

She nodded and turned away, but paused with a foot upon the first tread of the staircase.

"Be careful on your way home, Lord Hargrove. Brighton seems to be as dangerous as London."

CHAPTER SEVEN

A wakening around eleven, Glynnis's stomach was rumbling. She'd already consumed Lord Hargrove's other sandwich the day prior, long before the party, and today's picnic was still two hours away. Perhaps she should have eaten more of each course, rather than consuming such ladylike morsels. Even better, she could have attempted to bring some of the Regent's exquisite food home with her.

Ah well, it probably would have been stolen along with her reticule.

She considered whether she was brazen enough to walk to the Pavilion and present herself to Prinny for a quick nuncheon before the mid-afternoon gathering. However, Glynnis had heard he wasn't always as sociable when not playing host. It would be dreadful to do anything to raise his ire and risk missing out on the rest of the little Brighton Season.

While she could put anything from the hotel's teahouse on her hotel account, she decided to wait for the free meal. After all there was a slim chance when it came time to settle the bill, she would not have secured a wealthy fiancé to take care of it.

When Glynnis could stand her room not a minute longer, despite it being light, airy, and comfortable, she decided to go on her one errand. Parasol, straw bonnet with ribbons tied securely under her chin, a pale blue lightweight cotton dress, and a cream-colored silk shawl in case the breeze picked up—she was ready for the day's events.

Stopping at an apothecary, she purchased the smallest amount of both witch hazel and a soothing, chamomile salve. After all, the condition of her skin was nothing to risk. After hurrying past the delicious smells of the hotel's café, she was back in her room to apply both the treatments before going outside once again.

Not wanting to go too far in case she missed Hargrove, she remained on the oceanfront road, strolling next to the cliffs, past the fish market and the baths where she would be later, after the picnic, if the prince didn't change his mind. She crossed the opening where the Steyne met the sea and traversed the South Parade. In five minutes, Glynnis walked on the Marine Parade where the wealthier nobs had taken up residence.

To her surprise, just a few houses ahead of her, James popped out the front door, closing it behind him. As usual, he appeared mouth-wateringly handsome, or perhaps her mouth was merely watering because she was beyond famished. In either case, she was glad to see him.

"Hargrove," she exclaimed, and he looked equally astonished. "I had no idea your residence was so near to mine. Why didn't you tell me?"

He blinked. Maybe the sun was in his deep blue eyes.

"The address of my dwelling didn't come up in our conversation, nor did I see how there was any relevance as to where I was staying," he insisted.

"Hm." By his reaction, Glynnis had a suspicion he hadn't told her how very close he was because he was worried his proximity might present temptation. With him merely a few minutes down the road, if she were the immoral type, she

might find herself dancing Molly Pratley's gig on his feather bed.

A bold thought, yet she'd seen how his gaze had landed on her lips the night before. Pure desire had shone from his eyes, and she'd felt an answering sensation of yearning. Nothing would have seemed more natural and perfect than ending up swiving, despite knowing ladies didn't do such a thing outside of marriage.

More's the pity! In her heart, she knew he would have made her first time something spectacular.

"Were you out for a stroll?" he asked, such an innocent question when she was having such bawdy imaginings.

"I was, but mostly, I was waiting for you and for the picnic."

He looked surprised. "I had no idea anyone would be so eager to eat food on a blanket spread on prickly grass in the hot sun with all manner of creepy crawlies and flying things.

That dampened her spirits a little until she realized he was teasing.

"Your expression!" Hargrove said with a laugh, before taking her arm and escorting her back toward the Steyne and the Pavilion grounds. "Prinny may have blankets spread out, but he's just as likely to have tables and comfortable chairs on the grass on the western side, near where I caught Cumberry trying to kiss you."

He paused and she wished he hadn't caught her with three men who were unsuitable. It reflected as badly on her powers of sound discernment as it did on the quality of men hanging on to the royal coattails.

"In fact, I can't imagine him getting down onto a blanket. One of his legs looked a bit swollen last night. In any case, he'll have servants with giant fans to cool his guests and keep the flies away."

She laughed, but Hargrove added, "No, I don't speak in jest. He will. As for the crawlies, I'm not sure even the Prince Regent can do anything about ants."

"They shall have to fight me for the sausage rolls," she said.

"Don't tell me you skipped another meal."

"Of course not. I ate at the same table as you."

"I've had plum cake and a bracing cup of chocolate already and then a cup of tea with a brioche slathered in butter and jam."

Glynnis's mouth was watering again. "You knew how close I was. It would have been gentlemanly of you to invite me over," she said, feeling quite let down.

"That would have been the opposite of gentlemanly, and you know it. Besides, I was in a rented drawing room with salt-encrusted furniture, and I'm sure the sea air is purposefully blowing the aroma of dried seaweed through my window. You have that delightful hotel café at your disposal. I'm sure they have brioche there."

"Yes, of course," she said, glad when the Pavilion came into view. "But do you think we will eat presently, or will there be some sort of entertainment first?"

"Are you truly hungry?"

"It's no matter. My own fault. I got out of bed late and then had to go find something to soothe my scrapes instead of something to quell my appetite."

"Ah yes. I intend to have a word with that idiot Cumberry if he shows his face today."

A warm feeling flooded her. Hargrove was going to take the other man to task on her behalf. A champion at last!

"Thank you," she said, "yet I believe it will do you as much good as shouting into the wind. After all, what will he do? Offer to escort me another time? I believe I no longer wish to be on his arm."

"You should never be alone with that man again. Regardless, I will give him a tongue-lashing. It would do him some good to think about his actions, especially where women are concerned."

She couldn't disagree, so she said nothing. And soon, they'd traversed the property and found the Prince Regent standing under a tree with a gaggle of courtiers around him. She was relieved to see tables already set up, and a steady stream of servants carrying baskets and trays out from the kitchen's back door.

Almost running, she went to the nearest table, reached over, and picked up a bread roll.

"No, no, Miss Talbot!" It was Prince George's voice, and she dropped the crusty bun as if it were made of hot coal.

Her stomach panged, having been so close to getting a tasty morsel. And all she could think of was the blasted plum cake Hargrove had mentioned. Regardless, she sank into a deep curtsy until the Prince Regent nodded for her to rise.

"A picnic is a casual affair, but we still have to wait until all the guests are here. Besides, you're at the wrong table," Prince George informed her. "I want you at my table with my friends. Mine is the one in the shade. I'm sure someone with your fair complexion you'll appreciate not having to hold your parasol through the entire meal."

"How long do you think we'll spend dining?" Hargrove asked, and Glynnis could hear the worry in his voice that another three hours of his life were about to be stolen from him.

"Don't sound so anxious," the prince said. "We shall get to the ocean's edge today, long before the sun goes down with plenty of time to bathe and maybe take a donkey ride. And we shall stay on the beach for the sunset because it is glorious."

All that sounded fine, but not until she'd had a solid meal.

"It's a lovely day for a picnic and for bathing, Your Highness," she prompted.

"Isn't it though? But then Brighton or as I first knew it, Brighthelmstone, has always been a delightful place. I think I love everything about it, the assemblies, the horse-races, promenading along our splendid English Channel, the weather." The Prince Regent turned his pudgy face toward the seaside.

"The gambling, the loose blowsabellas, being so far from his stodgy parents," Hargrove muttered in her ear.

She dug her elbow into his ribs to shut his mouth as Prince George turned back to them.

"The people here," he continued, "are universally of wit and style, and the ladies such as yourself have all the beauty of a fine painting and the enjoyableness of—"

"Roast chicken?" Hargrove interrupted.

"What?" the Regent exclaimed. "Are you comparing lovely Miss Talbot to a piece of well-cooked fowl?"

Her stomach squeezed at the mention of chicken.

"No," Hargrove said, "certainly not."

Glynnis could hear the mockery in his tone.

"I was merely wondering what was on the picnic menu. It seems ages ago we were dining at your table."

"Yes, it does, doesn't it?" Prince George said, sounding distracted. "And I am growing peckish, as I haven't eaten since breakfast except for a small noontime snack. If you'll excuse me, Miss Talbot, more guests are arriving. By the way, Hargrove, you'll be at that table over there."

And he pointed to one in the full sun.

"I hope you enjoy my picnic," the prince said to her.

"Yes, thank you, Your Highness." She curtsied again and watched him waddle off across the grass, using a sturdy cane. "That was rude of you," she said to Hargrove. "You were mocking him."

"He isn't here for the wit and style, any more than his courtiers are. Being here makes him feel young again, like he's twenty-one and seeing Brighton for the first time. Word has it, he came two decades ago to escape his father's disapproval. Now, he's here to escape the same sentiment but from most of the British people, and especially Londoners who don't think he's half the man his father was, except in size, of course."

She frowned and stared after the prince. "It's unlikely his father will recover, isn't it?"

Hargrove nodded. "I think you're correct."

"Then Prince George will be our king and shall need to fill his father's shoes."

"He will try." And Hargrove sighed, sounding weary. "While he empties the country's coffers."

She didn't know anything about such things, but trusted Britain's coffers would remain as plentiful as ever, along with those of her future husband, whoever he may be.

Hoping to start moving things in the right direction, Glynnis walked toward the table the prince had indicated, closed her parasol and leaned it against a tree.

Hargrove accompanied her. When her stomach grumbled loudly, her gaze flew to his.

"Good lord, woman," he looked around as if he feared someone would think he'd made the noise. "You might wish to eat upon a more regular basis. It sounds as though you have an animal caged under your skirt."

She grimaced and turned her back, and that's when she saw servants setting up the croquet wickets.

"Oh, sweet Mary," she muttered. *Food first, food first,* she chanted silently.

"We shall have a round of lawn croquet before we dine," Prince George announced.

The Devil!

"Did you just mutter an oath?"

Had she? Glynnis was sure she'd only thought it.

"Of course not!" And as the rest of the guests had arrived including some new faces she hadn't seen the night before, the prince divided them up into groups of four. He looked happier even than at his party the night before.

Closing her eyes, she took a deep breath. And then she went to her assigned team with Hargrove and another man and woman. They all greeted one another, and the play began.

By the luck of the draw, Glynnis's team went last, and as she waited for the three groups ahead of her to clear the first hoop, she realized without her parasol, her hat wasn't providing enough shade to keep her head cool. When they started, the other lady in their group handed her parasol to her partner who dutifully held it over her as she swung the mallet, sending her blue-painted ball through the hoop.

Managing to hit a ball from the team ahead of them, she yelled "Roquet," even though Glynnis was certain they were to keep their points and their score confined to their own four balls.

Glynnis didn't make it through the hoop on her first try with her yellow ball, but did so on her second, as did both the gentlemen. Naturally, the Prince Regent finished his fourteen points first about an hour and a half later, hitting the brightly colored winning pin.

By then, Glynnis's skin felt clammy and her heart was racing despite doing nothing more strenuous than ambling around the parched lawn. Licking her dry lips, she focused on the hoop, but it seemed to be moving.

"Stay still," she ordered.

"Are you well?" she heard Hargrove ask, but a buzzing in her ears made her wonder if a hive of bees was nearby.

She felt the mallet slip from her grasp, and then . . . nothing.

JAMES CAUGHT MISS TALBOT before she hit the ground. A chorus of concerned murmurings went up around them, but she was oblivious. He looked down at the lovely creature in his arms. Her eyelids remained closed with her dark lashes fanning her cheek.

After a moment, Prinny stepped closer and observed the scene.

"You may take her inside, Hargrove. The sofa in the main salon under the dome is most comfortable."

James nodded and strode across the lawn carrying Miss Talbot high in his arms against his chest. One often heard of fainting damsels, and in some of the stuffier ballrooms in London, he'd heard murmurings some lady had fainted by and by. But Miss Talbot was the first he'd seen do so close up. It was a strange thing to be holding so much female flesh out in public.

In a short while, however, they were indoors and alone. He set her upon the very sofa Prinny had mentioned. Naturally, it was red velvet with gold tassels. He couldn't recall ever laying a woman down without it being quickly followed by a kiss or the removing of clothing. Maybe that was why he felt so mesmerized by her shapely form and parted lips.

The cushion pushed her hat forward as he released her, and since it looked uncomfortable, he untied the ribbon and removed it. She stirred, and her eyes slowly opened.

"Oh," she moaned. "I feel ill."

A footman stood in the doorway. "Would you bring a glass of ale or lemonade?" James asked him.

Then he touched her forehead. It was clammy. After brushing a few tendrils that clung to her skin, he lifted her gloved hand and patted it.

"Just catch your breath a moment. I'm sure it was simply too much sun."

He watched the rise and fall of her chest as, surprisingly, she did as he instructed.

"I fainted," Miss Talbot declared, eyes widening.

"You did."

"That's my first time ever," she said, looking at their joined hands. "One minute I was concentrating on the yellow ball, and then, here I am."

"It was my first time catching someone who fainted," he confessed. "You added a measure of excitement to the party, I must say."

"I'm ready to sit up," she declared.

When she started to rise, he wasn't sure whether to force her to remain prone, but in the end, he helped her to a seated position.

The footman returned with a tray, set it down and poured a glass of lemonade, handing it to James, who in turn gave it to Miss Talbot.

"Drink it down."

She needed no second invitation, but slurped the beverage with gusto.

"Don't tell me," he said. "Not only didn't you eat anything, you haven't drunk anything either all day."

She merely shrugged before draining the glass. He was starting to feel annoyed by her. It appeared she couldn't look after even her most basic needs. *Did the woman need a nanny?* But her next question disarmed him.

"Do you think they've started the picnic yet?"

He couldn't help but grin at her. He'd been crouching beside the sofa, but he rose to his feet and offered her his hand.

"I believe some food will do you better than resting here."

"I do hope there are sausage rolls," she said. As Miss Talbot stood, her hat fell behind her onto the sofa, and James hurried to pick it up.

"Allow me," he said.

With her facing him, he placed it atop her shiny brown hair, which was plaited and pinned up. An irrational wish to unpin and unplait and run his finger through the thick skeins made him feel a little clammy as well.

"Make it straight," she ordered, referring to her bonnet.

Dutifully, he adjusted it while her soft brown gaze regarded him the entire time.

"Don't forget the bow," she said. "Without a mirror, I can hardly do it myself."

There were plenty of mirrors in the room, but he had no desire to relinquish her care to any one of them.

Drawing the silky cream-colored ribbon through his fingers, he set to tying the most perfect bow under her equally perfect chin, all the while staring into her eyes. When he finished and his fingers trailed along her chin, he couldn't help brushing a thumb across her lush lower lip.

She gasped, and he fell farther under her spell, utterly compelled to kiss her.

CHAPTER EIGHT

Helplessly, James leaned in and claimed Miss Talbot's perfect mouth, tasting the tart and sweet lemonade when he did.

With his hands going to her slender waist, he drew her close, feeling her breasts press against him. Her hands circled up behind his neck and rested there.

The familiarity of their kiss astonished him, considering how infrequently it had happened before. The jasmine and orange blossom scent clinging to her skin and her clothing filled his head, and he crushed her closer as he'd wanted to do since first seeing her in the café.

And exactly as in London, his body reacted with absurdly strong desire.

"Mm," she hummed against his mouth.

When he drew back, her brown eyes opened wide, her visage appearing shocked.

In truth, James was surprised too, believing until that moment he would be perfectly capable of ignoring the attraction between them. Even for a rake, it was rash behavior to do such a thing in the middle of the day *and* in the middle of a room with large windows.

Should he offer his profound apology despite not feeling the least bit sorry? Feeling quite the opposite and with her staring at his mouth with blatant interest, there was only one thing he could do.

Tilting his head to the other side, he fused his mouth to hers again, deepening the kiss. With longing coursing through him, James wished it wasn't broad daylight with Prinny and all his courtiers directly outside the Pavilion, probably awaiting their return. Elsewise, alone with her in the palace's cool interior, it would be tempting to test that comfortable sofa.

Sliding his tongue across her lower lip, she opened her mouth. The tip of his tongue charged in like the Royal Calvary to stroke and explore. When her fingers tugged on his hair, the sensations sent a direct tug to his shaft, too.

"Grr," she growled, astonishing him until he realized the noise emanated from her stomach.

Leaning away, he looked down to see her smiling ruefully, her cheeks pink with embarrassment.

"My apologies for such an ignominious sound."

"No, it is for me to offer mine. I know you're all but starving, yet I detained you." *Detained* was a mild term for dancing with her tongue and sucking on her lower lip. Yet if she wasn't going to refer to the inadvisable breach of propriety, then he wouldn't either.

"Let us hasten to get you fed, lest you fall into the sea during the next event only to be carried away into the Channel."

He would miss her if she did.

She chuckled softly, her gaze holding his.

"My bonnet," she asked. "Still straight?"

He nodded and offered her his arm.

SYDNEY JANE BAILY

When beauteous fair-ones to the beach repair,
To taste the wave, or breathe the sea-fraught air;
Or wait in turns, their lovely forms to lave,
And steal fresh beauties from the ambient wave.

– *Brighton. A Poem* by Mary Lloyd, 1809

GLYNNIS FELT PERFECTLY SATISFIED when the Prince Regent announced it was time to stroll down to the beach and the bathing area. She'd been thoroughly, toe-curlingly kissed! Hargrove was a master at it, and all she could think of was *"More, please."* She could easily imagine a lifetime of his kisses.

Beyond that, her satisfaction was due to filling up on Scotch eggs, cold roast beef, ribs of lamb, roast duck, and the sausage rolls she'd been hoping for. There were even pork pies, spinach pudding, and pickled vegetables, along with tray upon tray of sweets, as well as comforts coated in sugar.

She hoped she wouldn't sink to the bottom of the ocean floor.

And at the end of it, when she thought the picnic was surely over, servants rolled out two buckets filled with ice and salt. Inside each was a metal pot holding perfectly blended ice cream.

The ladies clapped, and even the men looked rather chuffed as they all stood and swarmed the servants under the shade of the largest tree.

"It's like being at Gunter's in London," Glynnis said to Hargrove, who appeared by her elbow. Even he couldn't be grumpy about Brighton when there was such a treat.

When everyone had their fill of the blackberry and the strawberry ice cream, trays of a sweet cold ginger drink were brought out.

"To aid the speed and ease of your digestion," the Prince Regent assured them.

"So we can all stuff ourselves again tonight," Hargrove muttered to her. She'd nearly forgotten there was another assembly that evening.

"I'm looking forward to bathing in the sea first," she confessed. "I have never done it."

"Never?" He seemed surprised although she had difficulty picturing him stripping off in a bathing machine and splashing about while being held by a dipper. It seemed undignified for a man, and yet everyone knew King George had enjoyed it as did his son and other members of the royal family. *So why not Hargrove?*

"I found it too cold off the coast near my home, although Swansea Bay is usually calm and the beach is soft and sandy," she explained to him her lack of experience. No point in disclosing how she'd never been invited by any of the London quality folk when they took excursions to the seaside or even to the Serpentine for that matter.

"Then I hope you will find it enjoyable," he said, trying to lead her away from the picnic area.

But she held back, scouring the base of all the trees.

"My parasol has gone missing."

He joined her in the hunt. The other guests had left as she and Hargrove circled the trees and even looked under the tables, before he asked one of the remaining staff who was cleaning up.

The man shrugged and said he would look into it.

Glynnis couldn't believe she'd lost two pieces of her personal property within two days. So far, this seaside trip had not gained her anything, certainly not a husband. She was out a reticule and now the only parasol she had with her. *Drat it all!*

"If we see it in the pilfering hands of some lady," Hargrove began as he offered his arm and they proceeded to follow the prince's party down the Steyne to the bathing area at its end, "I shall wrestle her to the ground in your honor."

That made Glynnis laugh. "I'm sure I shall be able to handle her myself, but I thank you. It seems you have become my protector."

And more than that if his kiss was any indication. She felt warm every time she looked at him. Her body had become molten liquid when his mouth crushed hers and his tongue had fenced with her own. Yet after that, he'd hardly looked at her, giving his attention to some fair-haired lady while she listened to the Prince Regent's tall tales.

If she knew anything at all about attraction, she would say Hargrove felt the intense pull between them and was fighting it tooth and nail.

And then there it was, Brighton's splendid beach if one didn't mind the rocks and flinty pebbles from the chalk formations upon which the town was built. From humble beginnings as a fishermen's village, the idea that bathing in the sea was good for one's health had been the beginning of its development into a humming town that bustled with the gentry and commoners alike.

The prince was already in his royal bathing machine, a sturdy horse having pulled it into the sea. Dippers awaited his exit out the back while someone inside the little hut on wheels helped him to undress. At the picnic, he'd said he wished old Martha Gunn were still alive as she'd been helping him to bathe in the Brighton sea since his first visit in 1783 when he was only twenty-one years old. Sadly, she'd passed away in May, and he would have to make do with another keeping him from sinking like a stone.

Glynnis faltered at the shore's edge, seeing ladies from their party climbing into the bathing machines, mostly by twos. Their maids had waited during the picnic for the sole purpose of helping them undress in the small confines of the wooden bathing machine. *Would she be brave enough to go alone?*

"Well, Miss Talbot, here is your chance to renew your constitution with the vitality and health of the sea. Did you bring your own bathing dress?"

Oh! She looked around the beach to see what people were wearing, but of course, on the sand, everyone was in their regular clothing.

"I was told the people who own the bathing machines provide something suitable for bathing."

"Undoubtedly they do. However, at the table where I was seated, the ladies were all discussing a certain Mrs. Bell, who has posted advertisements in a London fashionable magazine," Hargrove informed her. "She has created some novel garment called a bathing preserver, although whether it is designed to preserve modesty or your life in the sea, I cannot say."

Glynnis looked around again to see those waiting to enter the little huts on wheels. Most if not all of them had some small bag.

"Surely they don't have bathing dresses in their reticules."

"Naturally, I am no expert," Hargrove continued, "but during the picnic, I was forced to listen to talk of these bathing preservers made of such delicate, light materials a lady may carry the garment in her purse. And apparently it comes with an oil skin cap to keep one's hair dry."

"I didn't know any such thing existed," she confessed. Besides, she wouldn't have had the money for such an extravagant item as a dress made to wear merely in the sea. "I shall be fine with whatever the dipper gives me to change into."

"The ladies expressed distaste at wearing something others had worn a hundred times."

Glynnis hadn't thought about that.

At her distraught expression, he added, "But if seawater is a restorative for the body, surely it can also clean a bathing dress."

"Yes, of course," she agreed. Those other ladies were being overly fastidious because they could afford to be. Undeterred, she would take a dip. No one would see her, nor what she was wearing. After all the women were mostly at one end of the beach while the men were taking their dips in the other. Or so she'd understood. Now, while she took another look, she noticed those in the Prince Regent's party were scandalously mixing company.

"Are you coming?" she asked.

Hargrove had halted his progress a few yards from those awaiting their turn in the bathing machines.

"No. I prefer the pristine lakes near my country estate. I'll watch the fun from here."

She smiled at him, thinking he found the whole notion unbecoming, which it probably was. Regardless, there had been some handsome bachelors at the picnic and now they were heading into the sea, so she would do the same. Moreover, from what she understood, the men often wore nothing at all when they climbed down the ladder-rung steps on the other side of the bathing machine, facing the ocean and God.

"Shall I put your reticule in my pocket so it doesn't come to any misfortune?"

"Thank you." After handing it to him, she moved closer to those waiting their turn, knowing the Prince Regent had paid for all his guests. If she waited and came on her own, it would cost her one shilling and six pence by the half hour.

In a very few minutes, she had entered through the front door of the bathing machine and a horse had drawn her into the water before turning to face the beach, at which time, it had been quickly unharnessed. The dipper who'd accompanied her stepped out the back, a middle-aged woman with arms like tree limbs.

"I'll be right here waiting, miss." And then she closed the door.

With only the smallest cut-out square at the top to let light in, Glynnis removed her clothing as swiftly as possible and put it all in the bag they said was oilskin and, thus, waterproof. She put it upon the high shelf for safe-keeping along with her shoes and her hat and took down the folded bathing garment.

Shaking out an ugly dun-colored felt gown, she draped it over her head, tugged it into place before tying it in the front at her neck. With long sleeves and the hem falling to her ankles, she felt sufficiently concealed for her adventure. Then she dragged the bathing hat over her hair, which was already up in a twist.

Opening the door, Glynnis saw so many from the picnic already splashing about. Some were able to swim, most simply stood in the thigh-high water. Some, like her, had a dipper to hold her arm and keep her upright.

"It's most exciting," she said. "This is my first time bathing in the sea."

"You'll love it, miss," her sturdy dipper said, assisting her down the steps. "But you're *dipping*. The men are *bathing*."

"I didn't realize there was a difference."

The woman laughed. "No, miss, there's none at all."

When her toes touched the cool water, Glynnis almost lost her nerve. Since her bathing machine was at the end of the line of them, she could peer around it and still see Hargrove on the beach. He was chatting with another couple who also appeared to have no interest in the restorative water.

"Come along, miss," her dipper beckoned. "It only feels cold at first, and then it'll be fine."

With the woman holding her arm, Glynnis climbed down the rungs that disappeared under the water until she could step off onto the ocean floor. It was a little sandier than the shore, but still mainly pebbles.

"Sink right down," her dipper insisted as one of the other ladies splashed water in her direction. When it hit her sun-drenched cheeks, the sea felt like ice.

"Maybe just for a moment," Glynnis said. "I didn't expect it to be so bracing."

The dipper only laughed. "Good for you. Not merely bracing, but refreshing."

With that, she tugged Glynnis down so quickly, her feet went out from under her and before her bottom hit the pebbles, her head went under.

Stupidly she gasped, got a mouthful of foul seawater, as bad as the mineral water she'd tasted in Bath with Aunt Mim, and came up spluttering.

"There," her dipper said, while Glynnis struggled to void the ocean from her lungs and catch her breath, "I bet you feel warmer now."

She glared at the woman. When she finished coughing, she stood up again, but pulled her hand out of the dipper's reach.

"I think I'll remain here a minute and take it all in, and then I'll be done. I don't need your services any longer, thank you. I don't intend to swim."

The woman looked disappointed, but Glynnis didn't care. There must be some other person the dipper could try to drown.

"Isn't this fun?" said another of the guests from the picnic, and since it was the only time the lady had spoken to Glynnis, she hastened to answer.

"Indeed. Is it your first dip in the sea, too?" she asked her, noting with envy the other lady's pretty cream-colored bathing dress.

"Of course not," the lady gloated. "I come to Brighton to swim with the Prince Regent nearly every year." And then she stared hard at Glynnis's unsightly bathing gown before turning away.

Nearby, another lady floated on her back. It looked easy, but when Glynnis tried, she sank and again coughed up seawater. Suddenly, a man appeared beside her. Not exactly Poseidon in stature and dressed in a gown as ugly as hers, but still he had good breadth to his shoulders underneath the felt. Glynnis couldn't help staring since being close under these circumstances seemed so improper.

"Are you well?" he asked.

"Fine, yes, thank you. I seem to keep swallowing the sea." She gave a little laugh as if her words were witty, while knowing they weren't.

However, at least she had the attention of a man, although his gaze was fixed upon the fabric clinging to her breasts. *Nothing wrong with looking,* she supposed. Besides, with her hair under the cap, and the way she was squinting into the sun, she had no other assets for him to admire.

"You were at the picnic, weren't you?" she asked.

"Indeed. I am Lord Dodd. A pleasure to meet you."

"Thank you, my lord. I am Miss Talbot, daughter of—"

Before she could finish, he lowered himself down into the water.

"Do you swim?" he asked before swimming a few feet away and then back to her, showing off his form.

"No, I don't."

"Perhaps I could assist you if you care to learn."

He had kind brown eyes, and he could be an unmarried man, ripe for plucking. Or was he?

Deciding not to beat about the bush, she asked, "Are you married?"

He appeared startled. "No. Why do you ask?"

She smiled. "If you are to become my swimming tutor, I would hate to anger your lady upon the beach."

"Very thoughtful, but I am a bachelor."

Glynnis wished she could ask him if he was in good standing with his bank or whether he had caused the birth of many babes on the wrong side of the blanket. That would be beyond the pale. Therefore, despite no longer being able to feel her fingers or toes, she decided to let this man give her a swimming lesson.

"Start by crouching in the water thusly," he directed.

She copied what he did.

"And now reach your arm over and out and pull it back toward you. That will propel you forward, especially if you give a few kicks once you get going. You can keep your head up above the water the entire time. Try the other arm."

She did as he told her until her arms were going in and out of the water. At least she was warming up.

"Try to become horizontal upon the sea's surface by pushing off with your legs. Go ahead, I'll help you."

As she followed his instructions, he boldly placed a hand under her stomach and another on her back to keep her from sinking.

"Keep your arms going, Miss Talbot. I will support you."

She was actually swimming. It was invigorating, and she felt the glory of her success.

"Now kick your feet, as if you are fluttering them, up and down."

As she did, Lord Dodd gave her a little push and sent her farther away from the shore. Immediately, Glynnis panicked and let her legs drift downward. The ocean floor had disappeared until finally the tip of her toes touched it. With the water up to her chest, she felt more than a little alarmed.

Glancing toward the beach, her gaze sought out Hargrove, to find him watching intently, with his hand shading his brow under his hat. *Had he witnessed Lord Dodd's lesson?*

Sighing, she would rather have had the viscount's hands upon her, but that was out of her control. Moreover, the wind was picking up, as were the waves rocking everyone nearby. Her enthusiastic tutor paddled toward her.

"A good time to go in, I believe. The winds have shifted. There may be rain by nightfall."

And then his warm hands were upon her again, and a little more easily, Glynnis stretched out, using her arms and legs to propel her the few feet back to the bathing machine. The Prince Regent had already gone back inside his royal one, and a horse was pulling it to the shore.

All around her, ladies and gentlemen were also retiring.

"Will you be at the Castle Hotel assembly room tonight?" Lord Dodd asked.

A shiver went through her, perhaps because he seemed genuinely interested, perhaps because her blood had frozen in her veins.

"Yes, most assuredly I shall."

He offered her his hand to help her up the steps to the open back door of her bathing machine. No gloves, simply wet bare fingers against wet bare fingers. *How thrilling!*

"Thank you for the lesson."

"Perhaps we shall swim again, Miss Talbot. Or at least have a dance tonight."

"I would like that. I will see you later, my lord."

She closed the door and was plunged into darkness until her eyes grew accustomed. *First things first,* she told herself, yanking the string that caused the flag on top of the bathing machine to rise, indicating she was ready to be pulled in. It came away in her hand.

Drats!

To be sure the flag hadn't been raised, she opened the backdoor again and tried to see the roof, but she feared she couldn't without descending into the water and paddling away from the hut.

Not liking that option, especially given the thunderclouds on the horizon and the size of the waves now coming toward her, Glynnis popped back inside and opened the front door A flurry of activity upon the shore caught her eyes.

Two horses were taking turns bringing in each bather, and she was last in the line of machines, so she would simply have to wait. They seemed to be moving quickly and getting people to shore in a hurry. Surely, after the one next to her was taken, hers would be next, flag or no flag.

Seeing Hargrove, she gave him a jaunty wave and closed the door. Despite the waves now rocking the little hut, Glynnis began changing out of her wet dress. First, she removed the cap, displeased to find her hair was actually wet. Taking a moment to squeeze it out, so it wouldn't drip on her gown, next she whipped the felt bathing dress up and over her head.

Already shivering, she worked quickly, dragging her bag off the shelf and opening it. Sure enough, her clothing had not a drop of seawater on it. Feeling pleased and looking forward to being dry and warm, she lay everything on the small bench and had just started to draw on a stocking when a wave crashed against the back steps. Glancing out the door she'd left open for the light it provided, she could see how choppy and gray the sea had become. A shard of alarm sliced through her.

Luckily, she could hear and then felt a horse being harnessed to the front of her bathing machine. Another wave came over the narrow rungs of the steps, and this time flooded the interior covering her feet.

"Oh, bother," she said, as one of her stockings was now soaked. Recognizing the good sense of the Brighton bathing machine's architect in making the back door open inward, instead of having to lean out, Glynnis had only to give the door a shove and it closed. Quickly, she latched it and, feeling secure, began to draw on her other stocking.

A moment later, however, the sea rushed in under the door and flooded the little hut up to her ankles.

"Blast it all!" she exclaimed. At the same time, she was relieved to feel the hut in motion.

Then too many things happened at once for her to comprehend. She heard a booming clap of thunder that made her jump. A man shouted. The front end of the bathing machine lifted, and she knew at once the horse had spooked. Then the hut turned sideways to the shore.

In the next instant, one of the large wheels either went down a rut, snapped, or perhaps it encountered one of the infernal small boulders the dippers claimed were *mere pebbles*. In any case, one side of her bathing machine lurched lower than the other, and she was flung against the wall while seawater seeped in.

CHAPTER NINE

G lynnis could hear yelling, which seemed uncalled for since she was close to the shore. It wasn't as if she were out on the ocean in a tiny boat, capsizing to her imminent demise.

However, an especially large wave crashed against her bathing machine. More slowly than she thought possible, it began to tip farther and farther, causing her to scramble up the slanting floor. She watched as all her clothing fell into the water, along with her boots and her bonnet from the shelf.

"Dammit!" It felt good to swear aloud, knowing no one could hear her.

Water flowed in from the corner of the hut and under the door. The gathering weight of it snapped the smaller front wheel until the bathing machine went completely over onto its side, and Glynnis along with it. Worse than that, the window hole in the roof was now underwater, allowing the rest of the sea to rush in to the inky blackness.

The horse—still attached as she could hear while her head was above water—was frantically pulling and dragging but going nowhere. And then somehow, it had gone, perhaps cut free so it didn't drown.

Drown!

Panic sliced through her as the chilly water, seeming even colder in the darkness, rose swiftly higher. On its side, the seven-foot-long cabin was only as high as its width. Five feet she would guess, maybe four. And it was filling with water, even with both doors closed.

Scrambling toward the wall which was playing the part of a ceiling, she feared the hut would be completely underwater in another few seconds.

JAMES HAD NEVER CARED for bathing in the sea, at least not with others splashing around. If he were going to have a hearty swim, he liked doing so in a clear lake, stretching out over the yards at a good clip and back again.

He also most assuredly didn't like the feel of his suit becoming soaked with salt water, but that was precisely what would have to happen as he watched Miss Talbot's infernal bathing machine tip over. No one else was rushing to her rescue. All the dippers seemed more concerned with the blasted horse, which was undoubtedly an expensive part of their daily endeavor.

For his part, he could not imagine a world in which the saucy chit didn't return from her little ocean adventure to smile at him and twinkle those deep-brown eyes.

Tossing his hat up the beach, he rushed the few yards into the cool water where the submerged hut rested on its side. Both the sea and the hut came up to his shoulders. The front door had floated open by his knees, and it was easy enough to take a deep breath, dive down, and swim inside.

Almost at once, he collided with Miss Talbot's figure and grabbed hold. *By God, she was bare as a needle!*

Hauling her against him and dragging her upward, they were both bobbing above the water, catching their breath in the small, dark space.

"Don't panic," he told her.

"I assure you, I am not, but my clothing has all floated away," Miss Talbot said, and plainly her teeth were chattering. More than that, where his fingers touched her slippery-smooth skin, he could feel her shivering.

"I hope that hideous bathing costume has disappeared, too," he said, trying to make light of a somewhat frightening situation.

"That is not at all amusing," she hissed. "I shall owe the woman money for it!"

"Can you be serious? That hardly seems important."

Suddenly, the entire contraption moved, and he knew they were being dragged closer to shore. Light was even then coming in, meaning the water was below the level of the open door.

So close, she glanced at him, water dripping off her lashes and her hair, which was floating all round her. Unfortunately, her lips, usually a pretty shade of pink, were turning a little blue.

His hands ran up and down her arms to warm her before his fingers skimmed her waist, drawing her closer. Somehow, her body was curling toward him, and he clasped each cheek of her round bottom, tucking her hips against his.

"It's like I've caught my own mermaid," he quipped.

They stared at one another in silence. Then before he let himself think better of it, he leaned forward and kissed her.

The salty kiss didn't last long as they were jarred by the hut's movement across the pebbled seabed, and he didn't know if it helped her to feel any warmer, but heat had certainly shot through him. Holding her bare, silken body, he was fiercely aroused at a plainly inconvenient time.

Drawing back, he opened his eyes as she did, bobbing before him, and then, to his amazement—and gratitude— her breasts became visible above the lowering seawater, showing him her nipples like ripe cherries, pert and dark.

"Hargrove," she warned, but her tone was breathless, and she didn't release the hold she had on his arms.

"If you swim in the sea like a fish," he said, "you must prepare to be caught upon a man's pole."

Thinking himself rather clever—*especially as his cock was stiffer than a fishing pole, more like a flag pole!*—his remark was met with a rolling of her eyes.

"You must give me your coat at least."

"Sadly, my coat will cover your sweet arse," he said, "but not the front of you."

And as the water level dropped, he could see more and more of her, including a trim waist and the flare of her hips. She was quite glorious, but he didn't want the rest of Brighton getting an eyeful.

Looking around the cabin, he saw the infernal felt bathing dress floating nearby.

"Put this on again." Before she could protest, he tugged it over her head and helped her get her arms into the long sleeves."

"Oh!" she yelped.

"What is it?" He had probably tugged her hair by mistake.

"I felt something brush against my ankle."

That gave him pause, but he said, "Nonsense!"

A moment later, he thought he felt something graze his leg, too.

"I think we should get out of here and not wait for them to drag us up the beach. With all this heavy water, it will take them forever."

Turning in the small space, he ordered her, "Take a deep breath," and then put his hand on the top of her wet head. Quickly ducking her under the sideways door, he gave her a shove ahead of him before following. Both of them only had to be under the water for a few seconds.

He swam toward shore, tugging her along while she kicked and flailed her hands, until he could get his feet under him.

"You can stand now, Miss Talbot," he advised, but she seemed incapable of hearing him and continued to thrash. Sighing, he bent down and tried to lift her, thinking it an extremely chivalrous thing to do. He would be a hero, indeed, if he carried her from the water.

'Zounds! A wet woman in an ugly felt bathing dress was heavy! Of course, the ugliness of the garment had nothing to do with it, but it added to the general unpleasantness of the whole experience, as far as he was concerned.

Eventually, he managed to help her to her feet, and they walked out of the sea with his arm around her waist. Away from the water, he lowered her to the pebbly sand where she closed her eyes and breathed hard.

"Shall I perform artificial respiration?" asked a man whom James knew to be Lord Dodd. "Mouth-to-mouth," he added, "as recommended by the Paris Academy of Sciences, eh, wot-wot?"

Before James could answer, a dipper chimed in.

"Just toss her onto one of these horses, stomach down, her limbs a-hanging. Run it along the beach, and she'll be breathing in no time."

Miss Talbot's eyes popped open at hearing those words, and then she sat up.

A few people cheered.

Gazing up at James, she said, "Take me away from here, please."

He nodded, and pulled her to her feet. A few more people cheered.

"I hope I will still see you at the dance tonight, Miss Talbot," Lord Dodd said, and James was ready to send him flying with a punch to the nose.

"If the lady is up to it," he said. Undoubtedly, irritation had taken hold of him due to the impossibly uncomfortable sensation of wet hose, shoes, pants and everything else. He longed to strip it all off.

"Let's go," he said to her, thinking Miss Talbot's complexion looked good all things considering, but she was still shivering. He thought to remove his wet coat to drape around her, but that was senseless.

Instead, with her arm tucked under his, he started across the beach.

"My gown!" she suddenly exclaimed. "I was going to gather all my lost clothes, but you shoved me out of the bathing machine."

Could she be blaming him for the loss?

"I cannot believe I've lost my parasol and my clothes in one day," she continued.

"At least you didn't lose your life," he pointed out.

Suddenly, there was a cry behind them to wait. It was a female dipper. "This was still caught in the bathing machine," the woman said, and she handed Miss Talbot a sodden mass, on top of which was her ruined bonnet.

James examined it with her. "That's not your gown, surely."

"No," she agreed. "My stays and a chemise. Oh, and a single glove. Hurrah!"

"At least it's something," he pointed out.

Showing better sport than he would have imagined, she plonked the bonnet on top of her tangled wet hair.

"Thank you," she told the dipper before turning away.

"Here now," the woman added. "I'll need that bathing dress back. Or you can buy it from me."

James watched Glynnis halt. Then she looked skyward a moment, collecting herself. Finally, she said, "I assure you I have no interest in buying this fine garment, nor am I stealing it. As soon as I am properly clothed, I will return it to you."

"Well," the woman began.

"I shall vouch for her," James said, trying not to laugh at the ridiculous notion of Miss Talbot wanting to retain the hideous, shapeless frock.

He took her elbow, but they got hardly more than a couple feet farther up the beach when for the second time, she yelped.

"A pebble," she said, "right under the sole of my foot."

It seemed to be the straw that broke Miss Talbot's proverbial camel's back as she realized yet another loss.

"My shoes," she moaned, turning tear-filled eyes up to him. "Where are my shoes?"

He glanced back at the dipper.

"Did her shoes wash up?" he asked the woman.

Immediately, she called over her shoulder to one of her associates.

"Did you find this lady's shoes?"

After a brief hullabaloo, in which the word "shoes" was called up and down the beach, a boy ran over with a single leather slipper.

"Where's the other one?" Miss Talbot asked.

The boy shrugged. "Dunno, miss. Only seen this one."

James watched her take it with a shaking hand. Her lips were looking blue again, and she was shivering more fiercely.

"You have other shoes, don't you?" he asked, thinking it best to get her indoors quickly.

Looking miserable, she nodded. Wordlessly, she handed him the rest of her dripping bundle before she bent over, drew up the gown and slipped on the shoe, giving him a nice view of her slender ankle.

Glancing away, down at the garments, somehow the stays were on top again. He swallowed.

"How mortifying!" she exclaimed, snatching it back from him and beginning the trek over the pebbles again toward the street.

James remembered his hat.

"Just a moment, Miss Talbot," and he jogged back to where it still lay upon the pebbles and set it on his head. When he rejoined her, he felt less undressed.

"At least my hat was saved," he crowed, then wished he'd kept his mouth closed as her lips pressed momentarily into a thin line of dismay.

"What about my reticule I gave you for safekeeping?" she demanded, then held her hand out.

He blinked. Reaching into his coat pocket, he withdrew it. Slowly, he handed her the soggy purse. The fine silk, he warranted, was ruined.

"I hope as with your other reticle there was nothing of much value in it."

She gave a massively long sigh.

Just as they climbed to street level, she struggled to tug on her single glove and slide the strap of the reticule onto her wrist while still holding her stays and chemise.

"That's better," she declared.

He would rather be flayed alive than tell her it wasn't. In fact, she looked even stranger in her bedraggled state, her hair hanging snarled down her back, limping slightly because of the single shoe, wearing a bathing dress, a single white lace glove, and a reticule dangling from her arm.

Poor Miss Talbot!

GLYNNIS CONSIDERED HER LOSSES as she hobbled along the rather rough track atop the cliffs toward the Old Ship— a day dress, shoes, a bonnet, a purse, and stockings. And maybe her stays were ruined, too! And the loss of her parasol to boot.

She feared she would have to move from her current lodging into the Lanes, as the center of Brighton's old section was known. Not only flint cottages which housed the workers servicing the more prestigious areas of Castle Square, East Street, North Street, and, of course, the Steyne, the Lanes were also home to brick and cobble buildings filled with public houses and small shops. Perhaps she could get a room above the Cricketers Arms or the Black Lion, although she wouldn't be able to tell anyone in the Prince Regent's group of friends where she was staying.

A sob welled up in her throat, but since Hargrove was still by her side, she shoved it down again. The viscount had grabbed her person most improperly inside the overturned bathing machine, although she'd been relieved to see him while still deciding how terrifying her situation was. When his head had appeared in her underwater grotto, she knew at once she was not going to die.

Nevertheless, instead of making her all tingly with his caresses and then shocking her with a kiss as he'd done, she dearly wished he had helped her reclaim her dress and stockings before they had been swept out to sea.

Yet that kiss! It had been rather spectacular, warming her completely, at least for a moment. Looking at him out of the corner of her eye, she wondered how he could take such liberties without a by-your-leave beforehand, nor an apology after.

The answer was obvious—he was decidedly a rake, one who didn't mind kissing an engaged woman.

Perhaps he wouldn't mind helping her, too, yet she couldn't imagine how. The one thing she could never do was stoop to asking for money. Naturally, she would *accept* it if offered, but she would never lower herself by asking.

Besides, how could she ask anything of him while appearing so bedraggled, like something the cat dragged in? After all, Hargrove looked in shabby shape despite his dry hat, so she could only imagine how wretched was her own appearance. She wished she'd never thought dipping in the sea would be a good way to attract a man.

True, Lord Dodd had expressed an interest, but it had cost her greatly to secure a dance later that evening. *Almost her life!* And she couldn't go anywhere that night unless she paid the hotel concierge extra to supply her a hot bath. Her account at the Old Ship was growing to dizzying heights.

She spared her rescuer another glance. Lord Hargrove was whistling to fill the silence in his quaint, off-key manner. And then she had a most outrageous and wonderful thought.

"How many bedrooms do you have in your rented house, my lord?"

"Three," he answered without hesitation, before swinging his attention to her. "Why?"

"Do you have plenty of hot water?" she asked.

"Hot water?" He looked perplexed.

"Yes, for baths and such. The inn is woefully short of it. I fear if I have another cold bath, I shall become ill." She coughed delicately before adding, "You may have noticed my delicate health of late."

Frowning, he nodded. "I wondered at your pale complexion and your fainting spells. At first I attributed both to a lack of appetite. However, when I saw you eat so heartily, I knew it wasn't lacking, merely being ignored."

"Not ignored." Glynnis coughed again and looked at him from under her lashes. "I haven't felt well enough to eat at the proper hours. I am entirely unsettled. And the inn is drafty."

"That's a pity. I will speak with the manager if you wish. I'm sure we can get you a hot bath."

"Perhaps," she mused, then cocked her head. "I was just thinking that you have so much space while I have only a room. If I were to move into your house, I could have all the comforts of home and remain under your protection as the Prince Regent requested."

She'd hoped the suggestion would at least appeal to his baser nature. He might be able to capture another glimpse of her bare skin, which he seemed to have greatly appreciated inside the overturned hut.

Doing her best to seem appealing despite the ugly felt gown and her bedraggled state, she offered him a winsome smile.

For a moment, given his expression, Glynnis thought she might have succeeded in gaining access to the viscount's plummy residence.

CHAPTER TEN

"Absolutely not!" Lord Hargrove said. "That's out of the question."

"But why?" Glynnis was astonished a reputed rake, a rum buck, a libertine of the first order would refuse to put up a woman in his home. It must be the cursed bathing dress!

"Because as swiftly as the starling flies, I would be accused of ruining you, and we would be forced to marry. And even if we married, you would be looked down upon for the rest of your life as a woman lacking in common decency."

Glynnis pondered both his objections and wondered how to get around them.

"What if you hired a chaperone?" she asked.

"On short notice? Impossible."

He was probably right.

"What if we don't tell anyone? And when my fiancé arrives, he, too, stays in your home, which will prohibit any accusations against you, and even prove my continued virtue. If he accepts the situation, it would seem to have been prearranged. You could be a proper guardian, and I, your charge."

He gaped at her. "I am not a fit guardian for a woman of your age, and you know it. Nor is that what Prinny intended. You shouldn't even be considering such a thing. I cannot imagine the other thoughts in your pretty head. What's more, I don't wish to find out. But you may cease any designs upon moving into my house. It will not happen."

She could tell his mind was made up and fell silent.

Passing the porter, standing guard just inside the entrance to the Old Ship, she endured his long stare while she dripped across the foyer, along with Hargrove. They went directly to the concierge's desk. Mr. Melton rushed around it to greet them.

"Whatever has befallen you?" he asked. "Or is it you who has fallen, directly into the sea?"

Then he laughed. This was not his first attempt at humor since Glynnis had arrived, but she sincerely hoped it would be his last. She might demand they reduce her bill to compensate for having to bear it.

By Hargrove's expression, he didn't find the man funny either.

"This lady had an incident with an overturned bathing machine," her rescuer said. "She will need a hot bath at once. If she doesn't get it, she may become ill, and I would not want to hear of your hotel causing such a thing."

"Of course, my lord." Mr. Melton stood straighter. "A deep tub will be taken up to her room at once and filled with the hottest water."

Glynnis sighed. She might as well add to her bill. "I also need the services of your laundress for my garments that ended up in the saltwater."

"I'll take them now, Miss Talbot."

Feeling a little humiliated, she handed over her linen shift and stays.

The man glanced at her soggy bonnet atop her head, but obviously, he couldn't give that to the laundress, nor her single glove. When the concierge surveyed what he held, his cheeks flushed.

"I'm   not   certain   your . . . um . . . that is . . . undergarments, I mean the cotton shift, certainly, but your . . . um . . . corset . . . it has wood in it, has it not?"

Her cheeks must be scarlet. To think she was discussing her stays with a man while another listened.

"That is a corded corset without boning or wood. Except for the busk. Thank you for reminding me."

She reached over and withdrew the slender wooden dowel from its sheath nestled between the bust cups. Her busk seemed to be as solid as ever, undamaged by its short time in the ocean.

Both men were staring at her.

"I believe it to be made from juniper," she said into the uncomfortable silence.

Mr. Melton cleared his throat. "I shall get these laundered at once." He paused to look at her salty dripping gown. "And your bathing dress, miss?"

"No," she told him without hesitation. "I shall not pay to launder this, thank you. When it dries, I will return it to the dippers on the beach."

"How will you dry it?" he asked, looking down at the puddles forming on the carpet around both her and Lord Hargrove's feet. "There is nowhere in your room to hang a dripping garment. And we can't have you dangling it out the window of the hotel."

"I wouldn't dream of doing so," she declared as a shiver wracked her entire body.

Despite the man's promise, Glynnis felt no closer to getting her hot bath and feared she never would, not if she had to wait outside for the bathing dress to dry.

"I'll escort the lady to her room," Hargrove volunteered obviously recognizing her distress, "and she can change out of the dress and give it to me. I'll return it to the dippers myself."

"Would you?" she asked, and thought she had never been fonder of anyone in her life. "That's settled then. Please order the bath, Mr. Melton, without delay."

"Yes, miss," but his gaze followed them up the stairs, concerned either with damp spots on the hotel floor or with the inn's reputation over a single man going with her to her room.

"He's thinking wicked thoughts," she said over her shoulder.

"Well, he can stop thinking them. I will stay in the hallway while you undress. And do hurry. The salt is starting to dry inside my suit and is making me itchy."

So grateful for his assistance, she didn't even smile at the notion of salt in his breeches while she led him to her room.

"I will be quick. I promise." And she opened her door and closed it behind her.

With an odd feeling, knowing Hargrove was directly on the other side, she removed the bathing dress.

Donning her dressing gown, Glynnis had nothing to put the felt monstrosity into, so she simply opened the door and handed the sandy, salty, sodden mess to him.

"I very much appreciate your taking care of this," she told him, feeling daring standing there barefooted with nothing on but a whisper of cream-colored satin tied at her waist.

Naturally, his gaze took in her appearance head to toe, but he'd seen so much of her earlier, she hardly thought it mattered.

Except the light of interest in his eyes told her otherwise. His appreciation of her was evident.

When he didn't speak, she couldn't help wondering if he would kiss her again. Given her scantily clad body and the proximity of privacy behind her in the shape of a soft clean bed, she wondered where it would lead.

His dark blue eyes held hers, and she almost convinced herself in the space of a heartbeat that he was asking permission. For precisely what, she was unsure, yet she found herself debating whether she was prepared to give a rake unfettered access to her person when there was no one to force his hand to marriage.

After all, that was the only reason to let a man kiss her, wasn't it?

Suddenly she heard footsteps on the stairs, and Hargrove stepped back when the desired bathtub came into view, carried by a man with his sleeves rolled up and his eyes bulging under his burden. Over his shoulder was an oilskin.

A good-sized tub, indeed! Glynnis was grateful she would be able to submerge to her shoulders. She moved out of the way so the hotel employee could deposit it in the middle of her bed chamber. The man was followed by two women, struggling under the weight of a bucket in each of their hands, and the water was plainly steaming.

"I'll leave you to it, Miss Talbot," Hargrove said now the moment was lost. "Before the water loses any measure of heat."

Had she wasted an opportunity? They could have been caught in a passionate embrace by the hotel staff. Looking at the sweating man and the red-faced women, Glynnis doubted any of the three would have been prepared to demand Hargrove behave honorably. More likely, they would have simply ignored the inappropriate behavior the way good employees pretended not to see so very many infractions.

"More water is coming, miss," the man said, disappearing quickly back down the stairs while the serving girls emptied their buckets into the tub.

"I will collect you at eight for the Castle Hotel assembly," he promised.

"Thank you."

WHAT WAS HE THINKING? James had lingered at Miss Talbot's door and would have tried to kiss her again if the bathtub hadn't arrived.

He lounged in a deep tub in his own bathroom at his house, and tried not to picture her naked and slippery down the street. *Impossible!* She was all he could think of after having had his hands on her bare skin once that day.

Knowing she had a fiancé and had been a ruthless husband-hunter should be enough of a deterrence. Yet she wouldn't be the worst wife in the world. She had a lovely face, a luscious figure, and a quick wit. Not to mention a hearty appetite.

That thought made him chuckle to himself.

Miss Talbot probably also had a robust dowry, being a viscount's only daughter, although he'd heard the son was something of a nightmare. Regardless, if James were interested in marrying, he could imagine her in the role of Lady Hargrove—except he would never know if she'd had a particular interest in him over any other jackanape.

He recalled the man at his club in London and the other one in Lady Sullivan's billiards room. Both had been treated to Miss Talbot's wiles. It was clear she'd had a singular plan for being compromised, and cared not a whit who did it.

Sighing, he decided he should let her go to her Welsh fiancé and hope again the man turned up quickly before James did something stupid, like bed the chit.

But those nipples! And her lips! And her eyes!

He sank under the water to soak his head and stop himself from musing upon her.

A knock at his door was a welcome interruption The house had come with a staff, who were performing adequately, although he missed his own butler.

"Yes," he called out to Mr. Sparks.

"An urgent message for you, my lord, from the Prince Regent."

James sneered. Even in his tub, he wasn't safe from Prinny's tyranny.

"Come in."

The door opened and Mr. Sparks entered, keeping his eyes averted from the tub, even as James sat up sloshing water onto the tiled floor.

Shaking dry one hand, he took the missive from the silver tray, and the butler retreated. The note was brief:

Not feeling sparkish.
Canceled the Castle until tomorrow.

James stared at the squiggly mess that was Prinny's signature.

Canceled the Castle?

He hoped word had been sent to all the other establishments offering evening entertainment for some of them closed on nights when the Regent was holding a large event elsewhere. They ought to be given the chance to reopen.

Quite shoddy of Prinny to do something so last minute. But that was the prerogative of royalty, James supposed. Before sinking down into the bath once again, he dropped the letter over the side onto the floor, unmindful of how the ink ran as soon as it encountered his splashed bathwater.

Belatedly, when clean, dry, and seated in his own dining room enjoying a meal while reading the newspaper, James thought of Miss Talbot. *Had anyone notified her of the change in plans?*

Doubtful. Knowing Prinny, he'd sent his message out to a few key guests, expecting them to disseminate the information. The rest would turn up at the Castle Hotel to be sorely disappointed. Since Miss Talbot expected him at her hotel to escort her, she would be saved that embarrassment as long as she stayed put. Yet he hated to think of her getting dressed and waiting for him. He wouldn't like to be considered the type of clod who left a woman in the lurch.

Finishing his repast, James hurried back upstairs and let his valet ready him for nothing more than walking a few hundred yards to Miss Talbot's hotel and telling her their evening was postponed. Then he might head to the house of that flash mollisher with the luscious curves and enjoy a quick roll. *What was her name?*

When he knocked on Miss Talbot's door a little after eight, he'd had the uncomfortable experience of the nighttime porter giving him a sideways glance when he went toward the staircase. Since this was most definitely not a brothel, he supposed single men coming and going was unusual if they weren't registered guests.

Miss Talbot opened the door, and James could honestly say she took his breath away. Dressed to the nines, as his mother called it when she was at her finest. Nine what, he had no idea, but he knew a beautiful woman when he saw one.

Wearing a deep mauve gown with a lacy gray bodice and little cap sleeves that left her slender arms on display, he wouldn't mind starting at her wrist and kissing his way up to her delicate shoulder.

"Your fiancé is missing out on a vision of loveliness tonight," he declared.

"Thank you. And you cut a bosh figure, my lord." She turned from him. "Let me get my shawl and my very last reticule. It's already after eight, and I wouldn't want to be too late in case the champagne has been poured."

Then James recalled why he was there.

"I am afraid there is no champagne tonight. Prinny has called off the assembly."

She blinked up at him, looking immediately disappointed, and he realized he didn't want to leave her so finely dressed and go elsewhere—not even to tup a welcoming whore.

After all they were both ready for a night out, and the storm had passed and gone somewhere farther inland to the east. It would be a shame to waste the fair weather.

That was the only possible reason he said his next words.

"Why don't we go to the theatre?"

Immediately, her expression brightened. Before he could even consider retracting his invitation, she stepped out of her room and pulled the door closed behind her. Then she took hold of his arm and looked up at him.

"I feel so much better than when you left me earlier." She squeezed against his arm, causing her breasts to nearly escape the top of her décolletage. "And I'm exceedingly pleased to go to the theatre. Will there be food there? Or will you take me to supper afterward?"

He almost laughed. There was that hearty appetite.

"Sometime this evening, we shall find nourishment," he assured her. Even though he had just eaten, he wouldn't deprive Miss Talbot lest she faint again.

They made their way down the stairs, and James made sure to nod at the porter so the judgmental lout would recall how quickly he'd vacated the premises with the lady, not lingering for even a kiss at her door.

While strolling along Ship Street, he told her the little he knew from Prinny.

"I hope he holds the assembly tomorrow night," she said. "I have yet to go inside the Castle Hotel."

"And if you don't see it soon, you won't see it at all," James told her.

"Whatever do you mean?

"I believe it is the end for the Castle."

They turned right onto North Street. At the end of it, one could make out the distinctive roof of the Castle Tavern, as he thought of it, though it was, indeed, a hotel and public rooms, too.

"It looks to be in good state of repair from the outside," she said.

"Oh, it is," he assured her. "A confirmed rumor has it that Prinny is buying the Castle to enlarge his already stupendous home."

"You don't sound pleased."

Best if he didn't speak ill of the prince even in front of a woman of no influence. Despite not spending much time in Brighton, James thought it to be a damnable shame for the Regent to snatch up the well-liked business if he meant only to demolish it.

"The passing of an era," he quipped.

She laughed, covering her mouth with her glove.

"I mean no offense, but the building is reputed to be about sixty years old, hardly a classical antiquity. I wouldn't mourn its loss as, say, the Tower of London or Windsor Castle, would you?"

He shrugged, and they turned left onto New Road and came upon the Theatre Royal with its line of slender Corinthian columns heralding its entrance.

"Regardless, if Prinny regains his spark, then there shall probably be a ball in one of the Castle's assembly rooms tomorrow. It may be the very last one, and you and I shall attend."

She beamed at him, and he gestured for her to precede him when the porter opened the theatre's door.

The antechamber was cool with marble floors and impressive statues, reminiscent of the theatre at Covent Garden. Here, too, the antiquity she'd made fun of regarding the jolly Castle was equally false as the building dated back only to 1807, and the life-sized Greek-style sculptures were modern representations of comedy and tragedy.

A grand staircase and twin side stairs led to the boxes, as well as the prince's private saloon and box, and a lounge upstairs. They toured everything in the crowded theatre, as James guessed it would be. With Prinny canceling the premiere event, Brighton's quality folk had sought out any open venue. Inside the oblong-shaped auditorium, there was nary a vacant seat in the pit, nor in the boxes.

Naturally, there was always room for a viscount and his guest. Thus, in short order, James had the singular experience of sitting alone in a second-tier box with a lady who had no chaperone. *Absolutely outrageous!* But she seemed not the least concerned, taking in the setting like a curious child and becoming even more excited when the performance was revealed to be William Congreve's *Love for Love*.

"Not that I don't appreciate Shakespeare or even Sophocles," Miss Talbot assured him, drawing out a fan from her reticule and opening it with a satisfying swish, "but they are sometimes so very . . . ," she trailed off, looking pensive.

"Dramatic," he supplied.

"Exactly," she agreed. "And while it is soul-cleansing and heart-breaking to witness a good production of *Hamlet*, it's also a pleasure to be entertained by farce and comedy, is it not?"

"A time and place for both," James said, finding himself in full agreement. The seaside theatre didn't seem a place to watch the eventual piling on of bodies that ended many of Shakespeare's tragic plays.

During the intermission, she seemed to be as thrilled to enjoy wine and sugar biscuits as she had the first three acts. James couldn't take his eyes off of her as she bubbled over with commentary on the play and the actors. She made him laugh more than the play itself.

A male voice interrupted their intimate gathering of two.

"There she is, my swimming pupil, Miss Talbot."

CHAPTER ELEVEN

"Miss Talbot, you are an absolute vision of loveliness and have obviously recovered to splendid good health from your earlier ordeal."

Lord Dodd had come upon them and spoke without first acknowledging James, which immediately put his back up. Plus, the man's words were overly flowery, even oily, smacking of insincerity if he ever heard it.

"Yes, my lord, I am well," Miss Talbot replied, seeming to welcome Dodd's intrusion. "Thanks to my friend, Lord Hargrove."

Her friend? Is that what they were? He supposed she was correct. They enjoyed a temporary friendship secured by Prinny until Aberavon arrived to claim her, or James left.

At last, Dodd's attention took him in. "You were there at the beach, too, weren't you?"

James rolled his eyes. The man very well knew he'd been there. What's more, he could tell Dodd was sizing him up as a rival. Letting him think James was interested in her might provide Miss Talbot with a measure of safety from other bucks. On the other hand, when her fiancé turned up and people assumed she had been free with her favors, her reputation might suffer. Thus, he decided to warn the man off.

"In the absence of Miss Talbot's *fiancé*, I am happy to provide her with my protection, be it at the beach or here at the theatre."

Dodd blinked, taking in James's meaning.

"I see. How magnanimous of you to look after another man's lady," Dodd said.

"Lord Hargrove has been most helpful," Miss Talbot agreed, making James feel like a spinster chaperone.

"Where is the fortunate fiancé?" Dodd asked, and James wished he would take himself off somewhere, like into a deep well. He'd been enjoying his private time with her more than he cared to admit.

"Lord Aberavon shall reach Brighton sometime soon, I am sure," she said, sounding unconcerned. "Are you enjoying the performance?"

"Very much so. And you?"

"It is delightful," she said enthusiastically. "Are you here alone? Where are you seated?"

To James's horror, when Miss Talbot found out Lord Dodd was by himself, she invited him to join them for the remainder of the play.

"After all, there are empty seats in our box. I don't think anyone would mind if you switched your location."

James most certainly minded! After the past couple of days, he had thought she held him in a higher regard than merely any old nob. Yet it seemed she didn't mind the company of mangy, too-smooth Dodd.

"It would be my pleasure, Miss Talbot," Dodd said, as James knew he would. The theatre manager rang a bell, and people began to shuffle back into the auditorium.

To James's surprise, the interloper offered her his arm.

To his greater surprise, she took it.

"Let's go," she said, looking absolutely cheerful, even when Dodd shot James a vexing grin over his shoulder.

Suddenly, James wished they *were* seeing *Hamlet*. Then when the lights went down, if he timed it correctly, when he strangled Dodd no one would hear his cries blended with those of the actors. *Pity!*

GLYNNIS COULDN'T BELIEVE HER good fortune. First, she was escorted by Hargrove, making for a tingly and pleasant evening, and then Lord Dodd, a potential suitor, joined them.

Moreover, his presence seemed to bother Hargrove, making her wonder if that avenue to marriage was still open to her. Brighton was suddenly treating her well.

The remaining two acts were as good as the first, and she hadn't laughed so much in a long time. Terror over one's future tended to make one less inclined to frivolity and laughter. And having a handsome man on either side of her only increased her pleasure.

"Gentlemen, that was wonderful," she said, rising to her feet after the actors last bow and the applause was dying out. "I wish it hadn't ended so soon."

"The evening doesn't have to come to an end," Lord Dodd said. "There must be some place we can go."

"I wish you'd go to . . ."

Glynnis was certain Hargrove was muttering something rude.

"Lord Hargrove and I were going to take a late supper."

"Where could you possibly go?" Lord Dodd asked, looking perplexed. "With the fairer sex involved, options are limited to the hotel dining rooms or the public houses. None of the other restaurants will allow you entrance."

Glynnis looked at Hargrove. *What was his intent?*

"The Old Ship dining room," he proposed.

She wished it wasn't so easy for him to put it on her account.

"Perhaps the Castle Hotel?" she suggested.

"Nonsense," Lord Dodd said before Hargrove could respond. "We shall go to my house. It's on the Steyne."

Was it Glynnis's imagination or was Lord Dodd puffing up his chest like a stuffed partridge? It was sweet he wanted to impress her, even humorous, but Hargrove didn't look amused.

"We wouldn't want to intrude on short notice," Hargrove began, appearing all mulish and frowning.

"It's the least I can do," Lord Dodd insisted, "after you allowed me to join you in your box." He spread his hands in supplication. "I was going to eat anyway."

"But three instead of one," Hargrove pointed out. "That can put a cook in a very bad humor. Besides, it is not in the lady's best interest to be alone with two men in private should it be discovered."

Glynnis pursed her lips. He was determined to ruin this, and yet she was even more resolute in her wish to go to Lord Dodd's home. He was a perfect catch from what she knew. Granted, that was very little, but he was good-looking and well-spoken, and with a rented house on the Steyne, he had enough money to make her happy.

Or at least he might be able to remove that persistent nagging fear of insecurity she'd had since about the age of seven when she'd overheard her parents fretting over funds.

Before she could attempt to overthrow Hargrove's reservations, Lord Dodd smiled and fixed everything.

"It will be four instead of two actually. My aunt is staying with me, enjoying the sea air. She'll enjoy having your company and will make the perfect chaperone. What's more, I have an excellent cook and can guarantee it will be a better meal than at a hotel."

With that settled, they began the short walk to the Steyne.

"Why didn't your aunt accompany you to the theatre?" Hargrove wanted to know, still sounding testy.

"She has only recently arrived. The journey from London left her spent."

Glynnis pictured an elderly aunt sitting by the fire in Lord Dodd's drawing room, her feet on an ottoman and a glass of sherry in her hand.

"I look forward to meeting her."

However, a few minutes later when they entered the drawing room of his three-story home, the satin-clad woman who was stretched out on the sofa with her stockinged feet dangling over the arm at one end was anything but elderly.

"The aunt" was probably about the same age as Hargrove and Lord Dodd. Looking up with a wolfish smile at seeing company, the woman lowered her newspaper. Moreover, she didn't stand or even have the sense to look discomfited when being caught in a state of deshabille.

Glynnis glanced uncertainly toward Lord Dodd.

"There you are Isabelle," he greeted, as if he'd misplaced her. "These are my new friends. They've come to dine with us."

With her glittering glance taking them both in, the woman slowly swung her legs to the floor.

"I'm thrilled we have company," she said. Her tone was welcoming, yet her gaze swiftly passed over Glynnis to rest upon Hargrove. *Who could blame her?*

Then the so-called Isabelle held out her hand to Lord Dodd, who took it and drew her to her feet.

"Introduce them to me, Hugh," she said softly.

"This is Miss Talbot and that is Lord Hargrove."

"I don't believe I've met you before," she said to Hargrove. "Either of you," she amended, glancing again at Glynnis.

"No," Hargrove agreed. "I would have remembered."

Glynnis didn't like the way Isabelle and Hargrove were taking one another's measure.

"Were you in London of late?" Glynnis asked her.

"Not recently," she said, and nothing else, keeping her attention on the viscount.

"I hope we are not intruding," he said.

"No, of course not. As I said, I'm thrilled." With that, she let go her hold on Lord Dodd and moved directly to Hargrove, wrapped her arm around his and said, "I believe the meal is ready to be served. Let's forgo wine here and have it with our dinner."

And then with her free hand, she gestured for him to escort her.

Glynnis couldn't help but notice how Isabelle pressed her bosom against Hargrove's forearm. Then Lord Dodd took her arm.

"I knew she would be pleased," he said.

"Your *aunt*?" Glynnis queried, unable to help from sounding doubtful when trailing behind the swaying backside of the full-figured blonde woman.

"By marriage," he explained. "We don't share a drop of blood. It's a long story. Difficult to believe I am her nephew. Wot-wot."

"Yes," Glynnis agreed. "Difficult indeed." Thinking it rude to pry too far, she asked no more than, "What is her surname? Perhaps I know her family."

"Montrose," he said without hesitation. "Quite a few of her family about."

Glynnis nodded although she didn't know any of the woman's family. They took their seats at a long table, laid for four.

"I keep it ready for company," Lord Dodd explained, glancing at Isabelle.

She smiled. "And a good thing, too," the woman said. "One never knows when one will be fortunate enough to have company."

They were an amiable pair. After the gentlemen had drawn out the chairs for the ladies, Lord Dodd took one end and Isabelle the other, while Glynnis was seated across from Hargrove. She'd hoped to flirt all night with Lord Dodd and perhaps secure an invitation for a walk or a ride on the morrow. Seeing his home, albeit a rented one, she was still impressed, and so far, nothing gave her pause except his "aunt" staying with him.

"Disappointing about the prince's assembly tonight at the Castle," Isabelle said while they all received a glass of wine.

"Would you have felt up to it after your long journey?" Hargrove asked.

"Of course, why not?" She smiled at him.

"I only ask because you were not at the theatre tonight. Lord Dodd indicated you were weary from your travels."

"Pish," Isabelle said. "It was nice to stretch out, certainly. But mostly I don't care for silly theatre. If it had been something with gravitas, like . . . ," she trailed off, considering.

"Like *Hamlet*," Glynnis supplied, and shared a smile with Hargrove.

"Yes, exactly," Isabelle agreed. "Only a simpleton could find that froth by Congreve to be amusing."

Glynnis recalled how much she'd enjoyed it, glancing warily at Hargrove in case he agreed with Isabelle's opinion.

Reassuringly, he winked at her. "I thought *Love for Love* to be not only charming," he declared, "but also witty." Then he smiled, entirely unbothered by what Lord Dodd's aunt thought.

"Never say it," Isabelle said. Then leaning far over to rest her hand upon Hargrove's in a gesture of familiarity, she laughed. Her large breasts jiggled, and her nipples were plainly outlined under the filmy material of her bodice.

Both men's eyes were fixed upon them. *It was a good thing the woman hadn't been at the theatre,* Glynnis thought. If she laughed in such a fashion, the male audience would have been too distracted to watch the actors.

"I thought it very amusing," Glynnis put forth bravely. "Not Shakespeare, to be sure, but with the sailors involved, it seemed a fitting comedy for Brighton. Will there be fresh fish?" she asked Lord Dodd, deciding to change the subject.

"Yes," he replied. "One of the kitchen staff goes to the beach and meets the boats most every morning."

"Fish!" Isabelle said. "Is that our next topic?" She laughed again, and Glynnis thought her rude.

"Very well, Miss Montrose. What topic will you put forth?"

"Call me Isabelle," she said, a glint in her eyes, "and I shall call you . . . ?"

"Miss Talbot," Glynnis reminded her, with no compunction to become any less formal.

Hargrove's eyes widened slightly at the snub, but Isabelle only smiled.

"A proper, starched miss," she remarked. "I see how it is. That's all right. And what about you, Lord Hargrove? Are you mired in social etiquette and hamstrung by propriety?"

"Not at all," he said, his gaze drinking in the woman as if she were fine wine, and Glynnis wanted to kick him under the table if she could only reach. "You may call me James, if you wish."

"I do wish," Isabelle declared.

Glynnis knew she'd lost that battle, seeing as how Hargrove had not yet given her leave to call him by his first name. And now she wouldn't even if he did!

"As for a topic, let's discuss the Prince Regent and what you've already seen of him," Isabelle suggested, directing her questions to Hargrove as if Glynnis hadn't been keeping close company with Prince George, too.

Regardless, she was only too happy when Lord Dodd engaged her in a separate conversation, asking after her family in a friendly way. And in return, Glynnis found out more about his residence in London near Hyde Park.

"And do you always rent this house when you come to Brighton?" she asked.

Isabelle overheard. "I suggested Hugh would like it. I've stayed here before."

Glynnis bet she'd stayed many places, but she merely nodded politely.

"And I was right. He finds it to be absolutely perfect, don't you, Hugh?"

Lord Dodd allowed as he did. Glynnis wasn't sure she could marry him knowing he was related to this flash female. *What kind of man let his aunt rule his dining table and pick out his residence?*

On the other hand, Lord Dodd's cook put out a fine dinner from the pottage to the pudding course. And Glynnis was content by the time they returned to the drawing room. She dearly hoped Isabelle wasn't going to put her feet up again, and then realized the woman had dined *without* shoes.

If it weren't that she was waiting for some sort of sign of admiration from Lord Dodd, Glynnis would be ready to leave at once, eager to converse with Hargrove over what he truly thought of the outrageous Isabelle Montrose.

She decided on ratafia when asked, while Isabelle asked for brandy like the gentlemen, and then they played whist. Lord Dodd insisted on partnering with Glynnis, which she thought a good sign, particularly when he praised her when she won the first trick. Unfortunately, they ended up losing to Hargrove and Isabelle.

Finally, when they were all taking turns yawning, Glynnis looked bleary-eyed at Hargrove and he said they were going to take their leave. She thought it a good time and hoped at their next meeting, she could decide whether Lord Dodd was someone by whom she would like to be compromised, and then marry. *Moreover, was he the type of man who would step up if pressed?*

Perhaps she ought to try harder with his aunt, who might be a wealth of information as to Lord Dodd's character and his preparedness to take a wife.

"Will you be at the Castle Hotel assembly tomorrow evening?" she asked Isabelle.

"If Prinny doesn't call it off again, then yes."

"May I escort you to the assembly, Miss Talbot?" Lord Dodd spoke up, catching Glynnis off-guard.

Without thinking, she glanced at Hargrove. For a moment, she wished he would claim that privilege for himself. However, he did little more than shrug. It wasn't his place to grant his permission, nor was she asking for it.

"I would welcome such an occurrence, my lord."

"Although," Lord Dodd added, "I cannot imagine how you will possibly look as beautiful as tonight."

Luckily, Glynnis still had a few splendid evening gowns to carry her through.

"I'm sure Miss Talbot will be as perfect as tonight," Isabelle remarked, and Glynnis thought there was the smallest hint of tartness to her tone.

"And who shall escort you?" Hargrove asked her.

"Why, James, how sweet of you to wonder. I expect I will simply cross the street by myself. It's only a stone's throw, after all."

There was a moment's thick silence, and Glynnis was certain she and Isabelle and even Lord Dodd were waiting for Hargrove to offer to accompany her. He didn't, nor did he look the least bit uncomfortable.

In another few minutes, Glynnis had her hand tucked into the crook of Hargrove's arm as they strolled the Steyne back down to the oceanfront, and she had to ask the first question on her mind.

"Why didn't you offer to escort Lord Dodd's aunt—?"

"Aunt by marriage," Hargrove interrupted.

"That signifies nothing," she said. "Wouldn't it have been the gentlemanly thing to do?"

"She's an odd gander, that one," he said, and Glynnis instantly relaxed. She wished it wouldn't have bothered her if Hargrove had been complimentary over the lady, but it would have.

"I thought so, too. And she ate dinner without her shoes."

He laughed. "I suppose she felt comfortable in her own home."

"But it's not. It's Lord Dodd's."

"And he's an odd goose, too."

Glynnis was taken aback. "Whatever do you mean? He seems perfectly normal. Keeping a well-run household."

"Staying with a woman who is not really his aunt, but passing her off as such. Why?"

"What are you suggesting?"

He laughed. "I don't wish to shock you. What did she call you? A proper, starched miss." And then he laughed some more.

"I am not," she protested.

"Oh, I know that," Hargrove said too quickly. "Only too well."

She would have to let that go for now—mostly because whatever he thought she'd been doing in London, he would be correct.

"What are you insinuating about Lord Dodd?"

"I doubt he behaves as if he's her nephew, and I'll leave it at that."

If Hargrove was saying what she thought he was, then . . .

"Why would he offer to escort me to the Castle Hotel tomorrow night, and in front of Isabelle?"

Hargrove held the door to the Old Ship open and ushered her inside.

"For appearances, perhaps?"

"Are you implying you don't think he can actually be attracted to me?" Without thinking, she nodded to the night manager and climbed the stairs, assuming Hargrove would see her to her door.

"Of course he is! Any man with eyes is attracted to you," he said to her back, ascending close behind her.

Glynnis smiled. *How wonderful to hear him say such a thing!*

Then he added, "But any man with an ounce of sense will fight that attraction."

She grimaced, which he also couldn't see.

"Anyway, whether Dodd is attracted to you or not should be irrelevant. After all you're engaged. The question is, why did you accept his invitation?"

She hesitated, and they'd reached her door. Facing him, she leaned her back against it.

"I accepted because it seemed polite. He'd invited us to dinner and we all got along well. Lord Dodd knows I'm engaged, so he must have offered to escort me simply to be friendly."

"Perhaps to take the burden from me," Hargrove added, leaning an arm on the door frame beside her head.

"The burden?" Glynnis wanted to clobber him again. "How rude! May I remind you that *you* were the one who invited *me* to the theatre tonight?"

"Yes, I did, and I enjoyed myself."

She had a notion they could enjoy themselves quite a bit more if he weren't so wary of her. She sighed, and his glance fell to her rising and falling chest, before raising again to her face.

"As did I," she confessed. "I never considered I was a burden to you."

His gaze held hers. She thought he had something more to say, but he remained silent. Then this handsome man, tall as a tree, with shoulders that made her feel small and protected, this viscount who smelled like fresh laundered linen hanging outside on a sunny day, this nobleman with his perfectly tied cravat leaned toward her.

CHAPTER TWELVE

With his expression unreadable, Hargrove slowly took her mouth under his, and Glynnis closed her eyes.

The floor sloped beneath her feet. No other part of him touched her, but her entire body heated and tingled. When he tilted his head farther, the force of his firm mouth pressed her head back against the door. If she thought about it, she would swear Hargrove's kiss made the sensitive area between her legs start to throb.

Unable to keep from touching him another second, she raised her hands and managed to thread her fingers in the hair at the nape of his neck. That caused her breasts to lift. When her taut nipples brushed against the fabric of her shift, she moaned. Almost desperately, she wished to bare herself to his gaze, and then . . . *Then what?*

Glynnis wanted to feel his mouth directly upon her breast. Indeed, she could almost imagine how glorious it would be.

"Hargrove," she breathed against his mouth, and he insinuated his thigh between her legs.

Reaching around her, he cradled her bottom with his large palms and drew her up his leg, stimulating her womanly core.

Drawn away from the support of the paneled door, her head fell back, and he broke off the kiss to nibble a trail along her chin and down her arched neck. When the tip of his tongue touched her skin at the base of her throat, she shivered.

Glynnis was sure her heart was going to beat out of her chest. And no hotel staff carrying a bathtub would be showing up to interrupt the moment.

With no words passing between them, he removed one hand from her person, still balancing her upon his upper thigh, while he reached around to push down on the handle and send the door drifting ajar behind her.

As Glynnis's eyes flew open and she slid off his leg, Hargrove walked her backward into the room, his mouth claiming hers again, even as she heard him kick the door shut.

Well!

And then everything seemed to happen in a flurry of movements, as the back of her legs eventually touched the side of her tidily made bed. Without breaking the fusion of their lips, he shrugged out of his jacket, dropping it behind him, and then dragged off her shawl which was draped precariously around her shoulders. He tossed this over her head.

To see his reaction, she raised her hand and knocked off his hat, sending it flying against the far wall.

Hargrove didn't seem to notice. Instead, he slid the cap sleeve of her gown down her right shoulder.

This was going farther than she'd ever intended with any man who wasn't her fiancé. *Her real fiancé!* After all, only a kiss was necessary to be compromised if properly discovered at the opportune moment. But Hargrove seemed intent on much more.

After drawing down her other sleeve, he tugged at her neckline until the entire gown fell, exposing her stays and under it, her shift.

They weren't in a place where they needed to stop for fear of slippery sea creatures around their ankles, nor even an assembly host or hostess coming upon them. And as her heartbeat raced and her body turned molten, Glynnis wasn't sure she wanted the viscount to stop.

Or at least, not before she experienced what she'd imagined—his wicked mouth upon her nipple.

"Yes," she said.

To her delight, with the smallest rearranging of her shift, he gave himself complete access. When the night air caressed her skin, she felt her already-sensitive buds pucker.

"Mm," he said, the first she'd heard from him in many minutes, just before his mouth latched onto one of her pert nipples, teasing it.

How was it possible she could feel his ministrations as if he were doing the very same between her legs?

Growing damp, she started to squirm as the pulsing sensation increased. Feeling suddenly desperate to shed more of her clothing and fiercely wishing to tear his off as well, she started to work on the buttons of his waistcoat.

His mouth moved to her other breast, sucking her nipple into his hot mouth.

"Yes," she hissed again. With his vest open, she yanked upon his shirt until it was free of his breeches. Finally, she could touch his skin. Sliding her hands under the linen shirt, she splayed her fingers across his flat stomach.

His skin was smooth and warm, and she wanted to map out every inch of him. To that end, she sent her hands roaming higher over his tautly muscled stomach until she found his nipples, the tiniest of nubs. Gently, she stroked them.

Hargrove growled against her breast. She would have continued her explorations, but suddenly his hands went to her waist. In a swift motion, he lifted her backward, setting her onto the bed. She gasped.

While raising her dress and dragging her long chemise along with it, he stepped between her legs.

With her breasts uncovered and his hands gathering her skirts ever higher, his fingers scraping up her thighs, Glynnis—overwhelmed with sensations and passion, not to mention a healthy dose of trepidation—tossed herself backward onto the counterpane. Her legs dangled over the side of the bed, and Hargrove remained wedged between them.

"Will you ruin me?" she asked him, flinging her arm over her eyes.

WITH HIS COCK IMPOSSIBLY hard inside his breeches and his heart pounding, her words filtered into his lust-filled brain. James froze.

He had ruined young ladies before. Of that he had no doubt—usually because they'd willingly, wantonly, wonderfully pushed him too far, dangling their soft, curvy assets before him.

"I will not marry you," he'd told an eager miss while they were behind a tree at Vauxhall, away from her chaperone.

"I don't care a whit," she had declared. "Just touch me again, my lord. Yes, there!" And a minute later, when her skirts were up and she was bent over a stone bench, and he'd repeated his warning about marriage, she'd added, "If you would be so kind as to ease my ardent excitement with your rod."

James was always shocked by how much these marriage-aged daughters of the *ton* knew about amorous conduct, and even more surprised by how much pent-up tension they had. So much that even with the risk of being ruined, they let him penetrate their sacred passages. Naturally, after making sure they were satisfied, he always pulled out in time to avoid consequences.

Predictably, a handful of them began to push for an engagement as soon as the deed was done. Patiently, he would remind them a third time of his utter abhorrence to being roped into matrimony. After they'd arranged themselves and smoothed their skirts, he would escort each woman back to wherever she belonged and never see her again.

But this was Miss Talbot. He already knew she had a fiancé. Moreover, he'd managed to resist her before. If he were to wager a guess, he would say she was as passionate as he was and as attracted to him as he to her. Yet that didn't excuse him willingly destroying her chance of marriage with no more motivation than to relieve his curiosity and his stifled desire.

With the strength of Achilles, James drew back, stepping out of the warm, beckoning area between her thighs.

"I became carried away," he said quietly, wanting her more than he'd ever wanted any woman. He hoped it wasn't simple competition with Dodd that had spurred him to this mad behavior.

Miss Talbot rose to her elbows, still reclined on the bed. He darted a hand out and sent her skirts dashing back down to her ankles.

"I suppose we both did," she said, watching him with her big brown eyes. "Somehow, you stopped yourself from taking it too far for which I am grateful."

No female had ever uttered those words to him before.

"And a wee bit disappointed," she added softly, even as she realized her state of deshabille. Coming to a seated position on the edge of the bed, she hastened to draw up her shift, covering her lovely breasts before keeping her hands clasped over the sheer white cotton.

They were trembling.

"As am I," he admitted, since she was being truthful.

Beyond disappointed, in fact. The ache in his groin was only matched by the odd emptiness that blossomed in his gut. A minute ago, he was set to have an enjoyable time, slaking his desire while satisfying hers, hopefully more than once before dawn. Instead, he would go directly home, for he no longer had a taste for an experienced blowsabella readily available in numerous houses in Brighton.

"Where you are concerned, my raffish nature fails me, which is to your benefit."

She nodded, her brown eyes seeming bigger than before. Yet he refused to apologize for having gone as far as they had. Their brief encounter had been mutual, and he thought she deserved better than a hollow act of contrition.

Swiftly, he buttoned his waistcoat in silence before donning his jacket. *How had his hat ended up on the floor?* He didn't recall.

At the door, he paused only to say, "Good evening, Miss Talbot," as if nothing untoward had happened, wanting to return their relationship to one in which he could be around her without pouncing, one where he could look her in the eye without a drop of awkward tension. "I shall see you tomorrow at the Castle Hotel."

Since he didn't turn to her when he said it, he couldn't see her reaction. Still, she didn't speak, so he strode out, closed the door quietly, and crept down the stairs like a true cad, hoping no one saw him or guessed where he'd been.

For her sake.

GLYNNIS MOVED AS IF in a dream, or in a large bowl of sticky toffee pudding. Slowly, deliberately, she got off the bed and picked up her shawl from the floor. What a strange evening it had been. She was still trembling with how close she'd come to being taken from a maiden to a woman. She was relieved, but as she'd told Hargrove, she was also disappointed.

Never could she have imagined how intense the fiery passion of longing could burn. She had wanted him more than she'd wanted her virtue to remain intact.

Undressing, recalling his mouth upon her breasts, she removed her gown, then her stays and stockings. If she'd become so stimulated with a few kisses and caresses, how much more was there to experience when they were both bare and joining completely. She couldn't fathom the actual act, but with this small taste, she could well imagine why men sought out prostitutes to enjoy it and why women sometimes gave in before marriage.

Thinking she would never sleep, Glynnis was surprised the following morning at how quickly and soundly she'd fallen into a deep slumber. In truth, when she had rested her head upon the pillow, the last dregs of her energy dissipated, and she recalled nothing else.

The sun was already streaming in her window when she opened her eyes, and the noises from the street below were rising to greet her. Carriage horses clopping along, people talking, even the sounds of the fishermen on the beach calling out prices of their catch met her ears.

And she had a long day to get through before seeing Hargrove again.

She shook her head—that should not be her first thought. She had a long day to get through before the handsome Lord Dodd came by to escort her to the Castle Hotel for the Regent's next grand gathering. For despite knowing Hargrove would be in attendance, nothing could come of it. He'd made that abundantly clear. He wanted her, but he didn't want to marry her.

Somehow, by strolling around Castle Square and North Street looking in the shops then returning to her room to write a letter to her brother as if she were in Bath and to her parents as if she were in London, before taking a light nuncheon and a walk along the Marine Parade, Glynnis managed to pass the hours. She told herself she was on the ocean boulevard looking for other eligible gentlemen and not hoping to run into Hargrove. In any case, she saw neither.

At the appointed time, she got herself ready, not an easy task without a lady's maid, but she was getting used to dressing her own hair. And of course, she wore half stays *à la paresseuse*, the lazy girl's stays, so she could easily tie them herself. Hargrove had already seen them, as had the hotel manager who'd got them cleaned for her.

So far, she had been humiliated and humbled. Shaking her head, she vowed to do better. To that end, she was waiting in the Old Ship's lobby when Lord Dodd arrived. He looked very good, she told herself. True, he was not Hargrove, but no one was.

And she must stop thinking of the unattainable!

The fair-haired Lord Dodd carried himself well and wore a fastidious charcoal gray jacket over a scarlet waistcoat and pale breeches.

"You have exceeded my expectations," he announced immediately. "A female who is ready at the appointed time. A miracle!"

She smiled, took his offered arm, and let him lead the way.

"I confess I like how close everything is in Brighton. It's so manageable compared to London."

He gave her a surprised glance. "I think everything one would care to do or anyone one would wish to know is all in the space of eight acres in Mayfair."

"But Hyde Park," she pointed out.

"We shall add the Park," he agreed.

"Do you also have a country estate?" she asked when they were traversing the Steyne and nearly at the Castle Hotel. Carriages were letting off those who probably were renting at the farthest end of Brighton, on the Royal Crescent.

"I do, but at this moment, my favorite place is here with you."

Glynnis took a breath. *Was Lord Hugh Dodd going to be her husband?*

When they were indoors, he began tending to her needs at once. It was warm so he found her a spot by the open window of the tea-room being used as a reception room before the dancing started. Luckily, there was no tea, only champagne and lemonade for those who didn't imbibe. And Lord Dodd went off in search of a couple of glasses for them while guests were still arriving.

And then after a minute, she spied Hargrove, his head above others and his fine-looking face causing her insides to do an odd flip.

It was followed by a wave of resentment, for despite what he'd said the night before, he was, in fact, escorting Isabelle Montrose. And every eye turned to take in the woman's stunning appearance.

While Glynnis knew her own gown of green silk trimmed with silver ribbon was pretty, it wasn't eye-catching in the way Isabelle's was. For one thing, Glynnis would vow the lady wasn't wearing a petticoat or a chemise under the diaphanous light golden dress. As she walked, her *mons Veneris* kept appearing at the apex of her thighs, and from behind, Glynnis was certain she could see the shadow of the crack between her buttocks.

Close up, Isabelle's nipples must surely be on display. Knowing how Hargrove appreciated a woman's breasts, it was no wonder he'd hardly glanced her way. In any case, she feared she could not compete, even with her fashionably low décolletage.

Then she wondered at her own ridiculous wish to compete at all. She'd had him between her legs the night before, after all.

But would Isabelle have him in her bed that night?

Firmly taking hold of her wild imaginings, she forced her attention to return to Lord Dodd, gratefully accepting the champagne he offered her.

"You are precisely the type of person I've been looking for," he said, surprising her.

"Type?" she asked. "You mean *female.*"

132

They both laughed. "I mean witty, amusing, and, of course, beautiful. And top it all off, you're a viscount's daughter with all the benefits, I imagine, befitting your status. No wonder your fiancé seeks to bind you to him. I cannot fathom, however, why he would let you come alone to Brighton. Are you sure he isn't a madman?"

"Quite certain, my lord. Yet there are many suitable ladies on the marriage mart. I saw them for myself last Season. Why haven't you snapped up one for yourself?"

He raised his gaze upward, as if hard put upon. Then he looked into her eyes.

"Somehow, I didn't see you in time" he said. "And now it's too late. Having kept company with you, I fear now I shall never marry."

She appreciated his manners, although he overdid the flattery.

His gaze fixed momentarily just past her left shoulder. "Maybe Isabelle will not be as unlucky as I am, nor come away from Brighton empty-handed."

Glynnis turned and realized he was watching Hargrove and Miss Montrose with their heads a little too close, discussing something private. She glanced back at Lord Dodd.

"Is your aunt—?"

"By marriage," he amended.

"Is she looking to make a match?"

"Mayhap, yes. If she found the right man, I suppose. Why not?"

They both looked again toward Isabelle and Hargrove. Glynnis frowned. *Had they somehow got even closer?* They were behaving almost indecently.

Glynnis hoped the discomfiting claw of jealousy that gripped her heart was easily vanquished. It was unpleasant, not to mention futile. She had tried that path twice, and twice been thwarted.

Whereas Lord Dodd had practically declared he would marry her if she weren't already engaged. She might not even have to get him into a compromising situation because he'd stated he wouldn't be adverse toward being her fiancé.

Hargrove hadn't had anything bad to say about the man, not the way he had about Lord Cumberry, Lord Leilton, or even the married Lord Staunton, all with their egregious character flaws. Although to be fair, she and Hargrove hadn't really had much of a conversation about Lord Dodd, especially not while the viscount was kissing her senseless.

She looked at Lord Dodd again. He had gray-blue eyes and blond hair. Good cheekbones, too. Nothing round or pudding-faced about him. Instead of taking him for granted while mooning over Hargrove and sending Isabelle glaring looks of thunder, Glynnis knew she must pay the man better attention.

The Prince Regent chose that moment to enter the reception room. The cheering began as usually accompanied his appearance. For when Prince George arrived at a party, there was always the promise of a good time, high quality food, and plenty of wine.

"Do you know the Regent personally?" Lord Dodd asked her.

"Somewhat. He has been kind to me on two occasions."

Lord Dodd gave her a nod of approval. "Naturally. You are a beautiful woman. Why don't we greet him together?"

Finding his suggestion agreeable, Glynnis allowed Lord Dodd to take her arm and move in the general direction of the line forming near the Regent. She couldn't help noticing Hargrove and Miss Montrose ignored the prince, remaining in their corner of the room.

In a few minutes, she and Lord Dodd had made their way to the front. She curtsied to Prince George who looked genuinely pleased to see her again.

"I heard you had quite a mishap on the shore," he said. "But you look recovered."

"I am well, Your Royal Highness. Thank you."

"And your fiancé has shown up at last I see."

Glynnis startled for a moment, thinking somehow Lord Aberavon had arrived from Wales. Then she realized whom he meant.

"Oh no, sir. Lord Dodd is merely keeping me company. He is not my fiancé."

"Greetings, Your Royal Highness." Lord Dodd offered a generously low bow. "If Miss Talbot *would* accept me, I should gratefully take up the mantle of an engaged man in the blink of an eye."

Good, Glynnis thought. She was counting on it.

"I'm sure you would make a fine pair," the prince said. "I don't know anything about Lord Aberavon," he said to her, "but you could do worse than Dodd."

Glynnis felt her cheeks warm, and she spared a glance to the man beside her. He seemed entirely favorable to the idea.

"Worse indeed, like Hargrove," Prince George added purposefully, as Hargrove and Miss Montrose stepped ahead of the line and turned their party of three into five. Then she found out why they took such a liberty.

"Isabelle!" Prince George gushed, taking her hand. "I'm glad to see you. It's been a donkey's age. And here you are, trying to outshine all the females in Brighton. You have competition, I fear."

Glynnis had no intention of putting herself up against Miss Montrose. There was something outlandish about the woman, a trait that seemed unpredictable and erratic.

"I don't think Miss Talbot has to worry on that account," Lord Dodd said.

Glynnis wished it had been Hargrove who spoke in her defense, but the viscount remained silent until Prince George addressed him.

"I thought you were going to look after Miss Talbot, and yet I find you've taken up with another."

Hargrove sent her a glance with an unfathomable meaning swimming in the depths of his deep blue eyes. She flinched, awaiting his answer.

CHAPTER THIRTEEN

Now fashion's fairest daughters pace the lawn,
And Mars' gay sons the lively scene adorn.

– *Brighton. A Poem* by Mary Lloyd, 1809

Hargrove bowed to him before speaking. "I haven't taken up with anyone, Your Highness. I am merely enjoying the company of your guests while in Brighton."

"You are a rake, to be sure," the prince insisted, glancing between Glynnis and Isabelle. "But when surrounded by such lovely females, who can blame you going from flower to flower, enjoying their honey."

The Prince Regent was known for his ribald jokes and innuendo, but after what had passed between her and Hargrove the night before, Glynnis wasn't in the mood to be the butt of that type of humor.

"If you'll excuse me, Your Highness, many others wish to greet you," she said. "Thank you for throwing this wonderful party." After dropping into a curtsy, she stepped aside and hurried away.

"You are a delight," the prince called after her.

Glynnis kept moving toward the round refreshment tables covered in white linens and laden with all manner of finger foods, and then past them into the deep orange and yellow ballroom where the musicians were already warming up. Currently empty, revelers would dance long into the night, her included. And Hargrove, too, she supposed.

She sniffed. She didn't need Hargrove, and swiftly ordered herself to cease thinking about him. Instead, she would find a place to let Lord Dodd kiss her if he wanted to. If he didn't, so be it. More gentlemen had arrived from London, as evidenced by this party being much busier than the last assembly. Given the air of festivity, she was certain she would leave Brighton with a husband of good quality.

"Miss Talbot," Lord Dodd had caught up to her. "Did something upset you?"

She slowed her steps. Something had yet it should not have done so.

"I am well," she said, looking up at him. He had a kind expression.

"Are you going outside?" he asked.

She hadn't been, but perhaps that was his first move on the chessboard of mating.

"It *is* growing stuffy in here," she said. "Shall we stroll around the building before the dancing begins?"

"We can promenade around the lawn on the east side of the prince's Pavilion," he suggested.

"Very well." And just like that, she disappeared into the gathering dusk with a veritable stranger.

At first, they both remained silent, listening to the gentle, low calls of the wood pigeons in the trees and the high-pitched sounds of the swifts still flittering about, searching for the evening insects. At least, she hoped they were swifts and not bats.

Then Lord Dodd cleared his throat. "Are you desperately in love with Lord Aberavon?"

"Gracious," she exclaimed. "That hardly seems an appropriate question. Why do you ask?" She hoped he asked because he was already falling in love with her himself.

"Ever since I first saw you emerge from the bathing machine," Lord Dodd said, "I confess to being smitten."

"Oh." She had always thought she needed to trick a man into marrying her, yet this one was speaking plainly. Probably if he knew her penniless state, it wouldn't be the case.

"We—my fiancé and I—we did engage ourselves in a marital contract upon little knowledge of one another, to be honest." She congratulated herself. That sounded as if there were room for another man in her life, if one swept her off her feet.

"I understand perfectly." He sounded pleased.

There were other couples strolling in the warm evening air, some even pausing by a tree or against the Prince Regent's front portico. By the way they were wrapped around each other, she doubted any of them would interfere should Lord Dodd kiss her. There were no chaperones to be seen, nor matrons, nor stern hostesses. *Brighton was a different world, indeed!*

Suddenly, as they passed a large elm, Lord Dodd pulled her sideways, and they were hidden behind it from anyone looking out the many windows of the Castle. And the Pavilion was empty of observers since everyone was with the prince.

Without hesitation, he drew her into his arms and kissed her.

Glynnis tried to sink into his embrace, to ignore the thoughts in her head, and to let the sizzling and the throbbing begin.

Nothing. His lips were firm, his breath was clean, his nose didn't knock awkwardly against hers. Yet no part of her body heated and pulsed, and she couldn't stop comparing the kiss to Hargrove's. *Where was the blossoming passion?*

On the other hand, as Lord Dodd tilted his head in the other direction and resumed the kiss, she wasn't revolted in the least. It was a good, solid kiss. It wouldn't be the worst thing to kiss this man for the rest of her life. As they became used to one another, as their feelings deepened and she hopefully fell in love with him, and as they enjoyed the other things that husbands and wives did, then she believed his kiss would begin to move her, even to thrill her.

Thus, she was confounded as to why Hargrove's kiss already had the power to send her to the moon and had from the very first one. It was a conundrum.

Lord Dodd was breathing hard when he broke away, clearly more stirred than she was. *How she wished she felt the same!* In time, she would, she promised herself.

"I burn for you," he declared.

Enough to offer her his hand? she wondered.

"I am engaged, as you know," Glynnis said. "Thus, there is nothing we can do about your feelings. That is, unless you can think of some remedy."

"We shall see," Lord Dodd said, and nothing more.

As they approached the assembly room, she startled. Up ahead, Hargrove stood just outside the door, arms crossed. She would vow he'd been scanning the area for her.

"You look like a porter," Lord Dodd quipped and led her past him. Her gown even brushed the viscount's leg.

Glynnis would swear she could feel waves of anger emanating from him, and she was compelled to look back, catching his eye. Hargrove's gaze was decidedly condemning, as if he knew what she'd been doing behind the elm tree.

Inside, little had changed. Isabelle was still by the prince's side, a glass of champagne in her hand. But the Castle's master of ceremonies signaled the dancing was about to begin with a vigorous shake of a bell.

"May I claim the first dance?" Lord Dodd asked.

"Yes, of course," she said.

They began with a minuet, which was easily arranged in the eighty-foot ballroom. The space appeared even larger due to the strategically hung mirrors placed on opposite walls, with three lamps in every girandole sconce between each looking glass. The light reflected from side to side, creating a dazzling effect, and illuminated the Wedgewood cameos and delicate moldings around the room's perimeter.

Hargrove partnered with a blonde from the picnic, and Glynnis wished she wasn't so aware always of his location.

After the first dance, when Lord Dodd had finally excused himself, Hargrove approached her.

"Will you dance with me?" he asked.

"I'm surprised you wish to," she said tartly. "You haven't spoken a word to me all evening."

He pursed his lips. "How was your *stroll* outside?"

Unthinkingly, she put her gloved hand to her mouth, and Hargrove's gaze narrowed as his jaw tightened.

"You're playing with fire again," he muttered.

"Don't tell me Lord Dodd is a petticoat-pensioner or married or a terrible libertine."

"No," Hargrove bit out. "None of those things. Must I remind you that you are engaged. You are putting your future happiness at terrible risk."

What could she say to that? Glynnis shrugged.

Without another word, he swept her into his arms for a waltz, and she did two things. She sniffed the familiar scent—something expensive and custom-made for him from Floris on Jermyn Street, she guessed—and she started to tingle all over. Maybe she'd caught an illness the first time he'd kissed her, a germ from his mouth to hers that would forever cause her to react strongly to him. *Perhaps he was a curse to her constitution!*

She didn't know. All she knew was no one else made her feel this way, and that was a shame.

After the second turn down the length of the room, she asked, "Why did you change your mind about Miss Montrose?"

His blue eyes met hers. "I'm not sure I understand your question."

"Last night, you didn't care for her. Yet tonight you escorted her and fawned all over her."

"I didn't fawn," he insisted. "As it happened, I saw her crossing the street at the same time as I was, and it would have been beyond rude for me not to accompany her."

She fell silent. Maybe it wasn't his fault. There might be no conceivable way for a man to ignore a woman who was wearing a sheer gown with nothing underneath.

"What was terribly rude was Lord Dodd not escorting his aunt," Hargrove said.

"By marriage," she reminded him.

"He should have at least brought Isabelle across the street."

"Because she is a doddering old auntie?" Glynnis shot back. "In a translucent dress!"

Hargrove barked out a laugh before he could stop himself.

"That dress!" he remarked. "I think she would be more at home in Paris."

"Is that how they are clothed there?"

"The courtesans at the Palais Royal are." Then Hargrove sobered. "Anyway, why do you mind if I escort a woman to a party? It should be nothing to you."

"It's not," she insisted. "No more than my taking a lovely stroll to listen to the birds ought to be of any interest to you."

"With Dodd," he muttered.

"The prince said he was a good man."

Hargrove's eyebrows drew together. "Did he? I wouldn't count his recommendation for much. After all, Prinny has two wives and at least that many mistresses."

She shook her head. The Regent's father was considered above reproach, salt of the earth, and interested in agriculture and in hunting more than in affairs of state. And certainly not one to have any other kind of affair either. Yet he and his devoted Queen Charlotte had managed to sire more than one dissolute son. Now the eldest and some said the most unprincipled ruled the kingdom as regent, and the only thing he seemed to have inherited from his moral-minded father was a love of art and music.

"On the other hand," Hargrove said, "perhaps we shouldn't judge Prinny too harshly. Rumor has it he's turning this very ballroom into his own private chapel after he shuts the Castle's doors at the end of the year. Thus, one could give him high marks for his faith."

She glanced around her as he twirled her past the maroon sofas lining the walls, and tried to imagine them as hard wooden pews. Men were a mystery to her.

When the dance ended, Hargrove left her with a bow to go to the card room, the third largest of the Castle Hotel's public rooms. She danced a few more dances with men whom she couldn't imagine as her husband, and then it was time for dinner in the hotel's dining room, which Prince George had rented out in its entirety.

As if by magic, Lord Dodd appeared by her side to escort her to dinner and be her partner. He was attentive and thoughtful. He drew out her chair, then naturally looked over her shoulder and down the front of her gown as he pushed her in. If he hadn't, she would have been worried.

The tables had been pushed together into three long rows, and Hargrove and another woman whom Glynnis didn't know sat at the far end of a different table. She didn't bother looking for Isabelle, as she could not possibly care less.

Stripping off her gloves and laying them upon her lap, she picked up the already-filled wine glass and turned her full attention to the man whom she decided would become her husband.

142

ALTHOUGH MISS TALBOT HADN'T needed him to escort her into the dining room, James kept his eye upon her. He couldn't particularly say anything against Dodd. He didn't really know the man. He knew Dodd's father had married a much younger woman after he'd become a widower, hence the youthful "Aunt" Isabelle.

When Payton had joined him at cards earlier, James asked him if he'd heard anything alarming. The answer had been a disinterested no.

So why was he bothered by seeing Miss Talbot firmly attached to Lord Dodd all night? After all, he didn't know Lord Aberavon either, nor did he particularly care if the man were cuckolded even before his wedding day.

James's concern was all for the lady. He didn't want her hurt by some scoundrel, even if she were careless with her attention and her affection. Why on earth she'd let him into her room and almost into her bed the previous night, James still couldn't fathom.

Sighing, he gestured to a server to refill his wine glass and realized he was already tired of Brighton. With any luck, he could get Prinny to spend a serious moment looking at the art he'd managed to bring back from Paris.

Would he be dissatisfied and decide some nasty fate for James or pleased and send him back to London? A yea or a nay was all he needed to decide his future.

Glancing again at Glynnis, he thought the best thing would be to get away from the seacoast as quickly as possible.

"What about you, my lord?" came the voice from the woman beside him, and he wrenched his gaze from the dark-haired minx who'd captivated him.

"My apologies, I missed the question."

The woman sighed. He'd been apologizing to her throughout dinner, but he couldn't seem to remember to listen to her and was grateful each time she turned to the gentleman on her other side and talked his ear off instead.

"You, my lord, are a boorish dining partner."

That much he heard.

"Why didn't you make it a point to dine with that dark-haired lady if you were going to give her all your attention?" she asked.

He was being so obvious as if he cared about Miss Talbot. *Irrational, foolish—what was he doing?* He certainly wasn't behaving like the care-free and unattached bachelor that he was.

"I'm behaving like an ass," he confessed to the lady whose name he didn't know but who deserved better. "How can I make it up to you?"

"You can't. The pudding course has come and gone, and I'm glad we shall soon be set free."

On that point, he wholeheartedly agreed. When the Prince Regent rose from his chair, appearing overstuffed and uncomfortable, James quickly drew out the lady's chair and watched her flee from his poor civility.

Sighing, he looked once more toward Miss Talbot, but she was already showing him her back, striding away from the table on Dodd's arm. He knew he would have enjoyed the meal had he been seated beside her. So far, he'd liked most every minute he'd spent in her company.

And the longer she spent with Dodd, the more miserable he became.

"Why are you looking like a dog who has lost his dinner?"

James smiled at Payton. "Prinny asked me to keep an eye on a young lady so she wouldn't get into trouble," he confessed.

"And you desperately want to be rid of her?" Payton asked, scanning the room as if she would have a sign over her head.

"I desperately want to get into trouble with her."

Payton barked out a laugh. "So why don't you?"

"She's engaged. What's more, I like her. It would be cruel to ruin her just because I can."

Payton stared at him, then he crossed his arms.

"What do you mean you *like* her?"

James rolled his eyes. "As a person and as a female, she seems . . . ," he trailed off. "Never mind."

"Do I know her?" Payton asked, back to looking at the other guests.

"I don't think so. Miss Talbot—"

Payton's head whipped around, and he gawked at him. "Not *the* Miss Talbot, the one you said was a conniving wench?"

CHAPTER FOURTEEN

James felt his mouth drop open, then he snapped it shut. "I never said her name," he protested.

Payton grinned. "You did, after about five pints of beer and then a couple glasses of piss quick. With the blue ruin in you, you were 'Miss Talbot this' and 'Miss Talbot that.'"

James felt his cheeks grow hot. Had he truly drunk so much gin in the pub that he'd spilled his guts in such an unchivalrous manner? *Naming her!* He was appalled at himself.

"Don't look so horrified. It happens to each of us occasionally," Payton said, trying to comfort him. "So the woman who tried to trap you in the parson's noose has now caught your fancy. How rich!"

"Prinny said to keep her safe until her fiancé arrives."

"But you want to tup her instead?" Payton quipped. The whole thing was a joke to him.

"No," James said, belatedly determined to protect her. He never would have started the conversation had he known Payton knew his lovely torturer by name.

Payton chuckled again. "It makes me no matter, ol' chum. Just don't get in the middle of something and end up at the wrong end of her fiancé's pistol."

AT NOON THE DAY after the Castle Hotel assembly when the porter knocked upon her door to say she had a gentlemen caller, Glynnis quickly set a lightweight green hat upon her head, pinned it in two places, grabbed her gloves which she yanked on as she went down the stairs, and then stopped in her tracks.

"Hargrove!" She was thrilled and disappointed at the same time.

"Don't look so surprised," he said. "I wondered if you were hungry or wanted to take a stroll."

"I am," she said, "and I do."

How nice of him, but she'd been expecting if any man were to call upon her, it would be Lord Dodd to press his case.

"Let's stop in the café first and then," he paused, "perhaps walk all the way to the Royal Crescent. Have you seen the statue of Prinny?"

"I haven't," she told him. Suddenly, the day that would have been another dreary one filled with worry over money was, instead, filled with expectation.

After she made sure Hargrove was treating her to the nuncheon, she ordered the most expensive mince lamb pie on the menu and a pot of tea, as well as a rich cake and fruit trifle for dessert.

"So delicious," she couldn't help exclaiming. "Is that all you're having?" Hargrove was eating like a single lady at a London dinner, trying to impress the gentlemen with her dainty appetite.

"I ate not too long ago," he confessed, setting down his half-eaten wafer before idly sipping his coffee.

How strange! She paused with a spoonful of trifle topped with clotted cream halfway to her lips. "Then why did you invite me for something to eat?"

He smiled. "Because you're always hungry, aren't you?"

"Yes, but you . . . ," she trailed off, rendered speechless by his kindness. If Lord Hargrove wanted to buy her a meal, she wouldn't protest. Sticking the spoon into her mouth, she enjoyed the remainder of her dessert. But the spark in his eyes was disconcerting. She could only hope she had no cream upon her lips.

After she swallowed, she asked, "Do you know anyone renting at the Royal Crescent?"

"Not renting, no, but I know someone who lives there. You may've been introduced to him the first night at the Pavilion. Lord Payton?"

She shrugged. The name meant nothing, and she'd been keeping careful track of whom she met.

Thus, after the meal which Hargrove paid for in full, he took her arm, and they began the long walk up toward the Royal Crescent. In the front of the shallow arc of terraced houses facing the sea, at its heart was a statue.

They walked around it, observing it from all sides.

"It's Prince George, is it not?" Glynnis asked.

"It is. Paid for by Mr. Otto, a man from India and of some wealth, who wished to impress His Royal Highness and obtain an invitation to the Pavilion."

Glynnis took another long look. It was impressive, she supposed, at least for its height, which she guessed to be about seven feet. And it was set upon a pedestal that was much taller than her. But the flaw was obvious.

"Why does it only have one arm?"

Hargrove roared with laughter, until she caught his humor and chuckled, too.

"We shouldn't," she said. "If the prince saw us, he'd be angry."

The viscount nodded, but it took him another few moments to catch his breath.

"The sculptor, a man named Charles Rossi, was commissioned to make it from Coade stone, supposedly quite durable to the elements."

"Apparently not in this case," Glynnis pointed out. The entire statue had pits and a sad, weathered look.

"It displeases Prinny greatly," Hargrove admitted. "Because of the arm, people have started to mistake it for Admiral Nelson." He laughed again.

"Oh my," Glynnis murmured, thinking how annoyed the Regent must be.

"I'm sure Prinny will order it removed soon. And as far as I know, Mr. Otto fell forever out of the prince's favor."

Glynnis had stopped listening for she'd noticed a lady strolling back from town. And the closer the woman came, the more certain she was of one thing.

"That woman has my parasol!"

Hargrove followed the direction of her gaze.

"How can you tell? It looks like every other parasol."

"Mayhap it does, but I believe it is mine," Glynnis insisted. The lady drew closer, nodding to both her and to Hargrove before making a circle of the statue.

"It used to look much nicer," the woman declared. "I live right there," she boasted, pointing to one of the exquisite homes standing parallel to the road. Each was faced in black-glazed mathematical tiles, and where the sun hit them, they shone with a brilliant iridescence.

But Glynnis could only stare at her parasol.

"Were you at the prince's picnic?" she asked.

"I beg your pardon?" the woman replied.

The lady lived in one of the nicest homes in Brighton, second only to the Pavilion itself, or maybe Mrs. Fitzherbert's home. And yet, she'd snatched Glynnis's precious parasol, which she'd been unable to afford to replace. Her dudgeon was high.

"What kind of person helps themselves to someone else's parasol?" she demanded.

The lady's jaw dropped, then her mouth compressed into a thin line.

"I'm sure I have no idea, but perhaps you have been out in the sun too long and ought to procure a parasol with all due haste." She turned to walk away.

"Miss Talbot," Hargrove began. "Surely, you are mistaken." He looked uneasy, when she'd hoped he would stand up for her and demand the return of her personal possession.

Darting forward, Glynnis snatched at the silk umbrella, ending up grabbing it by one of its tassels.

The lady exclaimed and stepped back in fright. When she didn't relinquish her hold, the tassel broke off in Glynnis's hand

"Oh!" she exclaimed at the same time as the woman. "I love these tassels." Her fury rose at the damage, even though she'd caused it herself.

"Bertram!" the woman yelled, far more loudly than Glynnis could have imagined. Perhaps the sea air did strengthen one's lungs as it was purported.

"Just let me have it back," Glynnis told her. "Even with the loss of a tassel, I want my parasol."

"Miss Talbot," Hargrove warned again, But Glynnis didn't look at him.

The woman's eyes widened. Slowly, with her gaze snapping between Glynnis and Hargrove, she started to back away.

"Bertram!" she screamed again.

Glynnis made another lunge for it, but the well-dressed lady used it as a foil. Like a prize fencer, she thrust it toward Glynnis's stomach before she turned to dash across the Marine Parade.

Glynnis moved to follow but Hargrove's arms came around her.

"Stop this at once. Even if it's yours, your dignity must be worth more."

Sadly, at that moment, her dignity was as valuable as her only parasol, given the strong coastal sun. Thinking quickly, she relaxed in his arms, enjoying for a moment the feel of him at her back, solid and comforting. However, as soon as he loosened his hold, she slipped easily from his grasp, chasing after her quarry who had already crossed the boulevard and was racing toward one of the four-story homes.

Its door opened under an ocean-facing balcony trimmed in cast-iron railings, and a man, probably Mr. Bertram, stepped out.

Glynnis was undeterred by the doubling of her foes. As the lady closed the parasol, beginning to tell the man her troubles, Glynnis simply reached out and snatched it by its straight wooden handle.

Wooden? Oh dear!

She stared at it, unable to believe what she was seeing. Sighing, she looked up into the shocked faces of the couple.

"This isn't my parasol," Glynnis mused aloud.

"Of course not," the lady said. "How could it be?"

Hargrove arrived at her side. "Please excuse my . . . friend. She's had too much sun, as you noted earlier." Then he turned to her. "Give it back, Miss Talbot. Now."

Glynnis, her cheeks burning, tried to hand the silk umbrella back to the lady, but she flinched, lifted her chin, and went inside.

Hargrove took it from her and gently handed it to the stunned gentleman.

"And this," Glynnis added, giving the man the torn tassel. "Please give your wife my sincere apologies," she said, her voice raspy with humiliation.

The man still said not a word, staring down at the tassel in his palm as Hargrove grabbed her by the arm and pulled her away.

"Leave them in peace," he ordered.

"I'm terribly sorry," she called over her shoulder. Then she said to him, "Well, it certainly looked like mine."

His face was set in stone until they'd walked a few hundred feet, and then he turned to her, a mirth-filled expression.

"The look on that man's face!" And the viscount started to laugh.

Glynnis was glad he wasn't angry with her, but she still didn't have her ivory-handled parasol with its fashionable twin tassels.

"Perhaps you should send the lady a basket of apples or some flowers to make amends," he said.

She cringed, thinking of the cost. Then she smiled at him.

"If you wish to do so on my behalf that would be most welcome."

He stared at her.

"I am of the firm belief it would be better coming directly from you."

She made a face. "Very well." Although she had no intention of doing so.

She realized they'd left the area of the Royal Crescent without stopping.

"What about visiting with Lord Payton?"

"I thought it best if we weren't seen by the Bertrams entering one of their neighbor's homes."

Deflated, Glynnis wished she'd had the opportunity to see inside. It might have been her only chance.

"I am exceedingly thirsty," she declared. "Will you buy me a barley or lemon water?"

After managing to also get Hargrove to open his plump purse for a large sticky bun studded with raisins from Perry's Doughey, a nearby bakery, Glynnis let him escort her back to the Old Ship.

"No assembly tonight," she reminded him, wondering how she would fill her time.

"Even Prinny needs a night off," Hargrove said, "although I'm sure he'll carry on as if he's hosting a gathering."

He hesitated before leaving, although since they were in the public foyer, there was little he could do or say of a private nature, nor could she imagine what might be on his mind. With a smile and nod of his head, he left.

Clutching the sticky bun wrapped in waxy paper, she watched his broad-shouldered form turn left toward his own home, wishing she had a reason to call out to him and make him stay—a reason beyond her heart caring for him above any man she'd ever met.

Sighing, she climbed the stairs and entered her room, stepping upon two missives that had been slid under her door. With excitement, she set the bun on her bed, stripped off her hat and gloves and bent to retrieve the notes.

The first one had the stamp of the Old Ship upon it, and its contents made her blood chill. Her account was coming due in two days. She stared at the sum, knowing it was more than she had. Swallowing her panic, she tossed it onto the bed next to the sticky bun and opened the second folded paper.

What met her eager gaze was an invitation from Lord Dodd to his home the following night. She closed her eyes and thanked her good fortune before running back downstairs to beg a single sheet of paper from the manager. Then, seated at the small writing desk in her room, she accepted his lordship's invitation, noting that it was only for the two of them.

Improper but intriguing.

Obviously, he was going to propose marriage. With one of her last copper ha'pennies in hand, she brought her response downstairs to the porter, handing him the coin to ensure delivery to Lord Dodd's home on the Steyne.

THE FOLLOWING DAY, GLYNNIS made her way unescorted to the Theatre Royal in the middle of the afternoon where the Regent had invited his "friends" to a puppet show. She was half expecting a booth to have been set up center stage with hand puppets to amuse them. Instead, a company of *fantoccini*, or Italian marionettes, performed a comic opera.

She sat in the pit, along with everyone, including the Regent, who was in the middle of the first row. A scaffolding built across the top of the stage with a red velvet curtain tacked on front created a hidden platform for those who handled the marionettes, and no one sat in the boxes overlooking the stage as the view there would spoil the illusion.

Beside her was a single gentleman who enjoyed the opera immensely, laughing so heartily, he brayed and snorted. Glynnis didn't mind in the least, for in the back of her mind was the thrilling notion she was going to be proposed to that night. And while she'd dreamed the night before of Hargrove, it would be Dodd who finally fulfilled her wish.

To her amazement, at the performance's conclusion, Prince George made his way onto the stage and voiced a large wooden puppet fashioned to look like him—or, at least, an improved svelte version of him. His entire speech, performed standing to the side while a puppeteer handled the marionette, was one of naughty jests and lewd innuendo. Glynnis wished Hargrove was there to see the spectacle, but alas, there was no sign of him, nor of her dinner host, Lord Dodd.

Afterward, she wandered alone toward the shops on North Street, wishing she had a few spare coins to buy herself something fine and lacy to celebrate the upcoming event.

Suddenly, making her heart instantly race was the dash-fire viscount, wearing a frown as he strode in her direction. When his gaze landed upon her, however, he smiled, and her insides twinged with pleasure.

"Good day, Miss Talbot."

"Good day, Lord Hargrove. Were you shopping?"

"Nothing so frivolous, I'm afraid. I just left a letter at the Pavilion with sketches of the art from the Louvre, hoping they will entice Prinny to let me show him the pieces."

"You should have come to the theatre. It was enjoyable, and you could have shown him the drawings in person."

He made a face. "I wasn't in the mood for puppets. I thought it best to drop off something he can look at when alone, although that is so rarely the case, I may be in Brighton the rest of my life."

"There's Mrs. Fitzherbert," Glynnis pointed out, seeing that impressive lady strolling along in front of them, past the row of the most expensive shops. As a year-round resident since 1804 with such close ties to the Prince Regent, shopkeepers probably didn't dare charge her more when her former "husband" was in residence at the Pavilion.

"Why don't you see if you can get her to put in a good word for you? Isn't that how royal influence usually works? You go to those who have the prince's ear rather than to the prince himself."

He stared at her. "By Jove, I believe you're getting the hang of all this lickspittle toady nonsense."

She laughed. "Do you think you can charm Mrs. Fitzherbert?"

He cocked his head. "You're a woman. Do *you* think I can?"

Heat rushed to her core. "Most certainly, my lord."

Their gazes locked and held for the span of many moments until a couple had trouble getting around them on the pavement. Stepping aside, Glynnis dragged her thoughts from how much she admired Hargrove back to the task on North Street.

"Come, maybe I can help, too. At least, you won't be a single man accosting her."

Nodding, they fell into step, trailing along behind the prince's former wife and mistress.

"Tell her about the best pieces you have and where you think—" Glynnis broke off.

"Is something the matter?"

When Mrs. Fitzherbert had slowed down and turned to look in a shop window, Glynnis received a nasty shock.

"She has my parasol!"

CHAPTER FIFTEEN

"Nonsense," Hargrove said. "Put whatever you're thinking right out of your pretty head. You're here to help me charm the woman, remember? If you get in wrestling match with her, we shall both be sunk."

"I know my own property," Glynnis insisted.

Mrs. Fitzherbert was twirling her white silken umbrella while bending low to peer at something in the jeweler's window.

"Maybe it simply looks like yours, just like the last one." He glanced around. "See for yourself. Every one I see is the same." He gestured to others walking around them.

But the viscount was wrong. True, her parasol was the same white mulberry silk lined with white tussore silk as nearly every woman's on the street. However, it didn't have an ivory or bone ferrule, but rather a shiny brass tip, which she was plainly visible along with its fetching tan-colored tassels. The two of them whipped around in a dizzying dance.

And while she couldn't see the handle clasped in Mrs. Fitzherbert's hand, this time she had no doubt it was ivory with a spiral carving and not the wooden one of Mrs. Bertram.

"It is mine! I know it," Glynnis said, beginning to quicken her steps.

Hargrove put a hand to her upper arm and stopped her. "What do you think you are doing?"

She glanced from where his fingers branded her arm with his heat then back to his face, which currently wore a severe expression.

"I am going to demand it back," she told him.

"You are not."

"I am."

"Mrs. Fitzherbert might not have been recognized as a legitimate consort by Prinny's royal parents or by Parliament or even by the Church of England, but he adores her nonetheless. And she can be a little, shall we say, unpredictable. I don't want you angering her and then having her tell the prince about it. It could go very badly for you."

"But she has my parasol." Glynnis managed to keep the whine out of her voice with great difficulty. She was not wrong this time.

"Doubtful," Hargrove said. "Was she even at that first picnic?"

"I don't recall," Glynnis said truthfully, "but somehow she got her hands on it."

"Regardless, you cannot confront her. It's a damned umbrella, and you are behaving beyond all reason. Why haven't you bought another one?"

"More to the point, why does she even need it?" Glynnis asked, feeling spiteful. "She is a bit long in the tooth to worry about the sun damaging her face now."

"Hush," Hargrove bit out. "If you're overheard, you'll lose favor with her and then with him for certain. If it is yours, which I highly doubt, then probably someone picked it up and set it inside the Pavilion where she found it. She merely didn't want it to go to waste."

"Then she won't be offended if I tell her it is mine."

Mrs. Fitzherbert had moved on from the jewelry store and was getting farther from them, still twirling the parasol as she strolled. It was almost as if she were taunting Glynnis, who could see her little tassels waving to her.

"I will simply tell her I would like it back."

"No," he insisted. "It will embarrass her."

"Then what do you suggest? Do you see the strong sun beating down upon me?" she fumed.

"As I said before, let's go to a notions' shop at once, and you can buy another."

"I cannot," she said softly.

"Why?" he pressed.

Thinking of her situation of near destitution, she felt tears prick her eyes as the last glimpse of her parasol turned the corner and was lost to her.

He waited.

"I cannot," she repeated loudly and clearly, then spun on the toes of her shoes and began walking in the opposite direction. *What point was there to being on a street with shops when one hadn't a spare farthing?*

Hargrove caught up to her in a flash.

"Are you well?"

She considered her situation, even as they passed by Hanningtons, a large shop selling not only parasols but every other capricious or practical desire, from gloves, fans, hats, stockings, to painted feathers and fancy buttons. She sighed and peered at the clipping from the Brighton Herald stuck prominently upon one window:

"New and elegant Assortment of Goods . . . at unusual Low Prices."

"Better yet," Glynnis said, knowing she sounded confrontational, "let's go in here and you can buy a parasol for me."

Instead of being affronted, he laughed.

"You are always very free with my money. Did you enjoy your almond tart?" he asked by way of reminding her of his previous generosity.

She shrugged. "You have plenty, don't you?" she challenged. If she pricked his nobleman's pride, perhaps he would stop this pointless discussion and simply buy her a blasted silk umbrella.

But looking directly at her, he shot back, "I do, as do you. Don't you? Or do you race through the allowance of a viscount's daughter, like a spendthrift and now seek to go through my income as well?"

That remark was like a slap to the face.

"I assure you I am quite frugal." He had no idea. She could squeeze a penny until it cried.

"Then you ought to have enough for a trifle like a parasol," Hargrove persisted.

"Why are you being so unchivalrous and ungentlemanly and . . . and miserly?" She was ready to stamp her foot like a child.

But he laughed again. "I am not. But you are *not* my responsibility. It would appear strange for me to be buying you presents, would it not? Where is that wretched fiancé of yours who should be buying you baubles and bonnets?"

The tears threatened again and Glynnis raised her eyes heavenward for a second. When she believed they wouldn't spill over, she looked at him again. She wanted to tell him there was no fiancé and that she was facing the world by herself. But she couldn't. She knew what he thought of her actions in London. If he discovered she'd lied about being engaged, he would bolt so fast, she would see nothing but a blur of breeches.

"My fiancé will be here soon enough," she said, recalling her dinner with Lord Dodd that very evening.

In any case, for some reason, her words wiped the smile from his face.

"Will he?"

"Yes." She looked away, tired of lying to him and to herself. "Anyway, I don't need a parasol. My hat is doing the job perfectly and keeping my hands free."

"To do what?" he asked, offering a sly look.

"You are incorrigible. I'm going back to my hotel," she said.

"Not yet." And Hargrove opened the door of Hanningtons for her. "I cannot possibly pass up 'unusual low prices.' Let me buy my *friend* a parasol."

JAMES HAD THE SUDDEN and terrible notion that Miss Talbot really didn't have any money. It would make clear why she starved herself some days and moaned over the loss of a hat or a pair of shoes or even paltry gloves, for that matter. He didn't know any other ladies of the *ton* who didn't have a dozen of everything and yet ordered more of each on a whim.

However, she seemed truly distressed over a parasol and willing to incur the wrath of someone as powerful as Mrs. Fitzherbert, even if Prinny had moved on to sharing his bed with Lady Hertford. James would hate to see Miss Talbot given the cut direct by the Prince Regent over such a silly matter.

He would buy her a damn parasol if only to see her soft brown eyes look happy again, rather than glistening with tears. *And where was that damned fiancé?* Aberavon was negligent at best. Moreover, why was a viscount's daughter traipsing around unchaperoned and perhaps with insufficient funds to her name?

He didn't like it, not one bit.

Thus, he ushered her into the store, known for selling linens, mercery, haberdashery, and hosiery. Assuredly, it would have something to suit Miss Talbot.

"Why don't you choose a colorful one. Green or orange, perhaps?" he suggested. Then she might not lose it so readily.

She looked at him as if he were a simpleton.

"I would need one for every gown in that case," she said. "The best parasol is plain to match with anything at any event. Although I do like that blue one."

He watched her linger at a dusky blue parasol with frills before taking hold of a white one. It looked similar to the one she'd almost wrested from Prinny's one-time wife, except this one had not only two tassels but a small tassel at the end of each rib. He could see that additional bit of whimsy pleased her.

"A perfect-sized handle," she said, wrapping her fingers around it, giving him a flash of entirely inappropriate thoughts regarding her fingers around an equally hard part of his person.

"Not too heavy so as to be tiring," she continued, oblivious to his wildly libidinous thoughts, "not too thick as to be clumsy, nor too thin so as I might lose my grip upon it."

His mouth dropped open slightly. James had no idea there were so many factors to choosing such a utilitarian object as an umbrella.

When she was satisfied with her choice, he paid for it with ready coin from his purse before slipping it back into his pocket. Easy as that, they departed the shop.

"Thank you. It was very kind of you." She seemed sincerely grateful.

"I was glad to oblige you, Miss Talbot." He was. What's more, seeing her happiness, he wished he'd done it sooner before she'd been brought to the brink of tears.

As soon as they were on the pavement, she popped it open, and he stooped to peer under it, amazed at how brilliant her smile despite the sun no longer shining on her face.

His breath caught slightly. *How was it that Miss Talbot grew more enchanting each day?*

"What now?" she asked, as if they had agreed to an outing or to spending the day together.

"I was going to wait a few minutes and then call upon Prinny to see if he'll allow me to bring the art to him. Or to force him to look at my crude descriptions of what I've brought. I know he's disappointed, but I believe he will like something."

"I asked you once if I could help. Maybe if I saw the art first, then I could accompany you and express to the prince my enjoyment of it."

James hesitated. That would mean taking her back to his home. Alone.

Yet she looked so earnest, he heard himself agreeing. In less than ten minutes, they were at his front door, which remained unlatched until nightfall. He pushed it open and they walked into the foyer where they stood awkwardly.

He considered calling for the butler who came with the house. Mr. Sparks was probably in the back with his feet up drinking James's tea—*hopefully not his brandy*—as he was not expected back until later.

"Set down your parasol, Miss Talbot. No one will steal it here." In turn, he put his hat and gloves on the hallstand.

She had nothing else to remove, at least not if this was to remain a decent encounter. Therefore, he gestured toward the stairs.

"The art is in a bedroom."

"Oh!" she uttered.

That one little word and the way her cheeks pinkened were nearly his undoing. James wanted to sweep her into his arms and carry her up the stairs, although that was never as easy nor as romantic as one hoped. Usually, there was an awkward amount of huffing and puffing, occasionally a staggering at the top on the landing before that blissful moment when one could set the dead weight of a relaxed woman upon the bed.

These feminine creatures looked like froth and air and light, but they felt like a huge sack of unwieldy coal.

Watching her ascend in front of him, he could not return his wayward thoughts to civility. Rather, they were playing in the lowest level of impropriety, of lusty actions and wicked wantonness.

When they reached the landing, he said, "One more flight up, I'm afraid."

She turned and shot him a smile, as if to say that was no matter. And again, he followed her luscious figure, with her round bottom making the merest outline of an appearance at each step.

When she turned toward the front bedroom, he had to reprimand himself for almost allowing her to go the wrong way, which would lead to an entirely different showing than one of art.

"No, not that door," he said. "That's my room." He enjoyed the sea view and the breeze in the night. Swallowing his desire, he added, "The other end of the hall. The last door."

He went in ahead of her and considered the crated contents. With ease, he removed the wooden top of the first one and drew out one of the smaller paintings. Holding this up for her perusal, he waited.

While he hadn't expected her to adore it, he also hadn't expected the look of dislike, quickly shuttered over to one of neutrality.

"Maybe it's the way the sunlight is streaming in here so brightly, but the painting does seem to be rather dark."

He sighed. "Yes. They are all like that. But in a large room with some grandeur, it could be the perfect decoration."

She nodded, and he put it back, drawing out a vase of peacock blue porcelain and gold overlay.

Miss Talbot smiled, and he thought it worth more than the entire roomful of art.

"Now that should please him," she said. "How could it not?"

"Because he is the unpredictable Prince George. But I do think he will like some of these pieces. If not for here, then for Carlton House."

"They should be on public display," she mused. "As they were at the Louvre."

"If Prinny has them, they practically will be. He has so many parties, anything in his homes is widely seen."

"I suppose." Uninvited, she lifted the lid on another crate and peered in. It was one of the few statues he'd secured and also had a sheet over it.

Drawing this aside, she ran a finger over its marble arm, making him lusty again.

"That's rather splendid," she proclaimed.

She was splendid! But he came to stand beside her and raise the other edge of the sheet.

"I think so, too," he said. "No one has seen it outside of Paris or Prussia, except for me and you."

She glanced at him and gave her saucy smile. "I'm honored."

He wanted to kiss her, and the honor would be entirely his.

A fiancé, he reminded himself, dropping the sheet and moving as far from her as he could.

To his amazement, she followed him, getting too close, looking at his face with the same attention she'd given the pieces of art.

"Shall we?" she asked, and he would vow her voice had dropped to a purring tone.

"Shall we?" he croaked, repeating her words, unable to take his gaze from her upturned face.

CHAPTER SIXTEEN

Hauling her against him by her upper arms, James swiftly took her mouth under his.

"*Mm,*" she murmured, but he couldn't tell if she said actual words or just hummed with pleasure.

In the next instant, he sank his fingers into her hair, just under her jaunty hat at the back of her head so he could apply more pressure to the kiss. When she gasped softly, he swept his tongue between her lips and plundered to his heart's content.

Exploring, sucking, caressing, James fervently wished they were horizontal. He also wished his breeches were looser as his shaft had risen to a great length with painful rigidity.

"*Mm,*" she managed again. However, she didn't try to step back or put her hands upon his chest to push him away. Yet nor did she encircle her fingers into his hair the way she had before. He liked tremendously when she did that.

Finally, he stopped. They both needed to suck in large breaths, which they did, staring at one another.

"Shall we do so again?" he asked when she looked at him with a glassy gaze and reddened mouth.

"We can, yes, but I meant, shall we go at once to see the prince?"

It was his turn to utter that one small word. *"Oh."*

What an idiot! He lowered his hands from her head, dragging some errant locks of her hair as he did.

After another moment in which he was certain his cheeks were taking on a ruddy pallor, he said, "I apologize."

But she merely shrugged. "An honest mistake. It's something we do well together, don't you think?"

He did! Better than he'd ever done with any other woman in fact. He hoped she felt the same. He had no idea how much kissing Miss Talbot had done in her life, but he knew she'd done some. On the other hand, it was a question no one had ever politely asked him before.

"Yes, we do it very well together. But we shouldn't. Again, I offer my apologies. Let's put your new parasol to good use and go to the Pavilion. Hopefully, with you along, Prinny will agree to see me and at least talk about the art."

And the Regent responded as James's anticipated, allowing them access to his person after they were announced.

"I'm so glad you came by, Miss Talbot, even if you're back with *this* rogue. What happened to Dodd? Or your fiancé, for that matter?"

But Prince George didn't really want an answer. He started to laugh with good humor before she could say anything. They found themselves walking with him into his private apartments where he ordered wine for all three of them.

"Tell me," he said once they were seated, "are people enjoying my little assemblies?"

"Immensely, Your Royal Highness," Miss Talbot promised him. Then she shot James a glance, raising her eyebrow, then back at Prinny. "Before your next gathering, sir, wouldn't you like to install some new art to astound your guests?"

The Prince Regent made a sour face. "Take care not to put me in a bad mood over Hargrove's failure."

"Failure?" Miss Talbot exclaimed. "Oh, sir, you must see what he has brought you from Paris. The most wondrous paintings and sculptures."

"Not *the* most wondrous," Prinny pointed out sullenly. "He didn't get what I asked him to bring me."

"That may be true, Your Highness, but your guests won't have the pieces side-by-side to compare. They will see only your new acquisitions and marvel at them. I vow you will want to take them all back with you to London to display in your other homes."

"Perhaps," Prinny allowed, with the first perk of interest.

James proffered an invitation.

"Would you care to come to my house on the Marine Parade, Your Highness, to look at them?"

Prinny grimaced.

"Not really, unless you are on the Circle. Are you?"

"No, sir."

Prinny folded his arms over his large stomach that appeared to be bursting his buttons. "Then you must bring them here."

James felt the end in sight for the first time in months.

"When?" he asked, trying to keep the eagerness from his tone.

"Before the next party, naturally, as the lady said."

All hail the miracle-worker, Miss Talbot!

"I shall bring them by tomorrow, Your Highness." James wanted to dance a jig of happiness. As soon as the pieces were accepted, he could be on his way.

Glancing at Miss Talbot, his excitement quelled. He couldn't imagine her fending for herself in Brighton without his assistance. Perhaps he would stay until Aberavon arrived so he could be assured of her well-being.

"You must bring Miss Talbot back with you," Prinny commanded. "And not too early, not before mid-afternoon." Then he addressed her more softly. "I hope you will come. I'm sure you're more splendid than anything Hargrove has." He said it as if she had a choice. Then he added, "I trust you'll help me pick out the best location for each piece."

"I will, Your Highness. I look forward to it."

"Meanwhile," Prinny said, rising to his feet, and they both rushed to do the same, "you two must leave. Or rather, you may stay if you wish, but I have somewhere to go and someone to see." He smiled. "Brighton is far superior to London, I think."

James didn't respond, nor did Miss Talbot except with a diplomatic nod. Then Prinny walked out of his own private room, shuffling still but not using a cane, an indication his gout was much improved.

"That went well," she said, looking pleased with herself.

James wished he could hug her, perhaps swing her around in a merry twirl.

"Thanks to you, it did. All previous attempts to make him look at them were met with stern resistance. Until you."

She beamed a large smile. He would swear it surrounded his heart with its warm beauty.

"What are you doing for dinner?" he asked.

Her smile disappeared. "I nearly forgot. I'm going to Lord Dodd's home for dinner."

"Ah, I see." But James didn't. *Why was she toying with the man?* And if it wasn't that, then she must genuinely enjoy Dodd's company.

"I would invite you along," she began, her cheeks pinkening.

"No, you can hardly do that. Brighton is small enough that Dodd and Miss Montrose know where I am. If they had wanted to invite me, they would have."

She glanced away and then at the floor.

"Shall we go?" she said. "I doubt His Highness really meant for us to stay in his room in his absence."

James nodded, and they began the trek to the mundane world outside the Pavilion.

DISHEARTENED BY THE DRAGGING length of the day after enjoying herself with Hargrove and knowing she would not see him again until the following afternoon, Glynnis did the unthinkable. At least, it would be in London. She showed up at Lord Dodd's home *before* the appointed hour. Many would think it outrageous she hadn't asked for an escort, but his home was so close, merely around the corner and along the Steyne.

Perhaps on the way home, when it was dark, she would allow him to walk her back to the Old Ship.

Even more outrageous was the fact that Miss Montrose would not be at the dinner or the entertainment afterward. Lord Dodd's missive had pointedly invited her to a dinner for two in order for them to become better acquainted. Glynnis knew being alone with a man in his home for hours was indefensible.

With a start, she realized she had done precisely the same with Hargrove, but somehow that was different since he had no intention of marrying her. Frowning at her own tortured logic, she rapped upon the door, wishing it had opened as she'd approached. Standing on the step was a most unsettling thing.

Moreover, Glynnis knew Hargrove would be disappointed in her, perhaps appalled, if he ever learned this was to be a party of two. And lately, what the viscount thought about her had come to matter a great deal.

After a short wait, a maid not the butler opened the door. At first, Glynnis was not readily given admittance. She had to give her name and explain she was there for dinner.

"Dinner isn't being served yet, miss," the maid said doubtfully. And since she apparently wasn't used to tending the door, she didn't immediately invite Glynnis inside to wait in the small downstairs parlor or, more appropriately, upstairs in the drawing room where she and Hargrove had been entertained during the previous visit.

Glynnis had to ask, "Is Lord Dodd at home?"

"Yes, miss," but the maid looked behind her as if unsure.

"Then why don't I await him in the drawing room while you tell his lordship I'm here." And no longer willing to stand on the step—after all, she was a viscount's daughter—she pushed her way inside.

"Yes, miss," the girl said before disappearing down the hallway toward the kitchen.

Somehow, Glynnis doubted Lord Dodd was in the servant's area. After poking her head into the informal parlor where one might take breakfast or read the paper and seeing it empty, she mounted the staircase.

While Glynnis would never dream of going two flights up to the private rooms, at least not until she became Lord Dodd's wife, she decided to make herself comfortable in the drawing room. Hopefully, he would be made aware of her presence and come find her. They could have a glass of wine and get to know one another better.

As she approached the drawing room, she heard noises.

Pausing, she nearly fled back down the stairs. But alarmingly, the distinct sound of moaning floated through the closed double doors, and then she heard a male voice groan.

Gracious! Was Dodd injured? Perhaps a dangerous London light-fingered napper had accompanied the other people from Town and had broken into the house to pilfer valuables. If Lord Dodd had surprised the varlet, violence might have occurred.

Before she could think better of barging in, Glynnis did exactly that. Tossing open one of the cream-colored doors, she took two steps into the drawing room and halted in frozen disbelief.

She could barely credit her eyes. There, on the sofa where she first saw Miss Montrose, Glynnis now saw a lot more of her! Naked as a needle, Isabelle was straddling Lord

Dodd, who was fully clothed but with his breeches pushed to his knees. The woman appeared to be riding him, going up and down on his hips as if he were a horse.

Pausing, Isabelle stared directly at Glynnis. Then, without even the stain of embarrassment coloring her cheeks, she smiled before closing her eyes, putting her head back, and beginning to move her hips even more rapidly.

Meanwhile, Lord Dodd, whom Glynnis had thought to marry a mere few minutes earlier, craned his neck to see what the interruption was.

"Oh, blast!" he exclaimed upon seeing her. "Isabelle, stop. You must . . . stop."

But she didn't, and he groaned again. Glynnis realized the sound wasn't one of pain at all, but absolute pleasure.

Glynnis couldn't unfreeze her feet although she desperately wanted to. Yet it was as if observing a naughty book come to life. She watched as Isabelle Montrose continued enjoying herself, rising up and sinking down. Lord Dodd appeared helpless to extricate himself from under her, and in fact, aided her movements with a hand on either side of her waist.

The agreeable sensations were obviously too good for him to push her aside and end the love-making. His fingers dug into the soft flesh of the woman's hips, and he rose to meet her body, driving deeply into her core.

All the while, Isabelle's large breasts bounced in a mesmerizing fashion. And then she gave a full-throated scream, making Glynnis jump despite watching it happen. It was followed a moment later by a guttural cry from Lord Dodd as he performed a series of rapid thrusts before he finally stilled.

Only then did Isabelle open her eyes again and look at Glynnis.

"You are early, Miss Talbot," she said. "How shocking of you!" Then she grinned. "But I assure you, he's quite good. If you give Hugh the better part of a half hour, he'll be up to it again. Even better by the time you've eaten dinner."

Then Isabelle climbed off of him and unhurriedly took her gown from where it was draped over the back of the sofa. Holding it in her arms, barely covering herself, she brushed past Glynnis and out the open door.

By this time, Lord Dodd had swiveled his legs to the floor, fastened his breeches, and rose to his feet.

"I'm sorry you came in unannounced," he said as opposed to apologizing for any number of other egregious events.

"But she's your *aunt*," Glynnis pointed out, her voice hardly above a whisper.

He cocked his head. "Only by marriage."

As if that gave him leave to give her a good swiving.

Glynnis shook her head, still stunned. She couldn't deny seeing the act played out before her had been eye-opening in the extreme.

"Do you wish to wait?" Lord Dodd asked, confounding her with his meaning until he added, "Shall we put off our own enjoyment until after dinner? That had been my plan. My pole is at half-mast now, but Isabelle is incorrect. It will be stiff as a tree limb in far less than a half hour, especially if you undress for me."

"Undress for you?" Glynnis was sure she'd walked into an asylum. "Are you mad?"

He took a step closer. "Don't tell me you are now becoming prudish. Or are you feeling jealous of her?" He ran a hand through his blond hair, smoothing it. "I promise you, Isabelle and I are *not* a couple. She has lovers, I have lovers. When it suits us, we satisfy one another. It doesn't mean I desire you any less."

"I thought you wanted to marry me," she protested, instantly wishing she'd kept her naïve notion to herself.

His expression became one of astonishment. "But you're already engaged. That's what makes you perfect, Miss Talbot. I assumed you were looking for some excitement *before* the dreadful day when you marry a man you barely know and whom you seem so little interested."

That was why he'd asked if she were in love with her fiancé and whether she knew him well. She supposed some women would, in fact, consider this a good bargain—if one were none-too-happily engaged.

"Never mind all that, Miss Talbot. I haven't changed my mind. Are you up for the sport? I can give you a tupping to remember. More than one if we suit and decide to enjoy each other's company for the remainder of my stay in Brighton. That is, until your fiancé arrives. And even then . . . ," he trailed off with a lascivious smile and reached out to take her hand in his.

Glynnis dodged backward. Hargrove had refused to tup her *because* she was engaged. Lord Dodd *wanted* to swive with her for the exact same reason.

What strange creatures men were!

Without bothering to answer, she turned and walked out, down the stairs and back onto the Steyne. She was exactly where she had begun when she'd first arrived in Brighton, no worse for the experience, except she'd run out of money. She'd wasted all her precious time on Lord Dodd.

Tomorrow, she had to settle up with the Old Ship and decide what to do. *What a sorry plight she was in!*

Ahead of her were two ladies wandering along, and Glynnis almost called out to them since they seemed to be going her way. Then she realized they were harlots, and one was the frowsy blonde in which Hargrove had shown an interest the first night.

Other people were out, too, on this pleasant evening, but they were mostly couples. There were also a few young bucks who took notice of her, perhaps mistaking her for a lightskirt. Viscounts' daughters didn't walk alone after sundown in evening dress, looking shiftless and with nowhere to go.

Thus, she caused her footsteps to become purposeful, passing the trollops who had stopped at the corner. They tittered when she went by, and for a moment, Glynnis wondered if they were more fortunate, more intelligent than she. After all, they were selling themselves as she'd hoped to do. Whereas she was offering her body for a lifetime as a wife, they only had to give theirs for an hour, maybe less, although there was little security in their precarious positions.

Sadly, presently, she had even less. At least they had enough money to keep a roof over their heads on the Steyne, not to mention companionship. She had neither. Even if she started selling packets of shells for the popular passion of *shelling*, with genteel ladies in London fixing shells to frames, vases, and even their hats, it would be too late. She needed assistance immediately.

Which was why when she reached the Marine Parade, she turned left instead of right, toward Hargrove's home instead of the Old Ship.

For the second time that night, she stood upon a nobleman's doorstep. Taking a deep and steadying breath, Glynnis knocked.

CHAPTER SEVENTEEN

When Hargrove's butler opened the door, Glynnis faltered. Uninvited and standing on the doorstep about to ask whether the man's employer was home, she felt like little more than a bedizened beggar in fancy dress.

Immediately, the man stepped back. "Miss Talbot, do come in. Lord Hargrove is at home."

How kind of him to remember her and to give her entrance!

"Mr. Sparks, isn't it?"

"Yes, miss. This way." And as a proper butler would do for a proper young lady, even one *without* a chaperone, he led her up the stairs to the formal drawing room.

"I will tell his lordship you're here."

"He's not expecting me," she confessed.

Mr. Sparks barely faltered in his step. "I understand, miss." And he disappeared.

Glancing at the sofa, recalling what she'd just seen, she opted for the gray winged-back chair. Leaning her head back, she closed her eyes. Instantly, Isabelle's face—*and her breasts!*—and Lord Dodd's bucking hips came to mind, and Glynnis could almost hear the moans and groans.

"Miss Talbot?"

Her eyes flicked open. Hargrove, looking so very familiar and normal, stood just inside the open door.

"Did I forget we had a prior engagement?"

She wished they had an engagement of an entirely different kind.

"You know you didn't," she said. "I apologize for coming uninvited. I was . . . I was . . . ," she trailed off and tossed up her hands.

What could she say? Glynnis might confess the absolute base and terrible truth, that she had no fiancé and no money.

He looked at her curiously. "Are you finding yourself with time on your hands before your dinner with Dodd?"

She startled, having completely forgotten he knew.

"You do look to be at sixes and sevens," he added. "And beautiful, too, may I add."

"I am not dining with Lord Dodd as it turns out."

Should she tell him? She would be pouring a large cup of gossip-water if she did.

"Has something happened?" he asked, coming farther into the room but leaving the door open.

"Will you sit?" she asked. "You make me unsettled standing there like a footman."

That made him grin. "It's the hour for a glass of wine, don't you think?" he offered.

Glynnis was grateful he was being so hospitable. "Yes, I do. And thank you."

She waited while he tugged the bell pull and ordered wine from the swift housemaid before he sat on the sofa opposite her.

Oh, what could be done on a sofa!

"You're blushing, Miss Talbot."

Her gaze snapped to his.

"And now you're blanching." He rested his elbows on his knees leaning forward. "What on earth has got into you?"

She couldn't tell him she'd hoped to make Lord Dodd her husband, but everything else was fair game, she supposed. As soon as she had a glass of claret in her hand, she told him every sordid detail.

"With his aunt," Hargrove declared, not looking as shocked as she would have expected.

"By marriage," she reminded him. For even if the man was a licentious gadabout, Lord Dodd wasn't depraved. At least, she assumed not.

"Exactly the case," Hargrove said. "I knew it."

"You knew it?"

"There was something off about that pair, and no self-respecting aunt-by-marriage, meaning no relation at all in truth, would stay unchaperoned with a man about her age. And both of them single as sausages."

"Indeed," Glynnis agreed.

"You had quite an eyeful, I take it."

"Yes," she said softly and sipped her wine, beginning to feel soothed. "I wish I could eliminate that eyeful, too. It's not pleasant to have someone else's amorous congress floating about in one's head."

He was trying not to smile. It was obvious. He lost the battle with himself and laughed outright.

What could she do but shake her head?

Then her stomach grumbled loudly.

His eyes widened.

"You are dressed for dinner," he pointed out.

She nodded, hopefully.

"I could have another place set at my table," Hargrove offered.

She detected a little hesitancy.

"Were you eating alone?" she asked, settling back farther into the chair, with the promise of not having to leave for hours.

"Indeed, I was. I mentioned Lord Payton before. He was to dine with me, but he had a better offer at the last moment."

"A female?" she surmised.

"Indubitably," he agreed.

"Frankly, I am glad," she confessed. "You are my only friend in town, and I couldn't bear returning to my hotel after . . . after what happened."

Her stomach rumbled again.

"Moreover, as usual, you're hungry."

"Famished," she declared. "Naturally, I had saved up my appetite for Lord Dodd's dinner table. The food was good at his home last time, don't you think?" And she drained her wine glass, becoming pleasantly relaxed.

"Yes, he did put out a good meal. I hope my own Cook can do as well." He paused, then added, "You realize this is simply *not* done, a single man and woman dining together in private."

She shrugged, deciding not to mention how she'd been going to do the very same with Lord Dodd without Miss Montrose as chaperone. The ridiculous notion of that woman as a chaperone made her smile.

"I won't tell anyone," Glynnis promised.

"Not even your fiancé?" Hargrove asked.

"Especially not him," she said, recalling how she had to start over tomorrow with finding a new one.

"And you're not going to leave here later screeching to the world how I debauched you and then force me into marriage?"

Glynnis sighed, saddened that he still feared she might trap him into marrying her. "Still gnawing at that bone, are you?"

"It was a shockingly sneaky thing to do."

"I suppose." Regardless, she would have to try it again soon with another man.

"Very well," Hargrove said, relaxing a little. "Let's hope I can satisfy your endless appetite."

As soon as he spoke, she locked her gaze with his, and the meaning of his words changed to something altogether different, some suggestive innuendo she didn't entirely understand but which made her skin feel prickly.

After seeing Isabelle on top of Lord Dodd and how they'd reached a satisfying ending, she could only imagine how it would be if it were she and Hargrove.

Glynnis swallowed.

He cleared his throat.

"More wine?" he offered, and poured it from the crystal decanter.

"Thank you," she croaked.

But when she lifted the refilled glass to her mouth to wet her suddenly parched lips, her hand trembled and she spilled a little.

"Blast!" she exclaimed, seeing a few drops of red wine on her pale gray silk. It was stupidly clumsy, but Hargrove and his intense masculinity unnerved her. Hurriedly setting the glass down, she drew a handkerchief from her reticule and dabbed at the small stain.

Small or not, it was conspicuous. She closed her eyes a moment and wished it away.

"Are you well?"

"Another gown to worry over," she said quietly. "If it were a grease stain, I would use chalk or perhaps rectified spirits of wine—"

"Wine on a wine stain?"

"This isn't funny. For red wine on silk, I need gin and honey, I think."

"Are you drinking the dress or cleaning it?" he quipped.

"I don't suppose you have any ox-gall?"

Hargrove looked startled. "No, I don't. At least I don't think I do."

"That's extraordinarily careless of you," she admonished, "but I expect your laundress does or knows where the closest butcher's is."

"The butcher wouldn't be open at this hour in any case. Won't boiling hot water do the trick?"

She almost snapped at him but caught herself. After all, she didn't want to miss a free meal.

"One doesn't put silk in boiling water. No more than one ever submerges wool in water, not unless you want to have a version of your suit in miniature."

She pulled on the edges of the skirt, holding it up to examine.

"Salt maybe," she mused, "or urine."

"Urine!" he repeated, sounding horrified. "Let's go back to the ox-gall."

The tone of his voice would have made her laugh if the matter of an unwearable gown didn't make her wish to cry. Men were squeamish about the everyday things that women dealt with. Her last lady's maid in London could handle all manner of stains and kept Glynnis's clothing in perfect condition, but it was still somewhat of a mystery to her as she attempted to do the same.

Releasing the fabric back onto her lap, she accepted the fact she simply could not wear the gown again until she could get it to a professional. The Old Ship manager was too expensive, and she had no idea to whom he sent her clothing the previous time. All she knew was that he'd added an ungodly sum to her account.

Feeling subdued, she didn't answer when Hargrove asked her about whether the hotel was noisy in the evenings or early mornings.

She wanted to close her eyes and contemplate how she'd reached this point where a couple drops of wine were her undoing. Her brother would probably dump an entire bottle over his own head and laugh it off.

"Miss Talbot?" he prompted.

"It is not noisy," she said. "And it wouldn't matter if it were since I won't be there much longer."

"No?" he asked. "Where will you be?"

Because she was tired of being brave, she said, "I haven't the foggiest notion."

Her treacherous insides grumbled again.

Hargrove rose to his feet and offered her his hand, "Come along, Miss Talbot. Let's make some tooth music

181

and take the wrinkles out of your stomach, as they say. Then you can tell me why you're moving from the jolly Old Ship."

She took his hand, glad for it since all the wine had gone to her head and left her wobbly and feeling a little loose-tongued and silly. In fact, she wanted to toss herself at his feet and beg for assistance. Instead, as they walked into his dining room, her tears finally spilled over.

JAMES WAS SHOCKED TO his core as he realized Miss Talbot was silently crying when he drew out her chair.

Not sure whether to remark upon her distress or to wait out the awkward deluge, he did neither but handed her a handkerchief from his pocket. Then he took his seat.

Almost surreptitiously, she wiped her cheeks. However, ruining the graceful effect, next she blew her nose, sounding like a honking goose.

He could remain quiet no longer.

"Are you in financial distress?"

At first, she simply froze, the handkerchief still covering her face. However, after a moment, she lowered it and nodded.

"It seems I am."

Carefully placing his napkin upon his lap and wondering how much he should pry, he decided to speak forthrightly.

"May I ask how you came to be in this state?"

She sighed, and the sound nearly broke his heart. Yet he would have to wait to hear for the footman brought in the first course of bouillon. Before starting upon it, she stripped off her gloves and reached for a piece of bread, which to his amazement, she devoured, looking more like a street urchin than a lady.

When she'd swallowed all of it, every last crumb, she took another and this time, took the time to butter it before setting it on her plate. Then she fixed him with her glorious coffee-brown gaze.

"I thought it best I soak up the spirits before I continue," she explained.

"Naturally." Then he waited.

"In Bath, did you know it cost two guineas for a ticket to a ball?" she asked.

He hadn't expected that tact. "No, I wasn't aware."

"And five shillings for concert tickets!" she continued.

"I had no idea." He had no idea because he never gave it a thought. With a large income of over ten thousand pounds a year, James didn't concern himself with shillings.

"And the cost of food has remained very high despite the end of the war. You know we were promised costs would go down. The market is stuffed with goods and high production. Everyone can see that. I have a cousin on the Continent who says their economy has revived." She took a moment to take a bite of the buttered bread, relish it, and then swallow. He was mesmerized.

"But we British have to suffer the Corn Law keeping our food prices high."

James was as amazed by her discussion as by her lovely mouth chewing bread. She stated her complaint as if women spoke every day about Parliamentary acts designed to appease the farmers and the noblemen who owned the largest tracts of agricultural land at the expense of the everyday folks.

"A shilling for a week's worth of candles," she continued.

"A week's worth?" he asked, wondering how many that was. "Doesn't that depend on the size of your household?"

"Yes, of course A shilling for a two-pound package of candles, and not the best either. The smoky kind. Can you imagine?"

"No," James said. "I honestly cannot." His candles definitely didn't smoke.

"Coal costs three shillings a week, and a maid of all work—"

He waited for the dreaded pronouncement.

"She can cost as much as sixteen pounds a year!"

That didn't sound high, but by her expression, he knew he was supposed to react.

"Well!" he said.

She narrowed her eyes at him.

"Do you know the cost of bread, sugar, or tea? What about fish?"

To each question, he shook his head. She enlightened him until his head spun with numbers.

"And you know all this because?" he asked.

"Because, Lord Hargrove, I have to count every penny I spend. I scrimped until the day I had to let my last maid go."

"*Your* last maid? But you don't keep a house in London by yourself?"

"I managed my family's modest residence, north of Hyde Park, along with my brother, Rhys. Sometimes my parents came to Town for a few weeks and then I relinquished the task to my mother. Rhys is rambling around in it on his own now, and I don't know if he has a staff of even one."

She was fuming, and James understood her brother was at fault.

"I'm sorry to hear that. I know a little of your brother. Quite a swell, yet with more the reputation of a pigeon than a shark, if I recall correctly."

"Sadly, you do. He receives enough to pay for running the entire household, but he squanders it and lets someone give him a sound physicking at cards every week. And still my parents find no fault with him."

"That sounds terribly unfair. And thus, when I mentioned your allowance as a viscount's daughter—"

"Pittance," she said. "I do my best with what I have. When the creditors were tenfold upon the doorstep on a Monday morning, I left London and went to Bath."

"Bath is lovely," James began.

"Bath is also expensive and . . . ," she trailed off momentarily, her eyes taking on a faraway look. "And the slip-slops and cats."

"Gruel?" he echoed. "And cats?"

She shrugged. "I have an elderly great aunt in Bath. However, she could only introduce me to other elderly people, mostly women."

Now, James was confused. "Then where did you meet your fiancé?"

She startled, paused, drank some wine. *Was she embarrassed? Had she trapped the man into it the way she'd tried to trap him?*

"Lord Aberavon is a friend of the family. His ancestral home is not too distant from ours."

He supposed that was an answer, bespeaking of a long-standing promise between the families to wed the son to the daughter.

"Your parents will send you nothing more?"

"They think me still in London," she confessed, shocking him.

Miss Talbot was not only without a chaperone or a protector, her family had no idea of her whereabouts. This simply wasn't done in his circle. When a young lady went missing, the search usually began instantly due to the ever-present fear of an elopement to Scotland.

"Besides," she said, "and I hate to speak out of turn, but I shall although my father would be mortified and my mother, too. Our Welsh viscountcy is not as I understand some of the English ones to be. Yours for instance probably has a good income associated with it, not to be vulgar," she added. "And what there is to spare goes to the heir."

"The Honorable Rhys Talbot," James muttered, feeling outraged on her behalf.

She held up her glass as if toasting his astuteness.

"Then I say again, it is unacceptable for you to be in Brighton without a chaperone or even a maid, as I now discover. Moreover, it's unconscionable that your parents haven't discovered your departure yet. And what about your brother? Surely he has noticed you're not at home handling the creditors."

"Rhys believes me still to be in Bath." She lowered her gaze, and he had to admit she was a clever lady for having managed to gain her freedom with no one the wiser. Clever but foolish.

"And what of Aberavon? Doesn't he care that you are gallivanting around, close to drowning? Not to mention starving most days?"

"I'm sure he would care if he knew," she said. "When my fiancé gets here, all will be well."

And then she burst into tears again, but this time, they were loud, body-wracking sobs.

CHAPTER EIGHTEEN

James jumped up from his chair and came around the corner of the table. Drawing out her chair, he squatted down before her.

"Please Miss Talbot, don't cry."

She snatched up the napkin from her lap and used it as a handkerchief.

"Why not? You've got it all out of me. Yes, I am in financial distress. To put it plainly, my lord, I am at low tide. While my brother makes ducks and drakes at the gaming hells, the devil himself may dance in my pockets they are so empty."

The absurdity of a beautiful lady in an evening gown talking about her empty pockets and wiping her tears caused a flash of anger to tear through James. Of course, he knew how the world worked and that she couldn't earn money. He also knew how an heir could be a profligate spendthrift. But he couldn't fathom her parents allowing their only daughter to fall to this fate of insecurity.

"Your parents seem woefully negligent," he said softly, hoping it didn't make her start crying again.

She hung her head. "They didn't know how dreadful it was in London. I tried my best, and I thought I could . . . ," she trailed off, sniffed, and then started again. "I thought I might start over in Bath, but that wasn't to be. Then I recalled the Prince Regent's birthday and knew he was planning to come here this year. So I thought I would . . . ," again she trailed off.

"Await Lord Aberavon here in sunny Brighton," he supplied.

She looked at him and blinked her lovely eyes. "Precisely."

"I suppose it's as nice a place as any, less rainy than Bath and without the dreaded slip-slops." He hoped he could lighten her mood with a little jest.

She shrugged. "I can no longer afford even gruel. Nor can I pay the entire bill at the Old Ship, which is due tomorrow. I'm a shilling or two short."

"A shilling or two?" he asked, believing her because he now knew her to be careful with money and particular down to the penny. "What will you do now?"

She looked away, pursed her lips, and said nothing.

He recalled their first meeting and how she'd wolfed down the sandwiches.

"I am sorry I left you with the bill from the café."

Her gaze swung back to him and, wonder of wonders, she laughed, a lovely sound despite the situation.

"I was annoyed when you did it," she admitted, "but it doesn't matter now. That small coin wouldn't save me from—"

"From what?" he demanded.

"From whatever comes next. In truth, I am not sure. I have never been quite so low." She looked down at the soiled gown. "I cannot afford to stay another night, yet I cannot afford passage home."

"Besides, what would your fiancé think if you left now?" James reminded her, not sure why but reluctant to have her leave. Then he realized why. He would miss her presence in Brighton and had imagined he would be the first to go.

She gave another short laugh sounding more despondent than happy. Rising to his feet, he reached out his hand. They could speak more comfortably in the drawing room. But she hesitated and looked at the table.

"Aren't there other courses to come, my lord, and what about dessert?"

It was James's turn to laugh, and he did, then he went back to his seat and nodded to the footman, who had remained plastered against the wall, forgotten. And the meal commenced with a dish of mackerel seasoned with fennel and mint. Next came a fine roasted chicken and roasted vegetables bathed in a rich butter sauce.

James watched her enjoying every bite while letting her chat in between mouthfuls, and he considered the options. He hadn't known her long, and what he knew of her wasn't exactly innocent. She'd tried to trap him and then had been perfectly free with herself despite being engaged. And she'd let him kiss her soundly on more than one occasion and nearly tup her in her hotel room.

So why, after the last savory course had been cleared away and dessert was imminent, did he find himself making her an offer?

"If you wish, you may stay in my spare bedroom."

She gasped, apparently taking in a drop of the wine she was sipping, then coughed and recovered. Still, when she looked at him, her eyes were wide, not to mention a little red from crying as was her nose. Yet somehow, she was still beautiful.

What was wrong with him?

James ought to rescind the offer at once He ought to pay for her to stay at the Old Ship, but a lady remaining there alone without a private bathroom or kitchen staff or even a helpful maid seemed brutish of him to force upon her.

Finally, Miss Talbot said, "Yes, I would like that very much. And I am beyond grateful."

He didn't need or want her gratitude. That could spell trouble with a capital K-I-S-S!

"Very well," he said before he could change his mind. "After dinner, I'll return to the hotel, pay your bill, and bring your things."

"I must pack them myself. I have stuff everywhere, all over the room, stockings drying on the windowsill and a shift hanging over the chair and—"

She broke off at his expression.

"I don't need a list of your unmentionables." No, he didn't because then he pictured her in only her stockings or with her shift raised to her . . .

"We shall go together then," he compromised as the dessert of meringue floating in cream sauce with fresh berries arrived before each of them. "You may pay while I . . . I mean, I will pay your account while you collect your things."

Dammit! Now he was flustered like a youth about to be alone with his first female.

"I'll wait for you in the hotel foyer," he added.

Miss Talbot ate her dessert with her usual gusto and without any further tears, while James slowed down. He hadn't lost his appetite exactly, but he certainly felt the weight of trepidation. She was desirable, practically irresistible. But resist, he would. He liked to think of himself as a rake with honor, and since she was putting herself in a tremendously vulnerable position through no fault of her own, he would not take advantage.

Soon, they'd settled her account to the shilling, just as she'd said, claimed her things, and were walking conspicuously back along the Marine Parade. He nodded to other couples as if it were the most natural thing in the world to stroll along carrying a carpet bag with a footman behind hoisting a trunk upon his shoulder. And Miss Talbot held only her parasol and a reticule.

"I'm so relieved," she said.

"Yes, you've said that."

In fact, she had stated it about ten times already, and he could only imagine the strain that had been firmly resting on her slender shoulders. Her brother should be shot. Her father should be shot. Her fiancé, too, should be shot. Everyone deserved a good shooting as far as he was concerned.

And this jubilant, dazzling beauty walked beside him and up the steps into his home as if she owned the place.

He looked heavenward. It was time for brandy.

'Zounds! He could hardly go off to the small study in the rented house and drink brandy alone and leave her without company in the drawing room.

"Do you like brandy?"

"Yes, I do. After the first sip," she said.

After directing where her things were to go, avoiding Mr. Sparks gaze and pretending not to see the butler's ever-so-slightly raised eyebrows, James ordered brandy in the drawing room and let her precede him up the stairs.

He tried to keep his eyes off her swaying rump. *Really, he did!*

GLYNNIS COULD RELAX FOR the first time since arriving in Brighton. Actually, for the first time since leaving London for Bath. She reconsidered. Her tension went back farther than that. The last few weeks in London had been terribly strained, with her dodging creditors on the doorstep and shoving bills that arrived daily under the disinterested nose of her brother.

Her current situation might only be temporary, but it was a welcome respite from worry. That must be why she was feeling such tenderness for the viscount who had gone against his better judgment to allow her into his home.

It wasn't as if she intended to stay forever!

But she gladly would, if she could.

After an evening of brandy and cards, with Hargrove behaving so gentlemanly and stiffly, not a word could be misconstrued, no action misinterpreted, and almost no fun at all, she'd gone upstairs to find someone had arranged all her things in the spacious guest room. It reminded her of happier times when she'd been able to use her pin money for actual hatpins and notions and not to keep their staff employed, those plump-in-the-pocket times when she had a lady's maid.

Almost as soon as she had removed her shoes, there was a tap on the door.

Her heart raced in a burst of anticipation, thinking it must be—

"Miss?" came the maid's voice.

"Come in," Glynnis told her. "Were you the one who put away my clothes?"

"Yes, miss." The young woman was a few years older than Glynnis, with her hair in a tidy plait that had been wound upon her crown and pinned.

"I thank you kindly. Do you work for Lord Hargrove?" For some reason, she had a hard time imagining the apple-cheeked girl in London proper.

"While his lordship is here, miss, but I come with the house."

Glynnis thought it an odd way to put it, as if the maid were a piece of furniture.

"All the staff does, except his lordship's valet, who arrived with him."

"I see." Glynnis would get no information from this one about Hargrove's personal life back in London, nor whether he had an arrangement with any lady of the *ton*.

"I am here to help you undress and put on your nightgown, miss. I've had little work to do recently."

Glynnis shook her head. "You can't possibly be happy I'm here to give you work to do," she said, even as the maid stepped forward to lift the gown over her head.

"Oh yes, miss. Brighton is a fine town, but it gets lonely here when the Prince Regent is elsewhere and the houses are all empty. And then instead of a family, Lord Hargrove showed up. Not that I've been lollygagging about or twiddling my thumbs," she added, perhaps worried she would be accused of laziness.

"No, of course. I know there's always something to do. What's your name?"

"Polly, miss."

They fell silent as the maid worked swiftly, and soon Glynnis was in her night-rail with her dressing gown over the top. Polly took out the hairpins, and Glynnis's long dark-brown hair came down, some of it in braids, some loose as she'd worked a while to create the pleasing style before going to Lord Dodd's.

Without asking, the maid undid the plaits.

"Shall I brush it, miss, and rebraid it? I set your toiletry articles upon the chest of drawers."

"No, I'll do it."

"Very well, is there anything else?"

"No, Polly, I am quite self-sufficient. Thank you."

Despite having said that, the maid retrieved the soiled gown from the chair. "I'll get this stain out, miss."

"Ox-gall?" Glynnis asked.

Polly wrinkled her nose. "Oh no, miss. Salt and vinegar will do the trick."

"Thank you, Polly." The maid couldn't possibly know how precious each gown was to Glynnis.

"What time would you like me to awaken you?"

She was being treated like a real lady again. "Whatever time Lord Hargrove takes his breakfast, I should like to get up before and be ready."

Polly nodded. "I'll make sure of it, miss."

BREAKFAST WITH A SINGLE man in an intimate parlor on the ground floor of a rented house in Brighton. *What next?*

Glynnis wondered. Fairies might dance upon the tabletop, for that would be just as likely.

True to her word, Polly had awakened her from a sound sleep. After a quick wash, with her hair brushed and dressed again, and wearing a pale rose-colored day gown, Glynnis was led downstairs to the informal parlor.

When she saw Hargrove, head bowed while reading the paper, her heart gave an unexpected squeeze. She had grown so fond of him, even before this gallant rescue. Daily, she wished she hadn't been bone-headed in London and treated him so poorly.

When he saw her, he rose to his feet.

"You look well rested," he offered.

For his part, he looked dash-fire handsome, but she tried not to gawk.

"The bed was very comfortable, my lord, and my thoughts were at ease for the first time in a long time. I slept well indeed."

"And now you're hungry?" he guessed.

She smiled. "I like to start the day with a meal, although I know many do not eat until later."

"I don't know where you put it, Miss Talbot," he said, drawing out the chair from the small oval table.

"My lord?" She looked up at him.

"Your portions of food," he clarified, returning to his own chair. "You eat heartily, but you have a—"

He bit off his words.

"I have a what?"

He shook his head. "I am straying into territory I have no place going, and only because we've become so familiar with one another." He rolled his eyes. "And we shouldn't have become familiar, either."

"Tell me what you were going to say," she asked, pouring herself a cup of chocolate and taking a piece of toast from the small silver rack.

"I was going to say despite your appetite, you have a . . . a shapely figure."

In the middle of buttering her toasted bread, Glynnis paused. Looking down to hide her blushing cheeks, they were *not* the only thing infused with heat. Knowing he thought her shapely caused a happy warmth to rush through her.

"Thank you," she said.

"I should have considered my words before speaking."

"That's not necessary," she said. "I've told you so much about my situation. We can be honest with one another. I have come to appreciate frankness, particularly after the past few days, being kissed by a married man and then invited to dinner by Lord Dodd."

She helped herself to the crisp, thick bacon strips, two coddled eggs, and a large sausage, all on a platter in the center of the table.

"If I understand you, this is not your normal morning fare," she said, thinking how preferable it was to only drinking pale tea and nibbling on a few crackers as some did.

"I asked the cook to make an especially robust offering in your honor, knowing your penchant to being gutfoundered."

"I'm not a knight of the trencher. You happen to have caught me a few times when I was particularly hungry. It was a coincidence."

He smiled, not believing her. Plainly, he thought her a piggy female who liked to yam more than she ought.

"I'm pleased to be able to provide you with plenty of nourishment. Besides, in return, you're going to help me with Prinny and make him accept all the art and allow me to return to London, remember?"

Glynnis felt a little of her contentment seep away. She'd only just found a level of security, but when the Prince Regent accepted the art and Hargrove left, she would lose it again.

Unless . . .

She couldn't. *Could she?*

CHAPTER NINETEEN

In a few hours, with two footmen accompanying them, Glynnis and Hargrove arrived at the Pavilion in the viscount's spacious traveling carriage with what they could haul in one trip.

The Regent was out when they arrived, but expected back momentarily.

"Just like him," Hargrove muttered to the back of the retreating servant. Meanwhile, they set up the pieces in the main salon under the domed roof.

"Stop pacing," Glynnis advised him, and he came to a stop by the window overlooking the west side with the stables in the distance.

"I see him now," he said. "He's coming from the stables. Not quickly, either. He's ambling and talking to some other gentlemen." Then he glanced back at her.

"You shouldn't stand so close to that painting," he griped, gesturing at the dark Spanish landscape.

"Whyever not?" she asked.

"Because frankly, you outshine it, and he'll want *you* here instead of it."

She tried not to smirk, but Hargrove was still free with his compliments despite saying he ought to consider his words more carefully. If she didn't know better, he would turn her head and she would be in love with him within the hour.

If she wasn't already, and she sadly suspected she was.

In any case, she was about to do something that would make him distinctly angry, yet she couldn't imagine how else she could keep him in Brighton and keep a roof over her head. For despite having lost a measure of enthusiasm for husband-hunting, she still needed a wealthy one as her only way to survive. Or return to Wales and live her life as a spinster daughter.

With that bleak future, she shored up her resolve.

"What are you thinking?" he asked.

"Nothing at all," Glynnis said. Nothing she could tell him, at any rate.

"Poppycock," he declared. "Women are always thinking something, and you have a definite thought in your head. I can practically see it."

She shrugged. She didn't feel like lying to him. Instead, she took a turn around the room, admiring the decorations the prince already had in there, a leather-topped round table upon which sat a crystal vase of flowers, and a round mirror framed in gold. Hargrove went back to staring out the window giving commentary upon how slowly Prince George was moving.

"Blast it all! He has stopped completely to talk with that fellow with the garish waistcoat. I think the man even has a feather attached to his hatband."

She ignored him. Nothing could hurry the prince. Hargrove had said that himself. Better they should have requested tea and looked calm and confident.

"Why don't we ask for—?"

"He's coming now. Thank God. I'm sure he'll find everything plummy with you here to praise it, and I'll be heading home to all that's good in my life before you can hop the twig."

She nodded and waited. In a few minutes, Prince George entered, not with a stride, but with a shuffle, breathing hard.

"I say, what a morning! I'm exhausted. Yet here you two are. Maybe I'm too tired to deal with this art nonsense."

She would swear she heard Hargrove growl, a low rumble in his throat.

"Good day, Your Highness." She curtsied low. "Please, why don't you take a seat. I recall how comfortable that sofa is from the day I fainted. Such good taste you have in furnishings. And we can show you what we have while you remain in utter ease."

"Very good. You're a sensible female. Hargrove, have you greeted me?"

Looking a tad insolent, he moved away from the window a few feet and bowed.

"Good day, Your Highness. I'm glad to see you looking so well."

"I do, don't I?" And then the prince did as Glynnis suggested and sat heavily upon the red velvet sofa. "Miss Talbot, you may present."

"This is not the entire collection, sir. But these are certainly among the best." She approached a painting Hargrove had propped against a chair. "See the columns behind the winged cherubs. Don't they remind you of the columns around the front of the rotunda right here at your seaside home?"

She made a point of peering closely because the columns were barely visible and did little to make the painting look like the prince's preferred styles of oriental or classical.

As expected, the Regent leaned forward and narrowed his eyes.

"Perhaps," he said doubtfully. Then he glanced at Hargrove. "Why didn't you get Veronese's *Wedding at Cana*?"

"I tried, sir."

The prince made a face. "And yet all your trying led to fiddlestick's end."

"But the colors, Your Highness," Glynnis hoped to *seem* helpful, at least as far as Hargrove was concerned. "Don't you think they well match those already here? You favor the dark reds and golds, do you not?"

He sighed. "I do, but those are muted. I like rich bright colors."

Glynnis nodded and went to the very opposite of rich and bright.

"This one, sir, is very pleasant to look at, suitable for a dining room."

Prince George sighed. "I don't think it suits my dining room here at all. I suppose it could hang at Carlton House. Do you know I have 453 paintings in my collection at last count?"

Glynnis wasn't expecting him to agree to placing it in London.

She had to put the nail in that coffin quickly. "I had no idea, sir." She glanced at the painting again. "Despite the *humbleness* of the subjects, it would be perfect for the majesty of your London home."

Out of view of the prince, Hargrove shook his head at her commenting on the painting's subject, but it was too late.

"What are they doing?" Prince George demanded, no longer looking the least bit favorable as he viewed the scene. "Are those a couple of beggars crouched over crumbs?"

"It was painted by Velázquez!" Hargrove explained.

"I don't care. It's all brown! Except for that silly orange. Who would stick an orange in the top of a vase? No, it shall not do at all."

"Sir," Hargrove protested, "with that many paintings, what's a few more? Wouldn't you like to have 455? And as Miss Talbot said, I have more at the house I'm renting. I believe 460 is a magnificent number befitting your stature."

"No," the prince said, and nothing more. He turned his attention back to her.

"This one, then," Glynnis persisted, crossing to the only statue they could carry. "Only see how it reminds one of your own marvelous physique, Your Highness?"

Made of marble, the naked man with arm raised holding a staff had made both footmen puff and huff while carrying it in, despite it being only four-feet tall. They'd brought in its three-foot pedestal separately. After setting the sculpture upon it, the effect was quite grand.

James nodded and smiled at her words.

Prince George nodded, too. "Yes, especially in my military youth. Not that I cannot still sit a horse when necessary, eh, wot-wot?" And he tugged his jacket around his corpulent belly, although there was no hope of buttoning it closed.

She exchanged glances with Hargrove. Everyone had heard the prince's stories of his glory days, leading men into battle atop a charger despite having never been part of a military campaign or even once going to war.

"They say this is meant to be Napoleon as the Roman god Mars," she added, seeing James instantly slap his hand over his eyes. Regardless, she continued, "It is said he modeled for this smaller one before Canova created an even larger one, about eleven feet. Emperor Bonaparte thought it *too* athletic, if you can believe it."

The prince's face darkened, and Hargrove was shaking his head like a fiend. Everyone knew Prince George's jealousy over Napoleon's greater reputation for battle sense, not to mention the former emperor's well-respected courage. He'd earned actual glory while the Regent had received scorn for being a gourmand and a philanderer.

"I hate it," the prince declared, and he rose to his feet. "None of this is of any interest to me. Hargrove, you've disappointed me greatly. Take it away. And unless you have something much better still residing in your squalid rental house on the ocean front, then don't bring any more of it for me to see."

With that, the Regent strode out a little more solidly than he'd wobbled in. Glynnis knew he must have been in a tweague for His Highness hadn't even said good day to her.

"WHAT DID YOU JUST do?" James demanded, trying not to shout.

Miss Talbot had started off so well but managed to put Prinny off each piece. She merely blinked at him.

"Why didn't you let the art speak for itself?"

"I was only trying to help," she promised. "I thought he was going to take the paintings to Carlton House and keep the statue here."

"He would have kept the blasted statue if you hadn't mentioned Napoleon."

"*Pish!* Surely you would have had to tell him eventually."

"Would I, though?" James muttered. He would have vowed it was a statue of Prinny himself if it had helped matters.

"Now we have to cart this all back to my house, and then what?" he fumed.

Then what, indeed! He would have to take it with him if he was ever allowed to return to London, and then he would offer it up to whichever nobleman wanted it.

Still annoyed at the turn of events, it took him until they arrived back at his rented house to realize Miss Talbot seemed entirely unperturbed. Barely in the door, she asked his butler for a pot of tea and some biscuits, almond or lemon, if he had them. And then she went upstairs to the best drawing room and put her feet up on a tufted ottoman.

Fanning herself, she watched him pace.

"We shall try again with the rest of the pieces," she promised. "Have some tea. Everything will seem better afterward."

Stopping before the unlit, cold hearth, he stared at her. "Tea will not make this better. Prinny didn't even set a firm day or time to view the rest of it. Moreover, you already told him that was the best."

"Of the largest pieces," she clarified. "At least when we take the remainder, it will be easier to transport."

"Even easier because there shall be more room in the carriage as you will not be accompanying me."

She shrugged. "As you wish."

He hated to think she'd done it on purpose. Yet she wasn't arguing to go with him and plead his case. Instead, she sat upright, looking sunnier than Helios when Mr. Sparks brought in the tea and treats.

"We'll give it a few minutes to steep. Biscuit?" she offered, holding out the plate.

Leaning forward, he snatched one ungraciously and snapped off the edge with his teeth, not caring how the crumbs hit the carpet.

"What are we doing next?" she asked. "The assembly isn't for many hours."

"And now my art won't be displayed," he griped. "I am not sure I'm even going to bother attending."

By her expression, his words made her happiness dim a little, which panged him. However, while munching thoughtfully, she rallied.

"I shall go in any case. Every day, there are new people to meet. The queen will come soon, too, don't you think?"

Would she really go to the party without him? And probably get into all sorts of trouble!

"I have a pamphlet in my room," she said. "I picked it up at the circulating library—"

"I know how you like libraries," he interrupted sourly, thinking of the spectacle they'd created in Lady Sullivan's private library in London.

Unremorseful, Miss Talbot made a face. "Brighton's lending library, the one on the southwest side of the Steyne, is a gem especially with the dear cost of a novel. But this pamphlet is mine to keep. It tells you all the places of interest hereabouts. There is plenty to do if one has a companion, things I couldn't really do by myself."

She poured them both a cup of tea, and James sat opposite her, wondering how they'd so quickly got into this perfect tableau of domesticity.

"Such as?" he asked, unable to entirely banish the testy tone from his voice.

"There's the spectacle of a windmill in Preston that used to be here."

He set his cup down. "What do you mean by *used to be here*? Windmills don't just get up and walk away."

"It took eighty-six oxen to drag it two miles according to the guide book," she told him.

He shrugged. "If the oxen dragged it away, then it mustn't be worth seeing."

She laughed softly, and he liked the sound. It cheered him more than anything else had done in the past few hours.

"There is also a tea-room in Preston," she persisted.

He gestured at the pot and platter between them. "Unnecessary. What else is there to do?" he asked, wanting to humor her.

"There are some Roman ruins somewhere close by. I'll have to check the book."

James had been to Rome and didn't need to traipse around the coast of England to see their one-time conqueror's ruins on his home soil.

"I would rather go to Italy," he said.

"There's the remains of a Norman castle overlooking the River Adur. It was called Brambley or Bramber, something like that. Shall I go get the guide book?"

"No. We can overlook the entire ocean from upstairs. Why traipse over to a Norman castle. They call them castles when there's nothing to see but a pile of old stones."

"Are you always so amusing?" she asked.

It took him a second to catch her smile.

"No, I'm usually gloomy, can't you tell?"

He really must snap out of it. He was becoming a tedious boor, even to himself.

She tried again. "I suppose you also wouldn't care to view a partly demolished medieval priory?"

"That sounds the worst of the lot, but I promise, if you come up with something interesting, I'll accompany you."

Sighing, she said, "I haven't yet seen inside the prince's stables, and believe it or not, they made it into the tour book."

"Yes, of course they were bound to," he said. "They're truly magnificent."

"I think Lord Cumberry said something similar."

"Kissing Cumberry," James remarked.

Her eyes widened. "Excuse me?"

"He has earned the name," he told her.

"Not with me," she vowed.

"Because I whistled him down the wind."

"And I thank you. So, a stroll to the stables? You can be my tour guide."

James could see no harm in it.

"Very well. But pass me another biscuit first. Your hunger is catching, I fear. And then we'll retrieve your new parasol and take a walk."

Thus, James found himself again strolling the streets of Brighton with the brown-eyed minx whom he wasn't sure about. *Was she friend or foe?*

"Tomorrow, we can go to the boat races," she said, giving his arm a squeeze.

They were for all intents and purposes a couple, and it didn't bother him the way any other similar circumstance ever had before in London.

CHAPTER TWENTY

Or let thine eye with pleas'd attention roam,
To where the Royal Stables rear their dome.
Majestic edifice, with graceful pride,
Towering above each structure by its side.

– *Brighton. A Poem* by Mary Lloyd, 1809

They went up the Steyne, past the Pavilion and took a left onto Church Street. James wondered if Prinny were watching, but he was probably resting for the evening's assembly. The prince was hampered by the modest size of his Brighton home, which was why the Castle Hotel's assembly rooms had come in so handy and why Prinny intended to take it over and expand his Pavilion to far larger proportions.

Also, with Nash's help, it would better match the more fanciful, oriental style of the stables. After all, the stables were nearly bigger than the main house, and the prince's horses lived better than he did—or at least, that was the joke among the townspeople, as James heard in the tavern on his first night.

In fact, all talk was of the prince's expansion plans and its great cost.

"I can see the preparations are underway for tonight," Miss Talbot pointed with her parasol across the extensive lawn.

Given the fine weather, the Regent's party would be held entirely outside on the west grounds of the Pavilion, with lanterns and tables, musicians, and even a makeshift dance floor.

White tents had been raised and servants were scurrying in and out. The First Yeoman of Confectionery, the Clerk Comptroller of the Kitchen, the Head Table Decker, and many more would be bringing their expertise outdoors to make everything run smoothly.

It was a rehearsal for the main play, the masquerade ball that would be the Prince Regent's birthday party the following week. James had hoped to be back in London by then, but now, he simply didn't know.

"The stables seem to be as busy as the Pavilion," his companion pointed out, and he wrenched his attention back from the night's impending party to where people were milling around the doorways of the largest stables James had ever known.

"Prinny has a passion for horses. Here, unlike in London, he had room to build the stables of his dreams."

"Of any pampered horse's dream, by the look of it," Miss Talbot said upon entering the large roundhouse.

"If one had to be a horse," James agreed, "this would be the place."

Both speechless, they walked to the center of the massive circular building where grooms were leading some horses out to the open courtyard through one archway and some to the rectangular Riding House for exercise through another while other horses were being brought back inside.

But before one could examine anything at eye level, one felt compelled to look up, drawn by the rays of light streaming down onto the dirt-covered brick floor. Although

James had seen the massive dome before, he whistled at the sight of it rising above them.

"I thought the outside was spectacular," Miss Talbot remarked, referring to the building's oriental-inspired exterior design, "but in here, it's as grand as Saint Paul's Cathedral."

Her head was tilted back, giving him a glorious view of her pale, arched neck as she stared up at the many-windowed cupola through which cheery sunbeams entered.

"I had the royal tour a couple years back when it was first completed," James told her. "Ask me anything."

"The dimensions, I suppose, would be my first question."

"Really? I thought you would ask me about the cost."

"I'm not always concerned about money," she said. "But tell me what it cost."

"Over fifty thousand pounds!"

She clutched at her bosom, drawing James's gaze to the swell of her breasts.

"It almost bankrupt Prinny at the time," he added. "His father had to appeal to Parliament to clear the debts."

"If only my brother could do the same," she mused.

"If your brother were going to rule England one day as king, then I suppose he could." James looked up. "The structure took five years to build and from where we're standing to the top of the dome, it's sixty-five feet high."

"I said it was like a cathedral, and I was right."

He nodded. "Instead of pews, there are sixty-one stalls, twenty-three for coach horses and thirty-eight for all the other saddle horses, including the prince's prized hunters."

"How can you recall all that?"

James shrugged. "I have a decent memory, and Prinny made me look into practically every stall."

And then Miss Talbot did a slow turn to take in the size of the roundhouse.

"Each horse has its own room," she said, sounding amazed.

"Stall," he corrected.

"Those are not like any stalls I've ever seen. They have proper doors and windows."

He laughed. "You're right. I had never seen anything like it either. The horses at my family's estate near Lambourn would think themselves in a pigpen by comparison."

"If your horses *were* thinking, my lord," she teased.

"True," he agreed, and desperately wanted to kiss her because of the jaunty tilt to her head. Instead, he pressed on with his tour. "There are lodgings for grooms and stable boys on the upper floor," he gestured to the circle of windows on the second floor. "And elsewhere on the premises, there are coach houses, an engine house, forge and farrier, and, of course, harness rooms. Prinny stables are a completely self-contained palace for horses. And some say the whole thing looks an awful lot like the Paris Corn Exchange, but I'm not sure anyone would tell the Prince Regent such a thing. Not to his face."

"And *does* it look like a corn exchange?" she asked as they walked toward the Riding House.

"This is far lovelier. I suppose the dome is the only real similarity. Prinny's is a foot higher, by the way."

"Naturally. The builder knew with whom he was dealing."

"You are exactly correct, Miss Talbot." Then he leaned closer, caught the scent of her floral perfume, and said, "Somewhere hereabouts, there's a secret tunnel that leads to the northern end of the Pavilion."

"Where?" she asked, looking around as if there would be a sign.

He laughed. "I told you, it's a secret. I know *of* it, but not where the passage begins or ends."

"I heard a rumor," she said, "the tunnel was not anywhere near here but connected the main house to that of Mrs. Fitzherbert."

"Poppycock!" James said.

They strolled through the arched opening into the Riding House.

"This is magnificent, too," she said.

Instead of a dome, it had a gracefully arched roof buoyed by buttresses.

"What's holding it up?" she asked.

"The prince's determination," he joked. "It's impressive, isn't it? One never sees such a large unsupported roof. Some said it would fall when the scaffolding was removed. Obviously it hasn't."

They stood to the side, out of the way, and watched riders putting horses through their paces, taking the jumps that were set up with ease and grace. And then one performed a perfect jump over the cross rails, galloped to the end, and turned, before trotting slowly toward them.

"Payton," James hailed the familiar figure.

He dismounted. "Hargrove," Payton said by way of greeting before turning to Miss Talbot. "We haven't been formally introduced, but you must be Miss Talbot. Do you plan on riding today?"

James noticed her cheeks infuse with a pleasant pink and also didn't miss his friend's curiosity at seeing them together. Moreover, Payton could very well see for himself they weren't planning on riding by their clothing, unless he was asking something quite different altogether.

"Miss Talbot had never seen the stables."

"It's an amazing place," she spoke up. "And you are a wonderful rider, Lord Payton. Will you be at the party tonight?"

"If only to see you," he said with full-blown flattery.

James rolled his eyes. "Come along, Miss Talbot. With your kind words, Payton's head will grow too big for his hat."

Payton laughed, giving James a knowing look.

Dammit all if his friend didn't think him jealous!

After Payton took his leave, they passed through the doorway at the other end of the Riding House and into the open courtyard, also owned by the prince. From there, they exited back onto Church Street.

"A lovely outing," Miss Talbot declared. "Do you think there is somewhere we can get any fruity ice or ice cream? Somewhere like Gunter's? Besides the prince's kitchen, I mean. Or even a glass of lemonade."

She twirled her parasol and looked beyond fetching. James was starting to think he might have to have a word with her about the future and her fiancé and whether she might see her way clear to fall in love with a rake who was willing to reform and become devoted.

After all, he'd had his fun—as much as any man and more so. Back in London was his comfortable house, ready for a family. Also back in London was his mistress, ready for anything, but he couldn't work up too much enthusiasm over returning to her, not when he was holding Miss Talbot's arm.

"Glynnis Talbot," he said, feeling her startle beside him.

She said nothing for a moment, and then, "Yes?"

"Nothing at all. I was just trying out the sound of your name. It's a strong yet pretty name. It suits you."

"Thank you. I didn't think you even knew my Christian name."

He chuckled. "After our first meeting, I asked our host who you were, including your name."

"I see."

He waited. *Did she know his name?* Perhaps she didn't care. He had to remind himself she had tried to trap more than one man during the Season.

"I know your name, too," she said after a few steps. "James Lambert. It is a strong name, yet not at all pretty."

He liked hearing her say it, too.

"Let's go through the Lanes," he suggested. "We'll find ice cream and lemonade, I believe."

Indeed they did. And James had never had such a fine time doing nothing before. They looked in shop windows, spoke prittle-prattle, and laughed a great deal. And he found himself looking forward to escorting Glynnis to Prinny's garden assembly.

"Isn't it strange to be walking back to the same house to get ready for the party?" she remarked later.

"It is," he agreed, and when they were back at his house, he found it difficult to part with her.

She, however, was gleeful to dash upstairs. "Your maid is most helpful. I am sure she will make me look my best for tonight."

"You already look your best," he said, despite her having gone too far to hear him.

Glynnis Talbot . . . Glynnis *Lambert.* Viscountess Hargrove. *Hm!*

A PERFECT DAY, SHE decided. And there would be more because Glynnis had made sure the Prince Regent didn't give the pieces of art a second look. Hargrove wasn't going anywhere anytime soon.

Biting her lip, she had the decency to feel terribly guilty. *Poor James!*

She liked the name immensely. He hadn't exactly given her leave to use it, nor would she when she recalled how revoltingly forward and intimate Isabelle had sounded.

But she could think of him that way, while continuing to call him Hargrove to his face, the same way his friends did, including that dashing Lord Payton. The man sat a horse well and had a nice way about him. Although he couldn't hold a candle to James.

Sighing, she wished she could stop comparing other men to the viscount.

Poor James indeed! She'd done him a terrible disservice. Sadly, it had been necessary to keep a roof over her head. However, if Lord Payton turned out to be a potential husband and she fell under his protection, then she would do her best to convince the Regent he must enjoy every piece James had brought over from Paris. What's more, she would be as convincing as her fellow Welsh-born woman, the famed actress Sarah Siddons.

After Glynnis gave herself a scrub down in the tiled bathing room, Polly helped her into a clean gown and dressed her hair. Tonight, she was determined to conquer Lord Payton.

Descending the stairs, she faltered. Hargrove had beaten her to the ready. She nearly blurted out how attractive he appeared in his cream-colored breeches, blue silk waistcoat, and darker blue coat, but managed to snap her teeth closed on the words.

He must admire her first. And he did. She could see it in his glittering eyes.

"Miss Talbot, you have outdone yourself."

She tried not to look as pleased as she felt. "I'm sure it's all Polly's doing."

He shook his head. "Who on earth is Polly?"

"Your maid, of course."

"Not really *my* maid," he said. "She came with the place, you know. I'm glad she finally has something to do since she is paid weekly with all the staff."

"A few shillings," she teased.

He smiled. "You may say it's Polly who's given you quite the shine, but you're a well-rigged frigate without any help from anyone."

Their gazes caught, and she would have welcomed him drawing closer and kissing her.

Instead, Glynnis let him take the lightweight shawl from her hands and turned as he directed until her back was to him. When he draped the silk across her shoulders, she shivered at the touch of his fingers, which remained for the briefest moment on her upper arms.

Facing him once more, she considered how intimate their living arrangement was—for he hadn't yet donned his evening gloves.

Taking a pair from the hallstand, he drew each on with a quick tug. She swallowed. It was easily one of the most enticing things she'd ever seen, and her insides fluttered. What would it be like to be in his bedchamber when he was dressing? To see his bare throat before his cravat was tied? *Gracious!*

"Is something amiss?" he asked.

She had been staring shamelessly at his hands, imagining them upon her body. Daring to glance at his face, she seemed to get caught by the sight of his attractive mouth.

"Nothing," she said, licking her lips. "Just . . . nothing."

When she dragged her glance to his blue eyes, she saw a spark flare to life that matched the heat curling inside her, low in her body.

"Miss Talbot," he began. Then he cut himself off, gave a shrug of surrender, and drew her toward him.

"May I kiss you?"

CHAPTER TWENTY-ONE

G lynnis swallowed, unable to believe James was asking such a question. Nor could she fathom why he bothered instead of taking what they both evidently wanted. Perhaps he was testing her.

Should she say no and prove herself an upstanding lady? Should she say yes so he understood how greatly she desired him?

James's eyes narrowed slightly. Maybe he, too, was weighing the ramifications.

In the end, she couldn't help herself. Glynnis gave the slightest of nods, and he swooped in as if he'd been barely restraining himself.

She was thankful he didn't sink his fingers into her hair, for she would hate to have to go to Polly in disarray before she'd even made it out the door. But he did wrap his hands around her waist and anchor her to him. She closed her eyes in anticipation.

He claimed her mouth, melding their lips into a perfect seal of desire. Her hunger for him grew until she had to steal her arms around his neck, dragging her reticule up his chest as she did. Heat sizzled through her as she tasted him, mint tooth powders and a before-the-gathering glass of brandy, and sniffed his familiar scent of sandalwood and bergamot.

This was passion. This was heaven. This was . . . impossible! The only thing such a rake of a viscount would offer was a delightful tupping or maybe a position as his mistress, for he adamantly didn't wish to be married.

By the time he pulled back and she slowly opened her eyes, her heart was pounding and her head felt light. If he suggested not going to the lawn party but going upstairs to his bedroom instead, she would agree.

And it wasn't mere lust, although she recognized that to be a component of the mixed emotions swirling through her. But she knew her heart, and it had become well and truly attached to this man.

She drew her hands from him, and they stared at one another, breathing hard.

"I'm sorry I tried to trap you," she blurted before she could change her mind.

His eyes widened briefly, then he nodded, which she took as an acceptance.

"I am almost sorry it didn't work," James confessed. Then he broke the mood with a wide grin. "Shall we go and partake of Prinny's delights?"

A part of her wished he had decided to partake of *her* delights instead, but she was also grateful he wasn't treating her in a shabby fashion, like one of the Cyprian's at the prince's parties. If they'd given in to desire and James had taken her upstairs, everything would have changed. She could no longer claim the status of a virginal lady, making it that much harder if not impossible to gain a husband. Besides, she was loath to lose the viscount's respect.

In silent companionship, both of them seemingly deep in thought, they walked to the Pavilion. Glynnis made a point not to glance at Lord Dodd's house on the Steyne and hoped he wouldn't be at the party, nor Isabelle Montrose. She couldn't forget what she'd seen or the vulgar way they'd handled her untimely interruption.

On the other hand, if they felt the passion she felt for James, then she couldn't really cast shade upon their choice to succumb. It was only how basely and casually they treated the act of amorous congress that shocked her—that and seeing Isabelle's bouncing breasts.

Besides, if she and James were to make love, she could not imagine happily handing him off to the next woman a minute later. She would want to scratch out the eyes of any female who tried to take him from her. Thus, whatever she'd seen in Lord Dodd's drawing room, she was firmly of the belief it wasn't love.

Love! That word came to mind to describe her warm feelings for the man next to her.

"Don't think about them," James interrupted her thoughts. "Dodd won't approach you unless you invite his attentions. And if he does, I'll deal with him."

Lord Hargrove, her protector again!

Taking a left onto North Street, they entered the back "pleasure garden," as the Prince Regent called it, through the south gate. Musicians who had been placed near the orangery, were already playing a lovely tune, "Sweet Lass of Richmond Hill," purported to be a favorite of not only the prince but his father, too.

From earlier in the day when she and James had gone to the northwest end of the lawn, great changes had been undertaken.

Large canvas tents with hanging lanterns strung between met their eyes, reminding Glynnis of the fancifully lit gardens of Vauxhall. Boards had been put out over the grass, creating a crude but level platform for country dancing.

"No waltzing tonight," James quipped. "Impossible to glide smoothly on that."

"I think it's marvelous," Glynnis declared. "Dancing outside under the stars—what a treat!"

"And under the tents shall be enough nourishment even for you, I would warrant."

She rolled her eyes, but then she thought about it.

"Actually, my lord, I am a little peckish now. Do you think there are hors d'oeuvres set out already?"

He let out a great guffaw at her admittance of an appetite, but she didn't mind.

"I'm sure Prinny will have food and drink available all evening," he promised. "Let's get a little of both, shall we?"

Glynnis was glad James was in such good humor, especially after she'd sabotaged his dispersion of the works of art. Approaching the first tent, they removed their gloves—James tucking his into his pocket and Glynnis rolling hers and sliding them into her reticule. Each took a glass of champagne in one hand and a small fish tartlet in the other, easily eaten in two bites.

"There's Miss Talbot," the Prince Regent declared, gesturing with his hand for her to approach. The small group who surrounded him melted away.

She curtsied and rose to see him smiling.

"I thank you for inviting me, Your Highness."

"And I thank you for bringing your lovely countenance. I shall even forgive you for bringing Hargrove."

But his expression belied his words, and he smiled at the viscount. "I've had a very good day today, Hargrove, and thus, you may bring me more of your ugly art. Although none of it will suit the redesigning of my Royal Pavilion, I may keep everything you showed me today and send it all to London."

"To Carlton House, sir?" James asked.

"God, no! I might send it to Buckingham House as a gift to my parents." The prince drained the champagne he was holding and then handed the empty glass unceremoniously to James.

"I shall see you on the dance floor, Miss Talbot. Isn't it a clever idea?" Then Prince George turned away to welcome other guests.

James set the glass down on a nearby table.

"He is our future king," he muttered quietly, not to her but to the world in general.

Glynnis smiled. Prince George seemed a mercurial fellow to lead a nation, but since she'd never met King George, she had no way of knowing whether they were all so spirited and somewhat silly.

"In any case, do you feel more at ease?" she asked her companion. For her part, she didn't. If the prince said he wanted the art, then he also might dismiss her new landlord, setting him free to leave for London.

"Do I feel better because he stated at the beginning of a long night of drinking that he will take the art off my hands?" He shrugged. "Quite possibly by tomorrow, he will have lost his good humor over whatever cheered him today, or he will simply forget entirely about his promise. Regardless, I will show up with the blasted stuff tomorrow and hope for the best."

Glynnis was about to remind him she wished to accompany him when she saw Lord Payton enter alone through the south gate.

"There's your friend."

James waved him over, but before the man could arrive, she asked, "Is Lord Payton a bachelor?"

She would swear she saw James stiffen, or at least stand a little taller with rigidity.

"Yes." He fixed her with his blue eyes that had recently flecked darkly with desire for her. "Why do you ask?"

"No reason really. I don't recall him in London during the Season, thus I assumed he was a happily married man staying out of the ballrooms."

James nodded. By that time, Lord Payton had reached them and greeted them both.

"Champagne for everyone. My treat," he said, snagging a glass from a passing servant's tray.

They all laughed.

"Are you starting to see the charm of Brighton?" Lord Payton asked his friend.

James glanced sideways at her, and she felt her cheeks grow warm at his obvious interest.

Lord Payton coughed. "I meant outdoor parties in the zingy salty air," he clarified. "Prinny has brought the entire indoors out with the dance floor and musicians."

"It is a lovely idea," Glynnis spoke up, determined to get the man's attention. Probably, if he was a friend of the viscount's, he was of similar ilk, a certain degree of wealth, too. And as she now knew him to be unmarried, she intended to go after him full tilt like a knight errant. "Do you enjoy dancing, my lord?"

"I do, and I will announce now that we shall have the first dance unless this lout or the prince has already claimed it."

"No, indeed," she said. "Neither have claimed the first. I look forward to it." And because she knew the best thing was a little mystery, and also to avoid any strange looks from James, she added, "I am going to take a look at the aviary. I'll see you gentlemen anon." That gave neither of them permission to join her.

Instead, she picked up another glass of champagne and another tartlet and sauntered toward the two-story bird enclosure on the other side of the garden.

JAMES KNEW HIS FRIEND was going to make a comment.

"Miss Talbot is a rum mort if I ever saw one," Payton remarked as soon as she was out of earshot. "Are you going to add the minx to your list of your amorous conquests?"

James followed her with his eyes, making sure Dodd was nowhere near, but he answered.

"I am not." He hoped his tone put an end to the discussion of Miss Talbot.

"Whyever not? I've seen you with her on two occasions. Has she rejected your advances?"

"No, it's not that." *Why had he kissed her again that evening?* He hated to think it was merely because he had the opportunity, simply because she'd been standing in his foyer looking so lovely. After all, he didn't want to take up with her, so why was he tormenting himself. *Moreover, why was he teasing her?*

And again, he couldn't help wondering why she didn't rebuff him when her fiancé was on his merry way. In his gut, James feared it was because she was willing to cuckold the poor fellow.

"I'm watching over her as instructed by Prinny. The more I can obey our regent, the sooner I get home."

"Is that really all it is?" Payton asked.

James nodded.

"Then you don't mind if I dance with her and perhaps keep a little company with such a beautiful woman?" Payton asked.

"She's engaged," James reminded him, wanting to warn Payton off as much as he had Leilton or Cumberry and now Dodd, too. "You don't wish to get in the middle of that, do you?"

"No," his friend said. Nonetheless, he was looking where Glynnis was foolishly sticking a finger into the aviary.

She would be lucky if it wasn't pecked off. And James hadn't found her to be the luckiest person he'd ever met.

"Look at her," he said. "Like a child. I bet she would stick her hand out to pet a lion at the Paris menagerie, too." He took a step forward, but Payton put a hand on his arm.

"I'll go. I know what some of the birds are. Prinny told me in the spring when he appropriated them. That aviary is almost as nice for the feathered members of the royal household as the stables are for the equines."

With that, James was left alone while Payton strode off toward Glynnis.

His gut twisted uncomfortably, and it wasn't from the fish tart. He hated to admit it but he was already feeling horn mad over Glynnis's fiancé, and the man wasn't even around. And now he was going to have to deal with Payton making advances upon her.

In the end, however, she was not truly his responsibility. Thus, if she welcomed Payton, so be it. James snatched up another glass of champagne and downed it.

Luckily, Prinny had made sure to invite the same band of Cyprians, and James was soon talking to the blonde who'd caught his eye previously. Of course, there were other single ladies there besides Glynnis, but courtesans were far easier to deal with. They didn't manage to worm their way into one's head and heart, nor did they evoke protective feelings. The only thing he wanted to do with this rouge-cheeked woman was swive her soundly.

Except he would rather be talking to Glynnis.

Each time he glanced around the vast garden, she was chatting and laughing with the Prince Regent or with Payton or some other man—never with a woman.

What a flirt! James felt sorry for Aberavon.

When the dancing started, Glynnis partnered with Payton for the long opening cotillion. James didn't bother approaching her for the second dance. After all, in the end, she would be going home upon his arm at one or two in the morning.

As the evening progressed, he realized he was drinking too much, and enjoyed himself while doing so. He had finally decided to let go of the worry over the art and accept the far-fetched notion that all would be plummy in the end.

What choice did he have? He might as well stop fighting and enjoy Brighton for the time remaining. He would attend the horse-races and then Prinny's birthday party, and after that, one way or the other, he would get home to London.

Accepting another glass of wine from a passing servant, he made note of where Glynnis was, and then downed another. By the last dance, when he finally partnered with her, he thought the floor was moving like a ship's deck.

"You have had fun tonight," he said as they moved down the row between the other couples.

"You're shouting," she replied, and her brow furrowed when she looked at him. Then when he staggered and nearly tripped over some man's feet, she grabbed his arm to yank him back into the center to finish the promenade. "You look flushed. Are you well?"

James scowled and turned away to take his place at the end of the row opposite her. When the rest of the dancers had moved through and taken their places, he met her in the center and touched palms. Fervently, he wished her hand was bare, but they'd all put their gloves back on after the midnight meal.

Glancing at the motley group of toadies and harlots, James rolled his eyes. *As if gloves would reinstate utmost civility to the pagan outdoor gathering!*

Finally recalling she'd asked him a question, he tried to moderate his tone. "I am well."

For her part, she was practically glowing with happiness. Well fed, dancing with every man, her head having been close to Payton in some secret chat—*why wouldn't she be happy?* She was in her element.

James scowled again.

"Have you enjoyed the party?" she asked.

Of course she wouldn't know whether he had or not seeing how she'd barely given him a glance and had been partnered with his friend at the sit-down meal under one of the two large tents.

"I have," he declared although he would have enjoyed it more had they been keeping company. "Not as much as you, I warrant. You've been quite the gadfly tonight. Let's hope you're not arranging for another encounter like the one with Dodd."

The thought of walking in on such a scene of sofa-swiving suddenly struck him as incredibly amusing, and he laughed.

But Glynnis didn't even crack a smile. Her cheeks flamed, and she glanced around her, probably to make sure no one had heard.

Pursing her lips, she said nothing as they finished the dance. Everyone clapped when Prinny made a final promenade between the rows of dancers. And then they were dismissed.

To his amazement, Glynnis walked toward Payton, and then Payton came over to him.

"Are you in your cups, old man?"

"No!" James peered past his friend to Glynnis who looked downright dour.

Payton put a hand on his shoulder. "It seems you've been a bit of a guzzle guts tonight."

James jerked his shoulder out from under his friend's grip. "Ridiculous," he said, feeling tired.

Marching over to Glynnis, he said, "Shall we go?" And he offered her his arm.

She didn't take it. Instead, she looked to Payton with an uncertainty that gutted him.

"Take it," James said quietly, having never in his life felt the humiliation of a woman not wanting to be on his arm.

She shook her head. "Lord Payton will walk with us."

Fury raced through him. *Was he to have a nursemaid?*

"You will take my arm, or you will not return to my home."

CHAPTER TWENTY-TWO

Miss Talbot's perfectly wondrous eyes opened wide in shock. Then she lifted her chin. "Lord Payton will accompany me back to your house."

James nearly pushed the matter, following through with his threat to shut her out, but it would benefit him not a whit. Obviously, she would stay with Payton, and James would go mad with jealousy.

"Very well, but I'm not going directly home. I was only going to escort you there safely before going out for the night." James was lying like a child, but he couldn't stop himself. He wanted this engaged woman whom he didn't trust, and he could see no way to have her.

"I won't be back until morning." He would enjoy a doxy that night and satiate all frustrations and desires. It was the only way he could live with Glynnis and not want to pounce on her every moment.

Without waiting to watch her walk away with Payton, he spun about and stumbled toward the blonde Cyprian. She was talking to another fellow, but he didn't care. Grabbing her arm, he whispered in her ear an invitation for an exorbitant price. Anything so she would immediately walk with him. She did. She even leaned her head upon his shoulder and looked up at him adoringly.

He wished he knew her name, but it didn't matter. It would be Glynnis he was thinking of when he thrust inside of the whore. It would be Glynnis's name he roared when he climaxed.

GLYNNIS HADN'T FELT SO miserable in a long time, maybe not since James had rebuffed her soundly in Lady Sullivan's library.

He'd raged at her duplicity. It had been a pity since her desire for him had been real even then when she'd hardly known more about him than that he was wealthy and handsome.

Now, she knew much more, and she loved all she knew of him. *Except his behavior that night!* Her brother drank too much, another reason Rhys always lost at cards. She found nothing attractive or admirable in a foxed man whether he be merely a little wet or so drunk he was clipping the king's English.

Tearing her gaze away from where James escorted a blowsabella through the south gate, she looked up at Lord Payton. He gave her a tentative smile before offering her his arm.

As they started to walk, he said, "Hargrove's been under some strain lately. He had a bit of a mishap in London."

At first Glynnis thought he meant the incident with her, but realized that was impossible. James hadn't been sent to Paris to get the art for the prince until well after their kiss.

"A mishap?" she asked.

Lord Payton nodded but kept walking. They left by the closer north gate, giving them a longer walk along the front of the east side of the Pavilion and along the Steyne toward the sea.

She refused to let it go so easily.

"Will you tell me of the mishap, my lord?"

He sighed. "It's not fit for a lady's ears, Miss Talbot. Suffice it to say, he got in a spot of trouble with another man's wife."

She gasped softly, only because she'd come to think of James as being unusually reserved, even prim, in how he'd managed to stop himself from tupping her on more than one occasion. A married woman was safer for a rake, she supposed, as someone's wife couldn't force his hand into marriage.

"I see. Then he is better off with the woman he escorted from the party."

That seemed to cheer Lord Payton up. "Yes, indeed. To tell you the truth, I thought the two of you . . . That is, you and Hargrove have no arrangement?

"No. None at all. I am borrowing a room in his house and that is all," she said firmly, wishing it weren't the truth, but she may as well get credit for her still-sterling reputation.

"You needn't worry what he'll be like when he does return to his house. I know Hargrove. He will be apologetic for his boorish antics."

"Thank you," she said. Since her brother became, if anything, gentler when intoxicated, she hadn't considered the alternative "I'm not worried in the least about that."

Besides, he wouldn't be back until morning. Her heart pinched at the thought of him spending the rest of the night with that harlot. Thinking of him returning tomorrow satiated and back to his old companionable self simply because he'd made the two-backed beast revolted her.

"I don't suppose you have a suitable chaperone at your home, Lord Payton, and thus could allow me sanctuary there for a short while. I need a place to stay as funds from my family haven't reached me yet. Lord Hargrove was providing such a place, but I no longer wish to remain under his protection."

"I'm afraid I am a bachelor, Miss Talbot. If anyone else found out you were at Hargrove's it would be bad enough, but if they thought you'd gone from his home to mine, it would be devastating to your reputation."

Her cheeks heated. "Yes, I understand."

She'd made her bed and now she had to lie in it.

Slowly, they went the rest of the way. Before leaving her on the doorstep, Lord Payton paused.

"I wonder if you would like to go to the racecourse with me tomorrow?"

She didn't have to think twice. It was the first real invitation she'd had from a potential husband.

"Yes, I would."

JAMES HADN'T EXACTLY PASSED out, but he had certainly gone straight to sleep as soon as he'd stretched out on the Cyprian's bed. Regardless of doing nothing more than slumbering for a few hours, when he awakened, he left money on her bedside table. She snored slightly, wearing nothing but the previous evening's rouge, oblivious to his departure.

The streets were still quiet, except for the early-rising servants. Thus, no one who mattered saw his ignominious trek back home with his cravat in his pocket and his shirt half untucked, sticking out from under his waistcoat.

Feeling ashamed despite not having tupped the blowsabella, he couldn't fathom why precisely. That was, until he stepped over his own threshold and realized the cause was the desirable, clever, lovely woman sleeping under his roof.

If he was going to do nothing with a woman, he would rather have been doing it with her. He couldn't recall why he hadn't taken her home. *What had caused her to pull away from him?*

Then he remembered the look on her sweet face and how Payton had come to her rescue.

Blast the man! Payton was no saint. *Was he even then with Glynnis, either upstairs or at his own home on the other side of Brighton?*

Taking the stairs two at a time, James couldn't resist going to her bedroom door.

Pressing his ear to it, all was quiet. Still, he pushed it open a crack and peered inside. The curtains weren't drawn and both of the sashes were open to catch the breeze. In the early morning light, he could see her head on the pillow, her lashes fanning her face, her hair unbraided.

His heart squeezed. Seeing her sleeping peacefully caught him with unexpected tenderness. He drew the door closed quietly. Today, when she awakened, he would apologize, and they would take the rest of the art to Prinny.

WHEN GLYNNIS HADN'T APPEARED for breakfast, demonstrating the depth of her annoyance with him, he sent up a fully-laden breakfast tray as a sign of his remorse. While he noticed the maid carry it past the parlor to the kitchen a while later—quite empty—Glynnis hadn't followed it downstairs to accept his apology.

Instead, promptly at one, there was a knock at his front door, and the butler admitted Payton, looking well-heeled in gray and white.

Mr. Sparks sent the maid up to inform Miss Talbot of his arrival, and James's head felt ready to explode. Standing in the parlor doorway, the day's mail in his hand, he stared grimly at Payton.

"What in the hell are you doing?" he demanded from his smiling friend.

"I'm collecting your beautiful houseguest to go to the horse-races after we take a ride around the town in my curricle. I've got lemonade and sandwiches."

James knew his expression was one of astonishment. Before he could say anything, or even wonder how Payton knew how much Glynnis enjoyed sandwiches, his friend gave a shake of his head.

"You made a muck of it last night, old chum. I know you like the fair-haired types, but compared to Miss Talbot, that piece of tail you staggered off with was as common as a barber's chair."

There was no time for James to retort since Glynnis appeared at the top of the stairs. Payton was right. She was breathtaking in a filmy, soft cotton gown of palest blue with a short, snug white over-bodice.

Smart white gloves and hat as well as the parasol he'd bought her completed her saucy outfit. He wanted to forbid her to go with Payton. He wanted to punch his friend in the nose for being so damned perfect and gentlemanly.

And for bringing sandwiches!

In the end, all James could do was gape as she descended the stairs, refusing to look at him. She smiled warmly at Payton, who nodded to him by way of farewell. Then he took her arm, and then they left.

James felt like the butler in his own home.

Fuming, he could hardly swallow the envy that stuck like a croquet ball in his throat. Either she hadn't remembered her offer to help him convince the difficult prince, or she no longer cared to do so. Scrunching the mail in one hand, he considered his options. He could go to the racetrack on Whitehawk Hill, on the edge of the South Downs. There, he would sit on the grass or remain atop his horse as the old grandstand had long since burned down, and no one had built a new one yet. That didn't stop hundreds from watching the races. They were extremely popular, and Prinny was almost always in attendance.

Prinny! If James didn't hurry over to the Pavilion with the rest of the art, the prince would head over to the track, and another day would be lost. Hoping to catch him, he garnered the assistance of Mr. Sparks and the footman to load his coach with the remaining pieces.

Yet as he set out for the Pavilion, his hopes along with his spirits were low. Strangely, Prinny invited him upstairs to his private apartment and brought out barley water instead of wine.

"Good to take a break, don't you think?"

James agreed with him. The cold barley water was mildly sweet and refreshing.

"The ice house is one of my favorite amenities," Prince George said after James put the chilled glass to his forehead to stave off the last of his headache.

Feeling comfortable at last, he leaned back. About to close his eyes, he recalled he was in the presence of the next King of England, and thus, tried to sit up and look alert.

"Where is your Miss Talbot today?"

James shrugged. "She's not *my* Miss Talbot, Your Highness."

"Not to wonder after your chirping merry performance last night."

James startled. "Whatever can you mean, sir?"

"You were trying to out-drink me. And Miss Talbot most definitely did not approve. What's more, I noticed you left with Miss Maria, that scrumptious high-flier from Pall Mall. I cannot think why you bothered with her when she's easily available in London. Miss Talbot seems a rarer chick-a-biddy, indeed."

"Yes, Your Highness."

"Yes, what?" Prinny asked coyly.

"Yes, you're right. I shouldn't let a diamond fall through my fingers, certainly not for a shiny stone."

"By the way, I'm over my fit of the blue devils regarding the Louvre, so you can stop worrying."

James's ears perked up, yet all he said was, "I am not worrying, Your Highness. I didn't realize you were so upset. Your nature is to always be most calm and fair."

Prinny laughed so hard, he turned purple.

"Then why have you been dancing attendance at every gathering?" He sipped his wine. "Maybe we're back to Miss Talbot as the reason, eh, wot-wot?"

"In truth, sir, you know I wish only for you to be happy with the art." Then James sighed. "Or tell me what the bloody hell to do with it."

This time, they both laughed. Finally, Prinny yawned.

"I really don't want anything I've seen so far."

James's heart sank.

"But I have good news for you," Prince George continued. "Wellington wants all the Spanish paintings for Apsley House. In fact, he wanted them all along."

James frowned. "You mean I didn't have to bring them all this way?"

Prinny smiled, looking years younger than his age. He'd led James on a merry and cruel dance to be sure.

"I shall keep that vase you brought today. And you can take the rest back to our distinguished Wellington."

James nodded, hoping his grin wasn't too wide. "Thank you, Your Highness."

"Will you come with me to the racecourse? There will be hurdle races today."

His smile died thinking of Glynnis and Payton.

"No, Your Highness. I'm going to pack the art back into its crates."

Prinny shook his head. "You've become like a fussy old woman. That can wait. Come with me."

James heard the order in the prince's tone. He would go and be tormented by his own longing.

CHAPTER TWENTY-THREE

Or should the sportive Race thy fancy fill,
East of the Town, across the sunny hill,
Princes, and peers, jockey and rural swain,
All sorts and ranks, make up the motley train.

— *Brighton. A Poem* by Mary Lloyd, 1809

The murmurings and small cheers that arose when the prince arrived at the racecourse drew Glynnis's attention. Although the event was crowded, she and Lord Payton were not far from the royal tent, where chairs had been set up to shade His Royal Highness.

Immediately she spotted James. While not realizing she'd been watching and waiting, her gaze fixed upon his tall, handsome figure as he strode in with the Regent and his hangers-on.

Instead of taking a seat, James distanced himself from the others and began to meander around the edge of the track.

She was well aware when James passed by. Even though she turned so he couldn't see her fascinated glance, her skin prickled in awareness, knowing he had noticed her.

Earlier, Lord Payton had taken her for a scenic drive before they'd arrived at the track. He was good company, told interesting stories, looked at her with a warmth and vitality in his brown eyes, and with interest in her person, too.

So why did she keep thinking of James?

Knowing he was there, it was all she could do to focus on the racing. However, when Lord Payton placed a bet on a horse for her, she found it easier to focus her attention. Caught up in the excitement when people started cheering just before the finish, she welcomed her companion's next words.

"You have won, Miss Talbot."

"Have I?" she exclaimed. "How wonderful! Thank you!" She clapped her hands, wishing she could hug him.

"It's just pin money," he clarified, but beamed at her anyway as if he'd performed a heroic act.

For a brief moment, Glynnis considered whether she should take up betting to earn an income, then thought of Rhys. It was no different from her brother's incessant gambling with cards, and ultimately, she would lose on a day when Lady Fortuna didn't favor her.

"It's pin money I did not have," she said. Three more races were held on the course that had the horses galloping in one direction, only to turn and gallop back the way they came. Then there was an impressive display of hurdle-jumping, which made her hold her breath at each jump. Finally, they turned away and strolled with the crowd back toward where the carriages were parked.

Young boys had been paid to watch the horses, most of which quietly munched on the grass of the downs. Again, she found herself looking for James, and again, she found him swiftly despite the throng. Easily, she spotted his height and his gait, making his way to the prince's carriage.

However, he eschewed it and kept walking in the direction of the town.

With Lord Payton driving, they were going right past him in a two-seater "gadabout," as Glynnis thought of the spiffy carriage. She glanced at her companion, who also looked at James but shrugged.

"No room," Lord Payton said, looking a little too gleeful.

"Surely he can stand on the back somehow," she suggested. "It would be rude not to offer."

She didn't know why she cared. After all, he'd spent the night with another woman, and she'd lain awake for hours picturing it. And all the while she knew it wasn't her place to judge him, yet she did anyway.

They slowed down as they drew beside him.

"I say, old man," Lord Payton began, "wouldn't Prinny let you back in his carriage?"

James shrugged, barely looking up. "I prefer to walk."

"Really. I'm surprised you have energy after last night."

Glynnis nearly gasped, thinking he was commenting on James's swiving, but then realized Lord Payton was referring to the viscount's vast imbibing.

James glared at him. "You're holding up the others," he said.

Glynnis turned in her seat. A line of carriages had formed behind them.

"Miss Talbot thinks you might like to balance on the back axle, like my footman," Lord Payton spoke up, then laughed.

James, however, didn't crack a smile. Finally, he directed his gaze at her. "That's kind of you, but I am satisfied with the stroll. It's barely a mile, I think. I'll see you back at the house?"

He'd made it a question, as if he wasn't sure she would still be there. In truth, she wished she didn't have to be. It would be difficult to sit across from him at dinner, impossible not to think of his strong arms wrapped around that harlot and his firm lips kissing her.

A surge of jealousy rushed through her.

Thus, she didn't bother to answer. He would find her at his home when he returned. With nary another word, Lord Payton flicked the reins, and the matched pair trotted forward.

When Lord Payton dropped her off, he walked her to the doorstep as he had the night before and leaned close. Since carriages and pedestrians were going by behind him on the Marine Parade, she knew he wouldn't kiss her. Still, she held her breath, waiting.

"I would like to take you on another outing," he said. "If you're amiable."

She dredged up a bright smile. They could go on outings until the moon turned blue, but unless he asked her to marry him, it would do her no good. Reaching out, she touched his arm.

"Do you have a prior agreement with a lady, my lord?"

He was obviously surprised by her frankness. "No, I don't."

She considered. She must speak even more plainly. "Is your heart engaged elsewhere?"

His smile was genuine and reached his brown eyes. "No, I promise you. It is not."

Her last question might put the nail to the coffin. "Are you directly set against the institution of marriage, like a rake?"

His smile faltered slightly at the word *marriage*, but he didn't cower from the notion.

"I have it in mind to marry one day."

She supposed that was as good a recommendation for continuing with Lord Payton as any.

"And may I know your Christian name?"

"Yes, of course. It's Rufus," he said tentatively, which she thought rather sweet of him.

"Rufus," she echoed. "A nice name. Mine is Glynnis."

"Thank you," he said.

"If I haven't scared you off with my boldness, then yes, I will accept your invitation."

"Quite the contrary, I like how frank you are, without stooping to games or coyness."

Regret lanced her sharply. If only she'd attempted some measure of frankness with James back in London . . .

"I have work to do tomorrow on the Prince Regent's behalf, but I will gladly escort you to the assembly. I believe it's in your old place of residence."

She'd forgotten the next dance was at the Old Ship. Prince George liked variety, and thus, held parties alternately at each of the large venues in Brighton.

"Indeed, you are correct," she said.

The assembly room at the Old Ship rivaled that of the Castle Hotel. She'd wandered through it when exploring on her first day in Brighton before the crowd from London had arrived.

"Good." Like a gentleman, he took her gloved hand and bowed over it. "I'll be here promptly at eight o'clock."

They'd been talking so long that, when he turned to leave, James strolled the last few paces to his own front door. He was scowling at the two of them, yet Glynnis still thought him exceedingly handsome in a Gothic way. And while she preferred his easy smile, she no longer cared to invoke it.

"Hargrove," Lord Payton said with a friendly nod of his head, even walloping him on the shoulder.

"Payton," James returned, only slightly less friendly, watching him walk away.

"Miss Talbot," he greeted, then reached around her—making her suck in her breath—but all he did was push open the front door, then gesture for her to precede him.

With a last glance at the man she hoped would be her future, Glynnis went inside.

WHEN SHE IMMEDIATELY CLIMBED the stairs with James trailing behind, he could stand the awkward silence no longer.

"Please, Glynnis, won't you have a drink with me?"

She continued to the top, then paused but didn't turn her head.

"I've been out for hours, and I feel dusty from head to toe. I was going to change for dinner." Then she finally looked at him, and when her brown gaze skittered towards his, he felt as if he'd been kicked in the gut by the disappointment he saw.

"Moreover, I think you had enough to drink last night that you needn't bother again for a week." Her voice was tart. "Do you even remember?"

James ran a hand through his hair. "I wasn't so foxed I don't remember. It was a party, and I was having fun."

"It did seem you had plenty of amusement," she agreed before turning away.

"Dinner is hours away," he tried again. "Surely, you're hungry." He was famished for her company. And even though they'd last kissed just the night before, he was hungry for her touch. Even a friendly brush of her fingers as she slapped his sorry face would do.

She sighed. "I am a little peckish, and I would love a cup of tea."

With that proclamation, she changed direction and entered the upstairs formal drawing room. James thanked his good luck for the demands of her stomach and followed.

Plopping down upon the sofa, she removed her hat and gloves. *Such intimacies!* Quickly, he yanked the bell pull and gave their request to the housemaid who appeared.

Then they returned to the silence he didn't care for, so he broke it.

"Did you enjoy the races?"

"I did," she said. "Lord Payton placed a bet for me, and my horse won."

Blasted Payton! "That's wonderful. You're no longer completely out of blunt."

She pursed her lips. "There's not enough for a hotel room if that's what you're thinking."

"No," he said at once. "I wasn't thinking of you moving out at all." *God no!* She had become the only joy in Brighton. "I've come to appreciate our arrangement."

"Whatever can you mean?" she demanded.

Why was she being so prickly over everything?

"I simply mean it's nice knowing I'll have company at the meals and someone with whom to take a stroll. I missed you at breakfast."

That seemed to infuriate her, and he thought she was going to get up and walk out, but she remained where she was, making some sort of fizzing noise, like an angry bee. James was most glad when the maid reappeared with the tea tray and large slices of golden sponge slathered in raspberry sauce. If that didn't win her back, nothing would.

Slightly mollified, Glynnis leaned forward and poured them both tea, and he knew he should be grateful she didn't toss it in his face. After stirring in her sugar and taking a sip, all of which fascinated him as never before, she set down the cup and saucer before helping herself to one of the plates of cake.

With the silver fork, she took a goodly sized bite, seeming to relish the very first morsel of sponge cake.

"Mm," she murmured approvingly, and her gaze, appearing more friendly, finally returned to him. "The cook here knows her business."

For his part, James couldn't speak nor even swallow. A small smudge of raspberry glaze remained on her perfect upper lip, and he waited to see her rescue it.

However, when her pink tongue did make an appearance, she merely licked the crumbs off her lower lip, and he groaned before he could stop himself.

Again, her eyes locked with his. She said nothing, merely continuing to eat. Finally, when he'd stared at her for a full minute and through her consuming half her piece of sponge, she spoke again.

"Aren't you going to taste it? It's divine."

Nodding, he picked up the other plate and forked in a bite. Somewhere in his lusty brain he knew it was delicious, but it might as well have been horse feed.

Then he raised his tea to his mouth and drank it down without milk and sugar, just the way he hated it, all the while obsessed over whether the tip of her tongue would make an appearance. *Would its velvety tip stroke her upper lip?*

Finally, when she set her empty plate down and wiped the corners of her exquisite mouth while leaving the bead of sauce behind, he had to act. Leaning forward across the narrow low table between them, James reached for her.

She froze. "What are you doing?"

"I'm just . . . ," he trailed off while leaning closer.

She pressed her head into the high-backed sofa.

"Your lip," he explained softly.

With a final stretch, he managed to wipe off the luscious red sauce from her even more luscious upper lip before losing his balance and falling onto the table, upsetting the tray and the dishes—*and the hot tea!*—under him.

Worse, he had to brace himself by his outstretched arms on either side of her thighs, with his head landing most fortuitously in her warm lap.

"James!" she shrieked.

"Glynnis," he said onto her thighs, hoping he could catch her womanly scent before he did the only gentlemanly thing he could do. Pressing himself up and away from her, most ungracefully, he floundered a second on the table before managing to return to his seat.

Too late! He had tea and raspberry stains from his chest to his lap. He'd also knocked the teapot to the floor where the handle had broken, creating a brown stain on the rug, and he'd smashed one cup and saucer to pieces.

"What under God's heaven has come over you?" she asked, eyes wide while her hands brushed at her lap as if she could still feel him there. "You don't own any of this, do you? You'll be charged extra for the dishes and for cleaning the rug."

He had to smile at her worry over his finances.

"It was worth it." He held up his right hand and then stuck up his thumb in triumph. Upon the pad was the smear of raspberry sauce, which he now licked clean, feeling like a lion after it had hunted.

He was losing his mind!

And clearly, Glynnis Talbot thought so, too. She gawked at him, from the hand still hovering near his mouth to his soiled clothing.

"Have you been drinking?" she asked.

"I assure you, I haven't. Not a drop since last night."

"Then what has got into you?" she demanded.

"You," he said truthfully and with utter abandon for propriety.

"Me?" Her lovely brown eyes grew larger. And then her cheeks went red, not with a delightful blush, but if he were to guess, he would say with anger.

Her next words, spoken harshly, proved him correct.

"I think you're merry about the gills from swiving last night. Your entire temperament has changed. I've read that sexual release is good for a man, curing him of nervous tension and soothing his violent tendencies. But I didn't know it caused near insanity. You sent my breakfast up to me, as if I were yours to care for. And now you lunge into my lap like a . . . like a cock-a-whoop lad!"

His mouth had dropped open during her tirade. He snapped it closed when she finished.

"Being considerate with a breakfast tray is hardly madness," he pointed out, not liking the warm tea-soggy areas he could feel. "Are you saying I should have let you starve this morning because you were too stubborn to come downstairs and be civilized?"

"Civilized!" She rose to her feet, and he quickly did the same. "Is it civilized to stagger off with a whore, letting everyone know your business?" She was seething now, and he had a good view of her lovely breasts rising and falling.

"Besides, the Lord Hargrove I know, who didn't even pay for his own sandwiches, certainly wouldn't have considerately sent up a breakfast tray, not unless you were feeling tip-top satisfied and fine as five pence. And I attribute such a mood to your recent sexual conquest."

She was being unfair. He'd already apologized for not paying the bill in the teahouse. Yet before he could defend himself, she raged on.

"I suppose the word *conquest* gives you too much credit since you paid the trollop. It's not as if you had to win her over, or that she had any choice in the matter."

In high dander, Glynnis took a few steps away from the scene of destroyed crockery and toward the door.

"Next time you want to put your face in a woman's lap, I suggest you go back to the Steyne and find your blonde blowsabella!"

She stomped from the room.

CHAPTER TWENTY-FOUR

Glynnis thought her heart would break, but then realized it already had. That was the ache she'd felt since watching James leave the party the night before. It was one thing to know the man was a rake, another to watch him at his loathsome act of debauchery.

Wringing her hands, she paced her room, trying to console herself with knowing Lord Rufus Payton was already forming an attachment to her. He would escort her to the party the following evening. She merely had to get through the rest of today and tomorrow without clobbering the sloppy smile off James's satisfied face.

If he were to wear the same after making love to her, she would be over the moon.

Sighing, she sat on the end of the bed.

Rufus Payton was an earl's second son with a title passed down from his mother's father, as she'd found out during their carriage ride before the races. He was unpretentious, clever, didn't mind working on behalf of the Prince Regent, and was enjoying his post in Brighton. Instead of being grumpy as James had been, he was making the best of it.

After all, Brighton was lovely with cool sea breezes and the scent of saltwater and . . . an infernal painted whore on every street corner!

Tossing herself backward onto the soft mattress, Glynnis groaned. She had to stop thinking of the blonde woman who'd eased James's tension, had to stop imagining them together. But entirely unbidden came the picture of the blowsabella in place of Isabelle, her naked breasts jutting forth with James under her rather than Lord Dodd.

"Argh!" Glynnis put her arm over her eyes. She wanted it to be her! She wanted to experience the pleasures of a man and woman with James Lambert. Merely thinking of the act—of him under her or over her or beside her if that was possible—made her wretchedly hot.

Blast the man! He'd ruined everything by flaunting his raffish nature in her face, but she would salvage what she could, even if her heart was shattered.

GLYNNIS WAS PROUD OF HERSELF. For the better part of twenty-four hours, she had managed to keep frigidly calm each time she was in James's presence, avoiding both anger and tears. She'd shown up for dinner, noticing he had changed out of his tea and sponge-stained clothing. They'd eaten in strained silence, and then she'd retired early. He had not attempted to stop her.

That morning, she'd gone downstairs to breakfast, thanking him for the meal again, before quietly reading the newspapers she found stacked on the parlor table. He did the same.

She missed the former friendliness but couldn't trust herself to speak beyond the niceties lest she either beg him to reconsider the traditional institute of marriage or reprimand him for his lifestyle.

For his part, James no longer joked or teased with her, but trod upon eggshells, as the saying went.

Finally, it was the appointed time for Lord Payton to collect her. Glynnis waited in her room, not wanting to encounter James again. She didn't even know whether he was attending. Listening intently for her escort's arrival, she hurried down the stairs as soon as Lord Payton entered the foyer.

"Has anyone ever told you what a prime lady you are?" he asked when he spied her.

"No, I don't believe so. At least none so dashing as yourself have ever done so."

Although he hesitated, looking past her, perhaps for his friend, she already had her gloves on and her shawl in hand.

Offering it to him, she turned her back and waited. When he draped it across her shoulders, she felt . . . nothing.

Nothing that sizzled at any rate, but also no feelings of revulsion. Contentment at going out with Lord Payton was enough. Far better than the emotional turmoil of every moment with James.

"Slippers?" he asked.

"Drat!" she exclaimed. "Thank you for reminding me. I am terribly sorry for the delay, my lord, but I left them in my room."

"It is no matter. The party won't be complete until we're there." Then he winked, setting her at ease, and she dashed back up the stairs.

On the landing, she spied James coming out of his room, every bit the rum duke cutting a flash figure, and she cursed her own buffleheadedness at having to see him. So eager to get away without an unpleasant scene, she'd actually caused it by her nervous hurrying.

Halting, he stared. She kept on moving toward her bedroom door. As she passed him, she caught the faint scent of his cologne, and it made her knees weak, taking her instantly back to when he stood between her thighs.

In another moment, she'd snatched her slippers from where she'd carefully laid them out and forgotten them. Turning, he was in her doorway.

"I thought you'd already left, you were so quiet in here."

"Lord Payton is downstairs. I mustn't keep him waiting," and she headed straight for him. He must move out of her way.

But he didn't. Filling the space between the doorframe, James was a dashing devil in a rich blue jacket and waistcoat, with the brightest of white cravats and pale gray breeches. Coming to a stop in front of him, her breath caught in her throat.

"You look lovely," he said, his tone a little husky, making her toes curl. A familiar throbbing began between her legs. *Blast!*

She must resist. Staring at his cravat instead of into his sultry eyes, she answered, "Yes, I know. Lord Payton has already said as such. I'm a *prime* lady. Now let me pass."

He made a face of distaste. "Is that the best he could do? Rather uncouth, if I may say."

"No, you may not. Step aside, Hargrove. He'll think I am too dim to find my own slippers."

"I would have gladly taken you to the assembly tonight."

Sighing, she finally looked directly at him, their gazes locking. "I gave my word to attend with Lord Payton. I didn't even know if you were planning to go seeing as you hate everything about Brighton except the whores."

"I didn't tup her." He'd said it so softly she almost missed it.

"You didn't . . . ," she began but stopped herself. *How did he know that was what was bothering her so greatly?* But his admission, which she believed because he had no reason to lie, caused an immediate sense of relief to filter through her. She could stop imagining him at least with *that* particular female.

Ultimately, of course, it changed little. Besides, she could guess the reason his plans for amorous congress had been thwarted. He'd been half seas over, and thus the blowsabella could as easily have milked a pigeon as have got him to swive with her.

Tonight, after the assembly, the entire performance might be repeated by him and the whore, except with him drinking less.

"Frankly, Lord Hargrove, I don't care if you tup the entire female population of Brighton. I am attending the soirée with a gentleman, and thus your actions are of no concern to me."

He looked unruffled by her coldness.

"Are you saying if I stroke your delicate chin like so," and with his ungloved thumb, he did exactly that along her sensitive jawline, "it will be as nothing to you?"

Glynnis lifted her chin away from his touch. She swallowed.

"Yes, that's correct."

"And if I put my hands upon your waist and draw you close," and he did so, "you won't lean against me and tilt your head back for a kiss?"

She shuddered as their fronts touched and the heat of desire shot through her like lightning bolts. Forcing herself to remain rigid, she had no choice but to tilt her head to look at him.

"I won't," she declared.

"Actually, you are rather," he said.

"I'm not leaning against you in any way." She was amazed by the steadiness of her voice when inside, she was feeling decidedly fluffy, crumbly, soft, and even squishy.

He ignored her. "And if I bend low and kiss you, will you bite my lower lip and push me away?"

She sucked in a breath and waited. Agonizingly slowly, he lowered his mouth to hers. Glynnis reminded herself she didn't really want this, no matter how her body seemed determined to become molten liquid. She wanted a man who would marry her! She needed a husband.

But when his hands reached around to grab the round swells of her buttocks, she moaned against his mouth.

As he drew her hips against his, curling her into his body so she could feel his stark arousal, she wondered how this would end.

"I can send Payton away," he murmured, barely lifting his mouth from hers. "We'll enjoy one another's company, and then I shall be the one to escort you tonight."

Lord Payton! She'd almost forgotten him. A perfectly good marriageable man was awaiting her below. As much as she cared for James Lambert, she needed a future.

With determination she could only maintain briefly, she sank her teeth into his lower lip as he'd predicted, releasing him when he yelped. Then she made a fist and rammed it below his ribs next to the mother-of-pearl buttons on his waistcoat.

Glynnis probably hurt herself more than him, but he got the message and let go his inappropriate hold of her bottom.

"Step aside," she said as strongly as she could, "or I swear I will scream."

His nostrils flared and the muscle in his jaw jumped, but silently, he moved out of the doorway and let her pass.

Hurrying down the stairs, Glynnis saw Lord Payton chatting with Mr. Sparks. Her entire encounter with James had probably lasted only three minutes, so why did she feel as if she'd kept him waiting an eternity?

"I'm dreadfully sorry. At first, I couldn't find this particular pair, and then, there they were, under the bed." She tucked them under her arm as Mr. Sparks opened the door for them.

"As I said, Miss Talbot, we shall enjoy the party when we get there. There's no rush."

Knowing James was probably at the top of the stairs watching them, by the way the hair on the back of her neck stood up, Glynnis willed herself not to turn.

At the same time, she forced herself to forget she preferred him over every man she'd ever met.

JAMES STROLLED ALONG THE Marine Parade by himself. His mood would be worse except he had felt the shiver under his fingers when he'd held Glynnis. And her warm lips had responded briefly with passion before she'd bitten him like a hellcat.

He supposed he deserved it. Moreover, he was intrigued by her jealousy over a harlot. After all, she was engaged. *Why would she care if he enjoyed himself?* It was a mystery, but she definitely had been bothered.

Probably not as much, however, as he was perturbed by her newfound companionship with Payton. If she had to await Aberavon in the company of a man, why not do so with him? Why take up with another?

After watching Payton take his lovely houseguest by the arm, James had waited a few minutes, not wanting to be trailing upon their heels down the street to the Old Ship, although the view of her backside might have been worth it. He'd thought about having a drink to bide the time but reconsidered.

With his obsession—*which is what he would now call this unceasing desire for Glynnis*—burning through him, making him blatantly irrational, he didn't want a repeat of the previous assembly's indulgence.

He'd been spoony drunk by the time he got to . . . *Dammit all!* He'd forgotten her name again. He doubted the Cyprian would hold a grudge since he'd left her well paid, but it had been a waste of good female flesh and his own coin. He needed to show a little more restraint.

"Stop behaving like a spoiled whelp," he muttered to himself when he finally entered the assembly room on the ground floor of the Old Ship. Quite a goodly sized crowd had already gathered, but the high, white plaster ceiling kept it from growing too warm. With their gold-and-red-striped curtains drawn back, the windows were all open along one wall of cream-colored wallpaper as were the double doors at the opposite end, leading into the back courtyard of the hotel.

Above them, the royal box was empty since there would be no concert that evening. In the perfectly positioned, musicians' balcony, however, the sounds of a small orchestra were already flowing down to the ballroom floor.

Deciding to pay his respects first to the Regent, now that His Highness had all but set him free, James made his way toward the elegant royal retiring room added after one of Prinny's first visits to Brighton in 1787, supposedly to entice him back. As it turned out, he had needed no such enticement.

Approaching the double open doors off one side of the ballroom, James knew Prinny was already enjoying himself in the royal chamber, as evidenced by the tail-end of a ribald joke followed by his loud laughter, quickly joined in by those around him.

James supposed a jovial Prince Regent was better than a dour one. But sometimes, he might instill more confidence in the British people if he weren't quite so jolly at so very many parties, and if he took more of an interest in matters of state as he did in matters of music and art.

Prinny welcomed him with a smile and a nod, and James bowed.

"Here's my good friend, Hargrove."

James was taken aback by the warmth of the greeting and by Prinny's declaration to the tuft-hunters surrounding him like bees to a flower.

"Hargrove has brought me the most exquisite vase, all the way from the Louvre. You shall see it at my birthday party. Did I mention we're having a masquerade?"

And with that, the flicker of fame passed from James back to the prince and those who crowded close to give him early good wishes.

Having done his duty, he returned to the ballroom, trying not to look for Glynnis and Payton. He failed, spying them laughing over something on the other side of the room with two other bucks dancing attendance. *And why not?* She was easily outshining everyone else in the room, just as she had in London all those months ago.

And exactly like that first time he'd spotted her, a surge of longing went through him. Glancing around wildly for some other destination—Staunton? No. Cumberry? No! Dodd? For God's sake, no! He ignored the refreshments and then saw a dull but harmless fellow he knew from his London club. They could have a chin-wag over the last Parliamentary session or the price of tea shares.

Yet he couldn't help noticing when Glynnis noticed him. Her gaze tracked him crossing the room. Her cheeks stained pink, and he felt an answering tightening of his loins thinking of their recent kiss. How they hadn't yet danced the hornpipe jig, he didn't know.

"Morley," he greeted his acquaintance, and their conversation commenced.

It was many minutes later, maybe a good half an hour when he glanced over in her direction for the umpteenth time only to discover her missing.

While Morley talked about coal reserves, James scanned the rest of the ballroom.

She and Payton were dancing, and he wished with all his heart he was her partner.

James waited until the music stopped, and then he made his move. Her eyes widened as he approached. He almost imagined she thought he would grab hold of her and kiss her again. That's what he wanted to do.

"I think I like this room as much as the ballroom at the Castle," he said by way of beginning.

She said nothing, but Payton nodded. "I agree. There is something welcoming about this one. What do you think, Miss Talbot?"

"I think it's because the musicians are above us." She glanced toward the curved balcony that protruded into the room. "Their position caused the music to float all around us," she offered.

James looked into her eyes. "I believe you're right, Miss Talbot. It's the music. Will you allow me the next dance?"

"No," she said, unnerving him.

Would she truly offer such a public insult by refusing to dance with him?

"That is, I have already promised it to a Mr. . . . ?" She looked at Payton as if he were her chaperone, and thus keeping track for her.

"Mr. Caldwell," Payton supplied. "You know," he said to James, "the Earl of Ware's son."

James nodded. "Yes, I know him." He could accept being put off for an earl's son. But he had another question in case she meant to shun him the entire night.

"Are *all* your dances taken?"

Payton laughed, which annoyed him, but he tried not to show it.

"I ask because this lady is so beautiful, I can imagine I am too late." James's attention didn't waver from her face. His compliment was real, and in a way, he knew he was too late because of Aberavon.

"The dance after is free," she allowed, and his spirits lifted. She wasn't going to punish him all night.

"In that case, I will see you then."

"You don't have to hurry off, do you, old chum," Payton said. "Tell me what's happening with the cursed art, and what was Morley telling you? He always knows which way the wind is blowing when it comes to investing."

James hesitated. Strangely, he felt as if *he* were the one escorting Glynnis that night and Payton was the interloper. However, her stance, closer to his friend, belied his wistful notion.

"If the lady doesn't mind such talk," James said.

Glynnis hesitated only briefly. "Of course not. You two gentlemen talk. The dance is about to begin anyway."

As she spoke, her next partner arrived and took her away. James watched her depart, his gaze fixed upon her until Payton spoke.

"What is going on with you tonight? You don't seem yourself. Nor did you the other night, for that matter, with all that sucking the monkey until you were drunk as David's sow."

James ignored his friend's colorful way with words.

"Actually, I have good news," he said, deciding to address the main reason for his recent foul mood, *not* Glynnis but Prinny. "Our prince is going to take precisely one vase from the wagonful of art I brought him."

"That's good news?" Payton asked.

"Wellington wants the rest, and Prinny knew it all along. He was punishing me, and now he's finished. The sea air or Mrs. Fitzherbert or who knows what has made him forgive me."

"That's grand. Then you can leave this horrid place whenever you wish," Payton said, laughter in his voice.

"I agree I was hard on Brighton when I first arrived. It's not as bad as I thought." James's gaze swept over the dancers again to locate her, a vision in sunny yellow silk. The saturated hue set off her dark hair to perfection. "However, I believe I've not been given permission to leave until after His Highness's birthday masquerade."

"Ah, yes, when we watch Prinny become a little boy again, expecting everyone to fawn all over him and give him presents."

"You mean like every day?" James quipped. They shared a laugh and were back on their old footing. He glanced toward the dance floor once more.

"She's quite the gimcrack," Payton said, knowing where he was looking and at whom.

He stiffened, but the man was correct. "She is. Truthfully, she's what has made my banishment to Brighton bearable."

"Hm," Payton said. "Not the light-heeled jade you were with the other night?"

James rolled his eyes. It was none of Payton's business anyway.

"Don't get too attached," his friend reminded him. "I hear from a very good source that she's engaged."

"The jade?" James asked glibly

"Ha! That is rich."

James hoped Payton was taking his own advice and not becoming attached to Miss Talbot.

"I wouldn't have spent so much time with her had she not been engaged," he explained. "That alone made her . . . safe."

"Safe?" Payton roared with laughter. "I never thought I would hear such a ridiculous statement from your lips. No female of a certain age is a safe one. You know that."

James did. He considered them, especially Glynnis, to be the essence of temptation, put upon the earth to send men mad with their eyes and mouths and their smooth skin and luscious curves. And then they had to go and speak, sometimes praising, sometimes cutting a man to shreds.

They talked of other things until Payton said, "I believe it's your turn, old chum."

James turned. Glynnis was being escorted off the floor.

CHAPTER TWENTY-FIVE

Or wouldst thou wish to join the dancing throng,
Where pleasure gaily leads the hours along;
Where laughing love lights up his gentle fires,
While melting music every heart inspires.

– *Brighton. A Poem* by Mary Lloyd, 1809

Glynnis couldn't deny she was happy knowing she would be in James's arms, even if only on the dance floor. His admission of not having tupped the harlot had certainly smoothed her ruffled feathers. However, the realization he only abstained due to the amount of wine he'd drunk was little comfort. Tonight, for instance, he seemed perfectly sober and might pay the doxy another visit.

"I would love some lemonade before the next dance," she announced. "Do you think there will be five minutes?"

Lord Payton responded immediately. "I shall see what is being offered. No wine tonight, Miss Talbot?"

She glanced at James, then back at Lord Payton. "No, thank you, my lord. I'll stick to lemonade or barley water if that is what they're offering."

He went toward the refreshment table.

James watched him go. When he turned to her, he looked as if he had something to say but kept his mouth firmly shut. She didn't want to ask. If he was going to warn her away from Payton for some reason, she would ignore him. In fact, she had quite the opposite plan.

"Prince George seems happy," she remarked.

He nodded. "Almost his birthday masquerade. Every other assembly has merely been a rehearsal to the main entertainment."

"I can hardly credit it can be a more spectacular party than those we've already attended. So much food and drink have recently been consumed. No wonder the local merchants are always thrilled when the prince and his toadies come to town."

Lord Payton returned with a servant behind him carrying three glasses of orangeade.

"What a treat!" she exclaimed, after taking her first sip and then, while trying not gulp it, she drained the glass. It quenched her thirst and revived her flagging energy.

"Interesting," James said, tilting his back.

"Could be improved with a splash of brandy," Lord Payton suggested, "but then most things can be."

A single note was played indicating the dancers should line up. A thrill went through her as James took her glass and set it down before taking her hand.

"Let us dance," he said, catching her eye.

Her treacherous body went hot all over as she imagined them together, bare as babes, doing something more intimate than dancing. But dancing would have to do.

Lining up opposite him, when they stepped together, Glynnis forgot all else except James Lambert. And even when she briefly touched palms with another, she kept coming back to him, and it felt perfectly natural. It felt right.

Yet an hour later, when Lord Payton invited her to leave the ballroom to see the musicians' balcony and even tour the royal box, she tamped down her regret and went with him. Up the stairs in the hallway outside the ballroom, they went first to where the musicians were taking a break. Twelve men were eating and drinking in good humor. Still, they didn't mind the interruption for her compliments and praise.

Then they went farther around the perimeter of the second-floor gallery that circled the ballroom below, and came out in the royal box, overlooking the dancers.

"It reminds me of the upper-floor balcony of Marlborough House," she said. "I only went there once, but it was a unique view to be able to watch the dancers from above. Shall we stay up here until the music starts again so we can watch?"

Lord Payton wasn't looking at the dance floor but at her. "Perhaps the next time you are at Marlborough House, Miss Talbot, I shall be with you, and we'll remember this night fondly."

Glynnis felt the possibility of victory within reach.

"That would be lovely," she said.

He took her hand and gazed into her eyes. "I've enjoyed the past few days with you. I know we haven't known each other for long at all, but you are an easy woman to spend time with."

"Thank you. I feel the same way about you." Truthfully, she felt at ease with Lord Payton, extremely comfortable like donning her most well-worn nightdress.

All at once, the murmurings from below reminded her anyone could look up and see them, standing close. Then it struck her—that was exactly what she had wanted to happen!

Glancing out over the other guests, however, no one was taking any notice of them. Except one.

James's blue stare caught her own, and she would vow he knew what was in her thoughts. As if on a stage with an audience, she could grab Lord Payton by his jacket, draw him close, and kiss him. As long as she made some noise, perhaps a stamp of her foot, someone would look up and witness the act of bold indiscretion.

Yet with James watching, she couldn't do it.

"Shall we go?" Glynnis asked. "Perhaps obtain another glass of that delicious orangeade."

"Yes, of course." Lord Payton looked around as if just realizing where they were. Releasing her hand, he gestured for her to precede him. In the hallway, however, in the space between the royal box and the entrance to the musician's balcony, he halted.

"Miss Talbot. Glynnis."

"Yes?" She turned to him.

"After the Prince's birthday masquerade, what are your plans?"

Her plans? Did he not know about her supposed fiancé? She hadn't discussed it with him but assumed James must have told his friend.

"I might be returning to Wales," she said honestly. "My life is not entirely in my own control." That was the truth. It was not a fiancé but finances which controlled her.

"But you're not against staying in Brighton, are you?" Lord Payton asked. "It sounds as though you aren't longing for someplace else, such as London. Might you as easily be satisfied with a home by the sea, at least for part of the year?"

His words reminded her of James. He was the one who desperately wanted to return to London. She could be happy just about anywhere . . . with the right person.

"So far, despite nearly drowning and having my reticule stolen," both of which she'd already told him when they were having their carriage ride, "Brighton has been entertaining," she said.

"I had heard you were engaged," he admitted bluntly. "I know I should respect such a contract. But I've observed you without your fiancé, and you seem no worse for it. Is it possible you have no true affection for the man?"

"It is possible," she allowed, not wanting to elaborate on her lie.

"That was what I had hoped."

"And do we get along as well as you do with your fiancé?"

Again, she could tell the truth. "Most definitely, my lord."

Lord Payton took hold of her upper arms without warning, drawing her close. With even less warning, he kissed her.

Glynnis breathed him in, and he smelled . . . wrong. Not unpleasant, just not the way she now expected the man kissing her to smell. And he tilted his head in the opposite way to what she'd come to anticipate.

These were small things, and when she was familiar with Lord Payton's kisses, they would become entirely expected. She had only to get used to him.

Raising her arms, she put her hands on his shoulders. This mild kiss was acceptable, she determined, albeit wishing that place between her legs would pulse merely a little.

Even her heartbeat felt calm.

"Payton!" It was James.

As she and Lord Payton broke apart quickly, her heartbeat certainly sped up. They turned as one to see not only James but also two of the musicians and a lady from the party. They had all witnessed the kiss!

"You know what this means," James spat out, arms fisted at his sides.

Lord Payton nodded solemnly. "Of course."

Glynnis's head was spinning. This was exactly her plan, and it had always seemed like a good one, too. Obviously, it worked like a magical charm. However, she hadn't thought about how mortifying it would actually be at the moment one was discovered. A single woman of good upbringing should not be in the clutches of a man who was not her husband. Not in public, at any rate.

Her cheeks were hot, even though only the lady was still staring at her, clearly horrified. To spare her the embarrassment of her ruin, however, the men all kept their gazes firmly upon the man who had ruined her.

"Although it isn't my place to call you out, Aberavon isn't here," James continued, looking, if possible, even grimmer.

"You don't have to call me out because I will marry Miss Talbot and with pleasure," Lord Payton said. "That is, if she will have me and if her fiancé will give her up. I shall go tell Prinny the happy news now, and this evening can become another type of celebration."

"Don't tell Prinny," James said. "You must leave her fiancé a little dignity. When Aberavon arrives in town, Miss Talbot should break it off with him first, and then you can announce your engagement. Anything else will cast her in a bad light."

Glynnis wished one of them would address her directly, but she had a feeling she could slip away and they would keep on arranging matters just the same. Besides, since no fiancé was, in fact, coming to town, waiting for one could put her in a precarious position.

"I accept your proposal," she said to save face, even though no one had asked her. All eyes turned to her, the lady's with pity and the men's with a mixture of distrust, anger, and joy depending on whom she looked at. She decided to keep her gaze fixed upon her future husband.

"Perhaps Lord Aberavon has been held up. If he hasn't come by the time of the Regent's birthday masquerade, I believe we should announce it. As far as I know, my fiancé has abandoned me."

That was plausible. After all, she didn't have a line of suitors at her door. Both James and, she assumed, Lord Payton knew of her impoverished status, and thus understood her undesirability on the marriage market. They might even believe her fiancé had changed his mind because of it.

James frowned, fixing her with a discerning look. But Lord Payton appeared pleased with that idea.

"Truly, any man who can't find his way from southern Wales to Brighton in a few days doesn't deserve to be your husband."

That made her smile despite the serious step she'd taken. Finally, it was done! Her future was secure. She was to be the wife of an earl's younger son. She should be thrilled with the honey-fall. And yet, the relief was bittersweet.

JAMES WALKED HOME WITH his emotions swinging wildly from anger to regret to sadness. He had behaved out of character. If he'd handled his Brighton encounter with Glynnis in his usual raffish way, he would have compromised her a dozen times over, and he would have been the one about to slip the parson's noose over his head.

And gladly, too.

Didn't it gall Payton to be merely another man whom she'd kissed and happened to get caught with? For all they knew, that was how she'd captured Aberavon in the first place. Perhaps at a dinner at her family home, she'd followed him down a passageway and got him to kiss her precisely as her parents were coming around the corner.

If she had actually caught herself a fiancé. To James's way of thinking, it seemed likely because she was a beautiful, lively woman, but Aberavon's long absence made him less and less convinced.

In any case, now she had a real fiancé. *His own friend!* A part of him was curious to see how this played out on the night of the masquerade ball, while another part of him wanted to defy Prinny and head home at once.

In London, everything made perfect sense. There, he was certain of his desires and his wants, and he went after them as he pleased. Mistresses didn't trick him. They knew their role. But they also didn't warm his heart or move his soul or lift his spirits the way Glynnis Talbot did.

The devil take her! He wouldn't deign to greet her when she returned in the wee hours. He would be harbored in his room, probably foxed on his best brandy or dead asleep if he was lucky.

But he wasn't that fortunate. Much later, he heard Glynnis come in. Despite the hour, he could hear the maid—Polly, if he recalled her name correctly—chatting to her as they ascended the stairs. The girl who'd become Glynnis's willing shadow must have stayed up to help her undress.

Rising from the chair in which he'd been sitting by his window with his head back, eyes closed but unable to nod off, he began pacing. He would give his right arm to be the one undressing her.

Instead, he waited. When he heard the maid take her leave, James counted to twenty, then slipped from his room. Approaching Glynnis's door, he tried to make himself halt and turn around. A moment later, he gave a light tap on white-painted oak panel.

"Come in, Polly," Glynnis said, then gave a soft laugh. "What did you forget?"

Pushing the door open, James stood in the opening and drank his fill of her, a vision in nothing but a white chemise. Her glorious dark brown hair was loose over one shoulder, hanging down the front, drawing his gaze to where it draped across one of her full breasts. As for the other, covered only by the sheer, fine lawn, he could see a shadow of its curve and her outlined nipple.

For a moment, he forgot all his words. Then she coughed, bringing his gaze to hers.

"All your plans went well tonight," he said.

She pursed her lips and said nothing in return, only crossing her arms to shield herself.

"Payton is a good man." James hadn't meant to say anything like that, but it was true. The way she'd caught his friend in her scheming trap both disappointed him and made him angry.

"I believe so," she agreed, looking wary.

"And you have no remorse over trapping him?"

She shook her head. "I did not trap him."

"I was there. I saw you." James couldn't believe, after everything, she would still lie to him.

Sighing, Glynnis lowered her arms and lifted her chin. "What do you want?"

What did he want? That was easy. Unlike her, he would be completely honest.

"I want you. I think my actions have made that obvious."

Her expression softened. "Want *me*? What do you mean?"

He took a step into the room. "Will you now play coy? Yes, I want you—in my bed or on the sofa like Dodd and his so-called aunt. I want you up against the wall or in the bathtub if we had one big enough. I want you on the seat of my coach. Hell, I wanted you on the grass at the racetrack and in the middle of the Old Ship's dance floor."

Her eyes had widened at his raw words. Then she shook her head.

"I see. You're speaking only of the physical wanting. Of swiving."

Again, she sighed, and he wondered what she would say if he told her how he also wanted to lie awake in the moonlight and talk to her about the world. He wanted to introduce her to his family. He wanted to discuss the news in the mornings over coddled eggs and share books and chess by the hearth in the evenings. He wanted to escort her around London, proudly showing her off as his lady love.

Except she wasn't his. And he could not trust her if she was. She seemed happy to spin Fortune's wheel and take up with whichever man was at hand, and her heart apparently played no part in her choice whatsoever.

"You only want me now because it is too late," she said, her voice filled with outrage.

"It was already too late. May I remind you once again, you are engaged? Now to two men," he added.

She shrugged delicately and closed her eyes for a second to complete the message of how inconsequential was her engagement.

James could only wonder whether the promise to Payton would be equally meaningless as that to Aberavon.

He could test her—only for his friend's sake, of course! Or he could do the gentlemanly thing and leave.

CHAPTER TWENTY-SIX

S triding toward her, James saw her brown eyes glimmer, not with fear but anticipation. Her body turned to face him fully and her hands were holding onto him almost before he had her in his arms.

With something akin to rage, James claimed her mouth, harshly taking her lips under his. Yet she didn't shy away. She gave it back to him, pressing the length of her curves and valleys against his body and firmly kissing him in return.

With his hands on the soft flesh of her bottom, he curled her hips into his, grinding his aching shaft against her soft womanly core.

She was his!

When he had to touch more of her, he reached down and bunched her chemise in his fist, dragging it up until he could sweep his hand underneath. Caressing her thigh, he felt her shiver. And with his first touch across her soft curls, instantly damp, she moaned against his mouth.

Slipping a finger between her silken petals, he stroked her along one side of her nubbin and then the other while she trembled against him. And when he flicked her little bud, she gasped, practically sinking to the floor if he hadn't supported her.

Latching his mouth onto her nipple through the soft lawn of her chemise, he lathed it to a peak, still stroking between her thighs. Changing to her other nipple, he dipped a finger inside her slick channel, while continuing to caress where she pulsed. Her body tensed and her fingers grasped his shirtfront.

When she arched her head back and shuddered, he knew he'd taken her to the height of sensation. From start to finish, it had barely been five minutes!

It wasn't enough. He ached to explore every facet of amorous pleasure with her. He wanted to teach her what their bodies could do for one another. He would breach her virtuous defenses and take her.

Like a husband took his wife on their wedding night.

Except she wasn't going to be *his* wife. She would be Payton's!

Dammit! If it were any man other than a friend, he would lose his qualms about right and wrong in the face of this intense desire and have her mewling under him while he slaked his lust for her.

Hell's bells! She had already collapsed against him, her wet quim still resting on his hand. With frustration, he jerked it away, letting her chemise fall into place. Then, with determination, he lifted his head from her breast, just as her eyes fluttered opened. They were glazed with passion, her pupils dilated.

Twice now, he'd tormented himself. *And people dared to call him a rake!* When it came to this woman, he couldn't possibly treat her like a convenient canary, nor could he in good conscience crack her pitcher.

Unless . . .

"Are you an innocent?" he asked. Perhaps she was an experienced female, and all his torment over tupping her was for naught.

It took her a moment to gather her wits. Yawning, she belatedly covered her mouth and then, after a few seconds, folded her arms across her chest again, shutting out his view of the wet fabric clinging to her nipples.

Still, with large eyes staring into his, she remained silent.

"Are you a virgin?" he demanded.

Her cheeks blazed scarlet, which he would have thought amusing if he weren't aching between his legs.

"I am," she declared softly.

He believed her. *Of course she was!* She might be a conniving husband-hunter, but she was also a viscount's daughter and would naturally guard her virtue in case its loss destroyed any chance of honorable marriage.

And yet there they were. He'd touched her intimately. *Again!*

"Why do you allow me such liberties? Do you want me to ruin you as you asked before? It would end any chance of happiness with Payton once he discovered it, even if that didn't occur until after the wedding. Tell me why, and I shall gladly debauch you to the fullest."

Her expression darkened like a thunder cloud over the sun.

"You must leave my room," she said, her voice wavering. "There is nothing more for you here. I was merely caught up in the moment. I won't let it happen again."

With that, she turned her trembling back to him.

What else could he do? He left.

FINALLY, IT WAS THE night of the Prince Regent's masquerade ball. To much fanfare, Queen Charlotte had arrived the day prior. Her eldest son loved her for sharing his taste in art and even, to some degree, in decoration. When first showing Glynnis the Royal Pavilion, Prince George had mentioned how much the Queen's Lodge at Windsor had inspired him with its beautiful Indian wallpaper, its brightly colored embroidered chairs, and its cheerful and lively rooms containing the finest furnishings right down to the wall sconces.

Moreover, the people adored their queen for standing by her husband through all the king's difficulties and bouts of madness. No one could ever say a word about her being anything less than faithful.

Glynnis intended to have such a reputation at the end of her life. She would be true to Lord Payton, despite burning with desire for his friend. Once she said her wedding vows, she would forever tamp down the longing she felt for James, squeeze out from her heart every last drop of tenderness she felt for him, and she would never allow herself to be alone with him again. The temptation was too great, and always would be.

Lord Payton had been kind and attentive ever since they'd been caught in their embrace. In fact, he seemed pleased by the circumstances and not the least bit wary of her or regretful.

"I needed a wife. You are as fine a woman as any," he said to her when they went to the tea-room in Preston two days after the Old Ship Hotel assembly. "Think of our king and queen. They only knew each other for six hours before they married, and they've been happy all these years."

Except for during the king's episodes of madness, and his downturn in health of late! Those could hardly have been happy times. But she took his point. A good marriage could blossom from many circumstances.

Glynnis wondered if she dare speak for a few minutes with Queen Charlotte that night and perhaps ask her about marriage—and love—but feared, given King George's present ill health, her questions would be unwelcome.

"Lord Payton will be here any minute, Polly. Are we finished? I don't see how there can be anything more to do to my hair."

"No, miss. We're keeping it simple tonight with a nice twist at the back and a few curls at the front. Your pretty mask and feathers will be all they'll see anyway."

Glynnis loved the mask. She'd bought it at Hanningtons with money from her racetrack winnings. Its bold purple feathers and purple satin eye covering went perfectly with the amethyst satin and gold dress she was wearing.

Although she'd been to the boat races with Lord Payton and for many strolls and carriage rides, this was the first assembly since their fated kiss. She was curious to see what it was like to go to a party as a man's fiancée, even if no one knew about it as yet. She was still trying to figure out how to make him declare it openly. However, Lord Payton seemed determined to give her fiancé more time to arrive.

Tonight, Glynnis had decided to tell him there wasn't one. She believed she knew Lord Payton well enough to know it would make no difference. He was quite fond of her, and the absence of a prior engagement would remove the last impediment to their own.

Hearing voices coming through the door she'd left ajar, Glynnis locked gazes with Polly.

"It sounds as if your beau is here, miss," the maid said, reaching for the gold silk wrap where it lay upon the counterpane. She draped it over Glynnis's arm.

"Thank you for your assistance." Everything was about to change. James was leaving Brighton the following day, and Glynnis would stay on another day or two before traveling in a private coach paid for by Lord Payton, all the way home to Wales. He promised to join her there himself to speak with her parents.

"I'm very glad Lord Hargrove chose this house, and that you were here," she said, for Polly had been an ideal maid.

"Thank you, miss. You've been a very kind lady to serve."

With that, she gave a shallow curtsy, leaving Glynnis to take one last look in the tilted cheval mirror standing by the bureau.

"You've done it," she told her reflection. She had left London, intent upon securing her future, and she had accomplished it. Never again would she need fear Rhys's capricious and irresponsible handling of money. Her parents could give him the purse strings if they wished, and her stomach wouldn't have to clench in nervous worry ever again.

"You did the right thing," she spoke aloud.

Was she trying to convince herself? Ever since the night at the Old Ship's assembly, James had been coolly polite, but mostly absent. He'd attended whatever event Prinny invited him to for the past few days, but not once had he smiled at her or shared a jest with Lord Payton.

He was probably disgusted with her, thinking her a duplicitous, fortune-hunter. But he was wrong. She wasn't after Rufus Payton for his fortune, only for the security he brought by being her husband. She didn't care about the title or the fine house he had told her about in the outskirts of London or his father's earldom or his family's country estate upon which stood a little church he thought they should use for their wedding. She cared for none of that so much as no longer having to wonder if the next day would be a hungry one.

And in return for peace of mind, she would give him her utter devotion. She might not love him the way she loved James—*with her heart aching for him*—but she would show Rufus the loyalty and respect due a husband.

Nodding to herself in the mirror, she took a deep breath, smoothed her dress one last time and strode through the doorway.

JAMES LEFT HIS RENTED house before Payton arrived. He was not going to hold his friend accountable for the turmoil in his gut. After all, their friendship had been years in the making, and Payton had not stolen Glynnis from him. On the other hand, James didn't have to wallow in his envy by watching them together.

If anything, he should pity the man for getting involved with her. Not that he didn't know firsthand how enticing the lady could be. James was still somewhat amazed she'd used the same tired trick and that it had worked so well.

Even worse, he'd been the one to discover them!

If he had been the only one to come upon them, James would have spared his friend being forced to marry a woman who didn't love him, a woman who wanted only what was in a man's coffers. However, with the others coming upon the tenderly staged scene, he'd had no choice but to insist upon the honorable action.

Naturally, Payton had been only too happy to oblige, getting himself a beautiful lady in the bargain. And James was left stupidly wishing with all his heart to switch places with him.

Half a dozen times over the past few days, he'd almost told her that very fact, how she should tell Payton she'd changed her mind. Somehow, he had dredged up a degree of self-respect and held himself back.

With a black satin mask in place, James circulated through the interior of the Pavilion before going outside. Prinny's birthday party was easily the most well-attended event in August in Brighton, dwarfing the other assemblies they'd already had. That night, every public room as well as the entire grounds were being used for merry-making.

The food was mainly indoors, but since Glynnis, who would go straight for the buffet table once she learned of it, wasn't there, he went outside. Again, as at the last assembly, a dance floor had been fashioned over the grass, giving plenty of space for the country dances while keeping the guests cool.

James scanned the gardens, easily spotting Prinny, who was unmistakable despite his fanciful mask due to his shape and his style of dress.

"Many happy returns of the day, Your Highness."

"Thank you. I don't know who you are, but I shall guess." The prince sipped his champagne. "Let's see, dark-haired, tall, and wishing he were elsewhere. Why, it must be Hargrove."

He succeeded in making James laugh. "I promise you, I am perfectly content to be here celebrating the day of your birth. As are so many others." He looked around at the crowd again and couldn't help searching for Glynnis.

"So much fuss made on my account!" Prince George said. "Everything, every ounce of wine and morsel of food are superbious in the extreme. Who would have imagined it?"

James merely smiled. After all, the prince had arranged it himself.

"I noticed the vase on display when I arrived. I'm glad it fits in so well."

"It does, doesn't it? Far better than those Spanish paintings. Are you leaving tomorrow?"

"Does that mean I have your permission to return home?" James wanted to hear it directly from his lips so there could be no misunderstanding, nothing Prinny could later hold against him.

However, the Prince Regent again sipped his champagne, raising a royal eyebrow.

"As if you needed my permission." Yet his eyes said otherwise, and James was glad he'd seen this ordeal through from Paris to Brighton. Regardless, the next time Prinny asked him to do a quick favor, James would move mountains to avoid doing so.

"I noticed Miss Talbot came in with one of my trusted councilors. Have you been derelict or did Payton outflank you, wot-wot?"

James bristled. "Not at all, sir. She prefers Lord Payton's company, and thus, he is escorting her. I trust him with my life."

Prinny laughed at James's ruffled feathers. "And with your lady, it seems."

"Miss Talbot is not—" he cut himself off when he realized the Prince Regent was teasing him.

"My mother is here," Prinny announced. "She's inside, enjoying my new gallery. Unlike you, Nash exceeded my expectations."

"Yes, Your Highness. I shall go pay my respects at once."

"When you come back next year," Prinny added, "the other rooms will reflect my new taste, too. Lots more dragons and such. And the exterior will start to look very different. Nash assures me I can have as many minarets as I fancy. I look forward to your compliments."

"Yes, Your Highness," James said again, bowed, and walked away. Apparently, he was being summoned to Brighton next August, too. Perhaps Glynnis and Payton would remain and be welcoming a babe by then.

That depressing thought had him snagging a glass of champagne before he went in search of Queen Charlotte. As Prinny had guessed, she was in the new oriental-inspired gallery.

Approaching the small group paying her homage, he realized the vision in rich amethyst silk and gold was Glynnis. His breath caught while his heart squeezed, and he wondered how he would carry on without her when his longing grew daily. The purple feather attached to her mask was wagging this way and that as she talked animatedly about something that had captured her interest, or maybe merely an amusing tale for the queen. At her side was Payton, looking like the luckiest man at the party.

"Your Majesty," James greeted, bowing before the aging queen with her friendly face, half concealed by a silver mask with real gems pasted to the upper perimeter, giving her the effect of colorful, jeweled eyebrows.

She turned to him, and he quickly added, "It's Hargrove, ma'am."

"Lord Hargrove, my son's faithful friend! How lovely to see you here."

"Thank you, Your Majesty. It's an honor to see you in Brighton." She didn't often leave London any more. "You look well indeed."

The queen smiled a little sadly. "I wish my husband was with me, but I came to see the happiness of my eldest. I haven't always agreed with his choices, but my son knows how to follow his heart, which keeps him often in good spirits."

James considered that. Following his heart would demand he tell Glynnis she must not marry Payton.

He turned to the pair. "Payton." He nodded. "Miss Talbot." He nodded again.

They greeted him, although Payton more warmly than Glynnis's somewhat stiff curtsy.

"You all know each other?" Queen Charlotte asked. "Miss Talbot tells me she was presented at court two years prior, but I am sorry to say I do not recollect. So many young ladies come out each year."

"No one would expect you to remember any one of us," Glynnis said. "But Your Majesty makes an indelible impression on each who is allowed to come before you. I will never forget the moment I saw you at the palace."

James heard sincerity in her voice. He imagined such a day in a young lady's life bore the bell of exception. The only thing better might be her wedding day.

His romantic thoughts were becoming tedious, and he should very much like to drown his head in the ocean.

"It is a pleasure to see you, Your Majesty." James took his leave of Queen Charlotte, and after a glance at the other two, he sauntered off, realizing the trip back to London was going to be a hellish one, alone with his regrets.

CHAPTER TWENTY-SEVEN

The miracle to-day is that we find
A lover true; not that a woman's kind.

— *Love for Love* by William Congreve, 1695

Glynnis wasn't going to be able to go through with it. That horrid thought kept interrupting her, like a pesky bumblebee on a summer day. When she looked at Lord Payton, she felt guilt, not love. And when she looked at James . . .

She must stop looking at James!

When others came over to chat with the queen, they took their leave of the gracious lady.

"Let us see what the Prince Regent's cook is serving, shall we?" she suggested, feeling a pang of hunger.

"I'm happy to do whatever you wish." And the amiable Lord Payton escorted her into the blue room where platters of hors d'oeuvres had been placed. Later, there would be a buffet in the dining room, although there wasn't room for everyone to be seated, one of the reasons Prince George was redesigning his Brighton home.

And if she married Lord Payton, she would probably be there to see the Pavilion's growth into a grand palace.

Each with a small plate filled with savories, they strolled outside.

You must tell him, she ordered herself.

Then all would be as before, and she would have to tuck her tail and return to her parents.

She must stay the course, she decided, before instantly changing her mind for the umpteenth time.

"You have the look of a woman thinking a great many thoughts," Payton remarked.

"Do I? Perhaps it's simply my appetite." And in order not to have to speak, she took a bite of this and another of that.

Over the next half hour, she occasionally spotted James talking with nobs or even with ladies, but when the dancing started outside, he headed in the other direction. If she was correct, he was leaving the party astonishingly early.

Would he do so without even saying goodbye?

She partnered with Lord Payton for the first extended cotillion. Each time they came together, she nearly blurted out the awful truth.

Finally, feeling ill with the decision she had to make, she fled the dance floor as the last notes were played, striding toward the aviary. The caged creatures reminded her of her own plight. Should she voluntarily imprison herself in exchange for food and shelter?

"Miss Talbot," Payton called, following her. "Are you well?"

She turned to him, tears pricking her eyes.

"I cannot marry you, my lord."

He considered her a moment. "Have I offended you in some way?"

"Not at all. You've been most kind." She raised her mask, suddenly weary.

"I know what happened was a shock, and you may have concerns over taking a husband because of a single kiss, but

I assure you, I'll do my best to make you happy. You'll want for nothing."

"Thank you," her voice was husky. "But it wouldn't be fair to you. My heart belongs to another."

"I see." His jaw tightened. "I didn't realize. You've seemed happy with me whenever we've been together."

Every moment with him had been easy and pleasant, but absolutely passionless.

"I have very much enjoyed the time we've spent in one another's company, every moment, and I do so appreciate how you took me riding and to the races and . . . ," she trailed off as tears filled her eyes.

Kindly, he leaned forward and used his gloved finger to capture the first one that spilled down her cheek.

"I would never have spent a moment alone with you, and I certainly wouldn't have kissed you had I known you loved your fiancé. For some reason, I got it into my thick head, you had not formed an attachment to him."

"Lord Payton, I must confess—"

Before she could tell him it wasn't her fiancé whom she loved, she saw the very man, Lord Aberavon, in the flesh, and leading him toward her was James.

Her mouth dropped open, and all the blood seemed to rush from her head. In front of everyone, even the queen, she would be denounced as a liar.

"You've gone pale," Lord Payton began, then turned to see what had caught her eye. "I say Hargrove, I think Miss Talbot is ill."

"I hope not," James said. "I found her fiancé wandering around, and I'm thrilled to reunite the happy couple."

He knew. By the wicked expression upon his handsome face, he knew.

"Miss Talbot, you do look pale indeed," said Lord Aberavon by way of greeting.

He appeared as she remembered, a few inches taller than herself, yet appearing short between James and Lord Payton. He was perhaps a decade older than any one of them, with a welcoming countenance, a round head and a platter face that reminded her of nothing so much as a large turnip with sandy-colored hair.

"I fear I have had too much sun," she said.

"But you weren't outside today, were you?" James asked, enjoying her discomfit.

She glared at him, then softened her expression as she looked at Lord Aberavon again. "Then perhaps it was too much champagne"

"I think you've only had one glass," Lord Payton said helpfully. "However, perhaps you should sit." Without a by-your-leave, he directed her to the nearest stone bench, with James and her "fiancé" in tow.

Glynnis wished she would fall into one of those secret tunnels James had mentioned as being somewhere under the expansive lawn, but that would be far too fortunate for her. She must suffer utter mortification before the night was out.

Once she was seated, she closed her eyes. Mayhap they would all three disappear.

"Miss Talbot." This came from Lord Payton. "Seeing your fiancé has obviously been a shock to you."

"I bet it has," muttered James so everyone could hear.

"Hush," said Lord Payton. "Let us give them some time alone."

"What!" exclaimed James. "I thought you were going to marry her."

"I thought *I* was supposed to marry her."

When she heard those words from Lord Aberavon, she opened her eyes.

How did he know? By James's smirking face, she realized he must have said something to the baron.

"Lord Aberavon," she began and stopped. *What could she say?*

"You are lovelier than I recall," he said, wiping the smile off James's face. "When I last dined at your parents' home—"

"You know her?" James asked.

Lord Payton stared at his friend as if he'd lost his mind. "Of course they know each other. They're engaged to be married."

"But—" James started.

"Will you gentlemen leave us, please," Lord Aberavon asked. "I would like a moment alone with my . . . fiancé."

At this, Glynnis couldn't help her mouth opening and closing like a fish. She didn't know what was happening, but James's expression was a mirror of her own. Only Lord Payton seemed to have the right of it, even though he was in the wrong.

"Come along, Hargrove. Let's leave them alone and go have some champagne."

Still James gawked at her. Yet as Lord Aberavon sat beside her, he shook his head.

"Maybe we can find Prinny's good brandy instead," James muttered.

She watched the two friends walk off toward the house, ready to face the truth.

"I do not understand, my lord. We are *not* engaged, are we?" Glynnis had to ask in case her father had, in fact, made an arrangement that she didn't know about.

"No, but I can tell when a lady needs to be rescued, and you seem to be in the suds. Quite deep, too."

She sighed. "I suppose I am."

JAMES AND PAYTON SNUCK away from the other party-goers onto the second floor. With a few coins given to a footman who knew them both, they managed to obtain a glass each of French brandy and were seated in Prinny's private salon.

"Don't you intend to marry her?" James asked his friend after they both slumped into comfortable chairs.

Payton shrugged. "If she had wanted to, I would've been game. Someone like Miss Talbot could probably make any man happy. She has decidedly good humor and a lovely face."

"A *beautiful* face," James amended. "And a figure to match." He thought of her shapely curves that had fit perfectly into his hands. "She's clever, too."

Payton laughed. "It's a good thing I'm not in love with her because you are."

James sucked in the swallow of brandy and coughed. "Don't be ridiculous. Just because I hold her in high esteem and think her a right gimcrack."

"And because you think of her *all* the time and long for her and want to see her smile and hear her laugh."

James's jaw dropped at Payton's understanding of his torment.

Payton smiled wryly. "I was in love once."

This was news. "What happened?"

"That's another story," his friend insisted. "But I'm sorry to say you are not going to marry Miss Talbot any more than I am.

"I don't want to marry her," James maintained, but his words were hollow. At that moment, he wanted to have her as his own more than he wanted his next breath.

"I truly hope not. I would hate to see you get your heart broken." Then Payton shook his head. "You're an idiot and don't deserve her. You stepped aside and let me get into the race when you had the lead."

James took another sip. "She seemed to set her cap at you. She managed to entice you into a kiss so you would be discovered. Miss Talbot must have wanted you to be the one to marry her."

Payton looked at him as if he were a madman. "I give you my word, it was all my doing at the Old Ship. I took her on a tour of the second floor, and then I decided to try a quick kiss to see if we suited."

James didn't like the jealousy that rose upon hearing his friend casually testing out a kiss, even if he'd already seen it for himself.

"And I thought we did suit well enough," Payton continued. "It was a sweet kiss."

"Stop talking about kissing her." *Sweet?* And the man called *him* an idiot. Kissing Glynnis Talbot was like dancing in a lightning storm and being struck over and over. His body was always heated and charged and ready with the barest whisper of a kiss from her lips. There was nothing sweet about it.

"Anyway," Payton said, "she told me she couldn't marry me, and I know she won't be marrying you."

"Why not?" James demanded, thinking himself ready to duel the Welsh baron at sunrise.

"She is in love with Aberavon. She told me so just before you brought him over. She finished giving me the mitten and saying how she loved him. It was as if she were speaking of the devil, and there he was! I've never been so surprised in my life. Her either, I expect. That's why she was overcome, I tell you."

"I can't believe it," James said softly, speaking to himself more than to Payton. "When I ran into Aberavon, freshly arrived from Swansea Bay for Prinny's party, I thought as you thought. But when I mentioned how his betrothed was at the Pavilion, he seemed to think I was dicked in the nob."

"You *are* dicked! But what took the blasted man so long to come?"

"As far as I can tell, he encountered a series of unfortunate circumstances, including a lame horse, a broken carriage wheel, and a band of highwaymen."

"It's a wonder he got here at all, I suppose." Since they could see no decanter and didn't want to go to the trouble of asking a servant, Payton drew a flask from his pocket and poured them both another half glass. "But if one were in love and had Miss Talbot waiting—"

"That's just it," James said, swirling the liquid in his glass, "when I insisted Miss Talbot was expecting him, he grew quiet upon hearing her name. I vow he didn't know she was his fiancée. From his strange manner, I thought she had been lying all along."

"I heard him mention dining at her father's," Payton pointed out.

"As did I," James agreed. "I can only surmise they are truly engaged. And you say she loves him?"

"*She* said she did. It must be love to prefer him over me, don't you think?" Payton pointed out. He laughed good-naturedly, but James thought his friend was correct. Of the two, Aberavon did not have the superior physique or face. Moreover, he was only a baron whereas Payton was an earl's son.

Glynnis was in love with Aberavon. James repeated the words in his head a few times, trying to make them stick. Whatever he thought he'd seen in her eyes when she looked at him, he had plainly misunderstood.

Wrenching his thoughts elsewhere to try and escape the pain concentrated in the vicinity of his heart, James said, "Prinny has allowed me to depart Brighton for London with his blessing, and I shall do so immediately. I thought I might have to stay for your nuptials, but I guess I was mistaken."

"Ah well, at least it has all worked out for you," Payton said, not realizing James's emotional torment. "You've had the company of a pretty lady, you also had your fun with that blonde blowsabella, you've satisfied our prince, and now you can return to your fair mistress in London."

James nodded. When Payton put it like that, he ought to be pleased to have escaped Brighton unscathed. His friend was looking at him for a reaction.

James smiled ruefully. "As for the fair-haired doxy, recall I was rather foxed that night. Sadly, I presented her with nothing but a limp lobcock, my sleeping back, and some coins."

Payton laughed as James had intended him to, but he was already thinking of Glynnis again.

She loved Aberavon? He never would have guessed it, not when she had kissed him with passion and melted in his arms. And then there was the way she'd climaxed under his touch.

'Zounds! James could hardly imagine how she would sizzle if she actually loved a man.

"Aberavon is a damned lucky bastard," he said.

"Yes," agreed Payton. "He certainly is."

CHAPTER TWENTY-EIGHT

G lynnis was confounded by the appearance of her fictitious fiancé and even more so by his willingness to play the part for real.

"I didn't go to your father's home simply for the roast beef, Miss Talbot. I intended to ask for your hand when the time was right. It was the neighborly thing to do. However, you made it clear you wanted to experience a London Season and then another. If you fell in love, I was perfectly happy to step aside. But each year, you didn't."

He was wrong. She had fallen in love, deeply and irrevocably.

"I am not a passionate man, Miss Talbot. I am like our great yet ill king, a mild farmer, happy to have a wife who will be my companion and bear my children. I'm also not much for Town, but I will give you an allowance to go to London at regular intervals, as long as you don't embarrass me."

She wouldn't be so rude as to gainsay him, but from what she knew, King George passionately loved his queen. In Glynnis's brief conversation with Her Majesty, the queen mentioned her husband many times with pride, love, and sadness. Besides, Glynnis didn't think a farmer any less able to be deeply in love than a shopkeeper, a nobleman, or royalty, for that matter.

That was all beside the point. She had never imagined such a plain-speaking, agreeable marriage arrangement as what Lord Aberavon offered. She would have freedom *and* an allowance.

And then there was Lord Payton, who had offered something similar but would have wanted her heart fully engaged.

Everything she had ever wanted in security and comfort were being offered by not one, but two men. She shook her head at her own stupidity. Instead of taking one of their offers, and gratefully, too, she simply couldn't do it—she could not bind herself to a man for the rest of her life without loving him.

Either passion and a full heart, or no man at all!

"I'm sorry, my lord. It was all a mistake. Lord Hargrove was under the impression you and I were engaged, but I cannot marry you. As it turns, I have fallen in love."

Lord Aberavon's face took on a hound-dog expression. Then he shrugged. "No matter. I wasn't engaged a half hour ago, and it seems I am not now, either." He looked around. "My father asked me to pay my respects to Queen Charlotte and to the Prince Regent on his birthday, as he knew King George in better times. That is why I came all this way."

Glynnis startled. "My lord, the Prince Regent might also be under the impression we are engaged." She felt her cheeks warm. "I would ask you not to say anything that might discredit me or injure my reputation."

He looked her up and down. "Are you certain you are in love? Perhaps it's just indigestion. We can have a nice life in Swansea."

"I am certain, but I thank you profusely for your offer. You have been most kind and gracious. Exactly as King George would have been, I'm sure."

That seemed to lift his spirits. Nodding, he bowed over her hand before taking his leave.

Glynnis sat on the bench once more. The light-headed feeling of shock had dissipated, but a general melancholy settled over her instead. She had told not one but two men *no, thank you,* and had even confessed aloud her feelings of love, albeit to the wrong man

Perhaps she ought to tell James and see if it would make a difference. *Would he believe her?* And if he did, she didn't know whether it would make a difference. While in Lord Payton's company, as circumspectly as possible, she'd asked questions about his good friend.

James was a happy bachelor with a mistress of six months. Not that Lord Payton had outwardly declared the woman to be such, but she'd understood his meaning. Moreover, James had never been engaged, nor given any hint of having given his heart to any woman whom Lord Payton knew about.

When Glynnis wished to learn more than he would say, she'd returned to the lending library. London's news arrived quickly and hung around for months in the form of a plethora of morning and evening papers, including *The Sun, The Times,* and *The Gazette,* stacked on the shelves alongside French and English weekly journals, magazines, and popular periodicals.

In the society pages Glynnis perused, the gossip-mongers had spelled it out plainly—Lord Hargrove was a confirmed rake!

Besides his mistress, who was named in the papers since he occasionally took her out in public, he had been known to dally with young ladies of the nobility or even a young, joyful widow.

There had been the briefest mention of her own interaction with him. Nothing about an indiscretion, of course, as they hadn't been caught, but he'd danced with her more than once, and so tongues had wagged.

What was plain to her was that James had no mind for marriage. And while it was obvious to her by his kisses—

and more!—that he desired her, she had no intention of becoming his next mistress.

Sighing, Glynnis rose to her feet. She would bid the Prince Regent and his mother good evening and then— *Blast!* She had lost her escort, and she knew better than to traipse around Brighton by herself when such revelry was occurring.

Hopefully, Lord Aberavon would do her a good turn and take her back to James's home later, but she would have to stay at the party until then.

IT WAS ALMOST TWO o'clock in the morning, and Glynnis had decided Lord Aberavon was *not* a farmer! At least, he didn't keep farmer's hours. He had wanted to eat and drink and dance as long as he could, and Glynnis stayed with him. She'd seen Lord Payton once more in the crowd but decided to leave the man alone. She could hardly demand he leave the birthday celebration to escort her home after having led him on.

And James had disappeared entirely.

After Lord Aberavon finally deposited her on James's doorstep, Glynnis decided she would talk to the viscount that night while she was still armored in her finery, feeling attractive albeit weary. However, the house was silent except for Polly who'd insisted on sleeping on a cot in Glynnis's room so she would be readily available to help her undress and take down her hair.

It was kind but unnecessary, as Glynnis was well able to take care of herself and would soon, once again, be forced to live without any assistance at all. Regardless, Polly had hoped to hear about the food and the dashing men and what Queen Charlotte was wearing.

Instead, after handing the maid her wrap, she told Polly their chat would have to wait. Then she changed into house slippers.

"Now what, miss?" the girl asked, stifling a yawn.

Glynnis shivered with anticipation. "I need to speak with the master of the house. I think Lord Hargrove came home before me as I didn't see him toward the party's end."

Polly nodded. "Yes, miss." But then she frowned. "I mean, he did come in, and quite early, too, as all the staff was still up. I was having a cuppa with Cook."

She paused and yawned again. "But you can't speak with him, miss."

"Did he turn in?" Glynnis asked.

"No, miss. The master left hours ago."

"I don't understand." *Was Polly addle-pated with tiredness?* She wasn't making any sense. James hadn't returned to the party. Then Glynnis realized the worst. He'd gone to that blowsabella on the Steyne!

"Lord Hargrove went to London, miss."

Glynnis took a step backward.

"His valet packed his bags, rather hurriedly, too," Polly added.

The atmosphere of the house changed entirely, knowing James wasn't sleeping down the hall. Suddenly, it was a vast, empty place, and she wished with all her heart she was home in Wales.

However, unless she asked Lord Payton or Lord Aberavon, she couldn't even afford the coach from the Old Ship. Then she had an idea.

"What about the art? Did his lordship manage to crate it all up?"

"No, miss. Lord Hargrove left in his traveling coach, but the crates are going in a wagon, just as they came. Pity about their quality," Polly added. "I've looked at 'em myself a number of times. Some of it isn't half bad, if you like that sort of thing."

Glynnis laughed without mirth, thinking of the precious paintings that even the maid didn't care for. Sitting on the end of the bed, she let Polly begin to pull the pins from her hair. She would miss her.

She would miss James, too, but unknowingly, he would do her a good service one more time.

THERE WAS NO COMFORT in a wagon ride, especially a long one. Glynnis's backside was bruised and her back ached after merely a couple hours on the dodgy and rutted road. Luckily the trip to London could be accomplished in one day barring a broken wheel.

James's valet had accompanied his master, so Glynnis sat beside one of his footmen and another rode behind on horseback. Trying to maintain her dignity while being jarred right and left, she clasped her parasol in one hand and held the edge of the seat with the other.

Her companion was from Scotland and a talkative fellow, who called London "Romeville," and fervently wished he'd gone to sea to make his fortune.

"I never imagined I'd be driving a crude tumbler like a country Nevis," he complained.

"I never thought I would be riding on the dickey of a crude tumbler," she returned.

That made him laugh, as they commiserated over their low circumstances.

"At least with the fine weather, we won't hit no hasty puddings," he added, which she understood to mean *muddy roads*.

The footman kept up a string of prittle-prattle for hours, putting in his oar upon every subject imaginable, occasionally calling over his shoulder to get confirmation of some fact or story from the other man.

Glynnis thought she was paying attention until she awakened herself with a noise—something between a snort and a grunt—and only then realized her mouth had fallen open while she slept.

Glancing sideways at the footman, who was even then discussing buccaneers, she was relieved to see he hadn't noticed. Her parasol had drooped along with her eyelids, and she raised it overhead once again.

"Hold up," her Scottish companion suddenly said.

Glynnis thought he must be speaking to himself, for his command finally stopped his rattling tongue. Then she realized he was looking into the distance as he pulled on the reins, bringing the horses to a halt.

"What is it?" she asked, straightening her hat and peering forward.

"Could be a high toby," the footman said.

"A what?"

"A land pirate, miss."

Glynnis frowned.

"A rank rider, a rum padder," he said. "In short, a knight of the road."

He signaled to the footman behind. "A rider!" he called over his shoulder. "Get your barking irons."

"His what?" she asked.

The footman sighed. "Am I speaking English, miss? His pistols. I have a brown Bess, so don't you worry." While he drew a musket from under his seat, he knocked her shoe with its long barrel, making her jump.

Oh dear! Lord Aberavon had told her of running into thieves on his journey. However, in his traveling coach, he'd been safely inside with a pistol pointed out the window, and his driver and footman had both been armed with rifles.

They waited as the speck of a horse and rider drew closer and closer. Her insides were quivering. In all her young life, Glynnis had managed never to be the victim of a robbery. And now, while traveling with priceless artwork from the

Louvre, she might finally encounter that most exciting of creatures—a highwayman!

JAMES RECOGNIZED THE PARASOL before he could see the faces. And then Glynnis came into view next to his footman, Cuthbert.

What in blue blazes? On the other hand, how fortuitous!

He only hoped the talkative, high-spirited Scot didn't shoot him before he could identify himself.

"Cuthbert, it's Hargrove. Put away your weapon."

When the man did as instructed, and even Glynnis had lowered her parasol, he cantered forward.

"What on earth are you doing with my artwork?" he asked her.

"I thought it belonged to the Duke of Wellington now?"

Confounded woman! Yet when she smiled, he noticed the sun for the first time in days, and a warmth spread through him. He grinned back and dismounted, hobbling the horse before walking around to Glynnis's side of the wagon.

"Are you trying to sneak into Apsley House with the artwork and perhaps take up residence there? I believe you could pass yourself off as the loveliest statue in Wellington's collection."

"I was merely catching a ride to London," she said.

Feeling relieved he didn't have to duel for the lady, at least not immediately, he made a great show of looking around, searching.

"Where is your fiancé?" he asked.

"Which one?" she shot back.

"Either," he returned, holding out his hand to her, which she took, letting him help her down from the bench seat.

She slid down the front of him, and he was hard before her feet touched the ground.

"I haven't seen Lord Payton since I broke it off with him directly before Lord Aberavon arrived last night. And the latter left me at your door in the early hours of this morning. You had already left, and I'm exhausted, by the way."

"I'm rather fatigued myself," James admitted, having slept not a wink. "All this riding to London at a moment's notice only to get there and have to turn around again."

"Why?" she asked.

He gazed down at the woman he loved beyond words.

"I had to go back to Brighton at a desperate pace for I'd forgotten something dreadfully important."

She shielded her eyes from the sun while looking up at him.

"What was that?" she asked.

"You, of course."

Her lovely face split into a wide smile, and his heart clenched. If she didn't agree to put him out of his misery, he would never be happy again.

"I was running home to the life I thought I loved," he explained, wishing the footman wasn't listening with obvious interest. "But I no longer wanted that life, not without you in it."

She bit her lower lip and had tears in her eyes. He took that as a good sign.

"Then you're not engaged to Aberavon?"

"I think you know I never was."

"He was willing to jump into the farce though, wasn't he?" James asked, circling his arms around her waist.

Nodding, she secured her hands behind his head. He heard and felt her sigh.

"Yes, he was, the dear soul, but I told him I couldn't go through with it for the same reason I told Lord Payton."

"Payton said you were in love. He thought it was with Aberavon."

"I *am* desperately in love," she confessed. "So much so that I jumped in your wagon for the most uncomfortable ride of my life just to get near you. And it worked, for here you are."

He couldn't wait another second.

"Cuthbert, hide your eyes."

"Yes, my lord."

James claimed her mouth, letting the sensations flow through him. Heat, rightness, love, desire, desperation, relief. Like a whirlwind, he couldn't seem to fasten on any single emotion for too long.

"Since we're both so tired, Miss Talbot, I believe we should take a rest. I passed a coaching inn barely a mile back." He gestured toward London behind him.

"We have no coach between us," she teased.

"They will allow a viscount to have a room even without one." He eyed his footman who remained stock-still, one large hand over his eyes. "Cuthbert, ride my horse and I'll sit with the lady in the wagon."

"Yes, my lord." The Scot dismounted.

James helped her back onto the dickey, and she groaned. He got on the seat beside her.

"We both need a hot bath to ease our aches, and then I think a good rub down."

He flicked the reins, and they started forward.

"My lord, only think of my reputation. If I go to this inn alone with you, I will be well and truly compromised. You would have to marry me."

"Yes, Miss Talbot, I am well aware of that."

CHAPTER TWENTY-NINE

If this be not love, it is madness,
And then it is pardonable.

– *Love for Love* by William Congreve, 1695

R elaxed from the bath James had ordered, Glynnis
wrapped herself in her robe and waited while he took
his turn. He'd left the room when she'd stripped off and
settled in, but he'd returned to tease her with his eyes, and
then with his mouth and hands.

They'd sloshed so much water onto the oilskin that had
been placed under the bathtub, he would have very little
water for his turn.

When she'd emerged, he had groaned before handing
her a towel. Sitting on the end of the bed, she took down
her hair, loosening the plaits then combing through them
with her fingers.

And then she watched.

Having already removed his riding coat which held most
of the road dust as well as his boots, he now stood in the
everyday clothing of a gentleman. With his gaze fixed on
hers, he stripped off, down to his breeches.

She swallowed, fascinated by his chest and flat nipples, eager to see her first view of a naked man, but also slightly apprehensive.

When he unfastened his breeches, he shook his head.

"I don't think I've ever been anxious when undressing before a woman before. But I want you to like everything you see."

"I understand." For she felt the same way, hoping she met with his expectations. "I'm sure I will. Besides, I have nothing to compare you to except pictures in books and a statue of Napoleon as Mars."

That made him laugh, easing the tension, before he slid his breeches down his long, lean legs.

She stared at his manly parts. "You are *impressive*, my lord, if I had to choose a word."

"That's a good word," he said. "I like it. I'll be quick in the bath."

True to his word, James proclaimed his muscles soothed after five minutes, scrubbed himself clean, and rose from the water.

"You still look like a Greek god," she told him, appreciating every hard plane and firm muscle.

"Mars was a Roman one. But I appreciate the compliment."

Soaking wet, he stalked toward her and gathered her in his arms.

"Why did you cover yourself with this dressing gown?" He plucked at the neckline as if it were distasteful, but Glynnis simply scooted backward across the counterpane.

"Ruin me," she said, unable to keep from smiling.

"Gladly." James unbelted her gown, opening it to reveal her nakedness, before sliding it down her shoulders. The caress of cool air against her damp skin made her shiver.

They spoke no more as he pushed her slowly back onto the coverlet. Glynnis willingly parted her thighs to allow him room to settle between them, his hips against hers.

"Kiss me," she whispered, pulling him down by his shoulders before closing her eyes when he lowered his mouth to hers.

All her senses magnified so she could hear her own heartbeat while her body tingled with anticipation. On his tongue that slid between her lips, Glynnis tasted the wine they'd shared while waiting for the bath. Gasping when his chest touched her breasts, her lungs filled with the scent of him—not his familiar cologne but the inn's Pear's soap.

With her fingers pressing into his smooth bare shoulders, she dared to stroke his tongue in return with the tip of her own.

He groaned, and she felt his shaft twitch against her thigh.

"Hargrove?" she queried at the unfamiliar movement.

He was busy kissing his way down her neck to her breasts. With his mouth on her nipple, he spoke.

"My body is ready to ruin you."

Opening her eyes, she shivered again.

"But let me play a little first," he said, then flicked his tongue over her nipple.

She couldn't help how her hips bucked under him. Threading her fingers into his damp hair, she held his head close until he'd nearly driven her mad with licking and sucking and . . . biting! And then he moved to her other nipple.

"A little longer," he pleaded, "until your body is ready, too."

Glynnis was beyond ready to do what she'd seen in Lord Dodd's drawing room. Not only had a pulsing heat branded her body between her legs, but she could feel the dampness of her desire.

"I am ready," she promised, tugging at his hair.

"Ouch," he exclaimed.

But she'd got his attention. Lifting his head, he looked down at her, his lovely blue eyes dark with passion.

"I'm ready," she insisted.

"I don't want to hurt you," James murmured quietly. "And it can pain you briefly."

"How briefly?" she began, then shook her head. "Never mind." Lifting her hips against him, she confessed, "I have read about the pain. Let's hurry and get past it."

His expression softened. "No, we'll take it slowly, and I promise it will be good."

True to his word, James guided the tip of his shaft to her opening, but before he penetrated, he settled onto his forearms, staring into her eyes.

"I love your eyes," he said, pressing his arousal gently inside her.

Glynnis gasped.

"I love your nose, too," he added, pushing forward inch by inch, stretching her slick channel.

She forgot to breathe, her body quivering while she clasped at his shoulders again as he gradually filled her.

"And your smile, I especially love how your upper lip bows and your lower lip curves." Finally, he thrust.

Glynnis felt a pang, as if she'd set her little finger to the candle flame, and then the burning sensation ended. However, James remained motionless, his hard length fully sheathed.

"Good?" he asked, his tone husky.

"Yes," she said. "I think so. What's next?"

"I pleasure you and try to hang on until you've gained your release."

With that, he drew back, an arousing sensation as her body tried to tug him back. Then he glided easily deep inside her again. While Glynnis thought he did all the work, rocking his hips, thrusting in and pulling back, she silently hung onto his shoulders and closed her eyes.

Her entire world had shrunk to that room in a comfortable inn somewhere between London and Brighton, and to one adorable man who was magically stimulating her body to the peak of release.

"Mm," she moaned. It took a few minutes, but the heat between them and the way he filled her core and the movement of his manhood back and forth across her sensitive flesh—all of that conspired to make her delightfully light-headed. She gasped for breath, while her body clamored for something just out of reach.

"Please," she begged, her heart pounding.

"I love you," James stated softly, reaching between them to stroke her aching nubbin.

She wanted to reply at once, but her muscles tensed as the pressure between her hips built, and then—suddenly— she spent her pleasure, her hips rising over and over to meet him.

At last, she shuddered and stilled, feeling as if she were floating in a warm sea.

"I love you," she whispered, opening her eyes in time to watch him close his own, arch his neck, and plunge into her as he found his own scorching release.

After he stilled, James laid his forehead on her shoulder for a few moments before he rolled to the side, resting upon his back.

"Have mercy, sweet Lord," he muttered. "I am the luckiest man alive."

Glynnis giggled. "Being ruined was better than I imagined."

"I don't believe you can describe yourself as *ruined*, my love, since we are going to marry."

Her eyes pricked with tears, thinking of being his wife, and she sniffed.

"Did you *ask* me to marry you?"

He paused. "No, I don't believe I did." Sitting up, he looked down at her. "Glynnis Talbot, will you do me the honor of becoming my wife?" He trailed his finger tip down from her collarbone between her breasts, before resting his palm flat on her stomach. "I long to make you happy every day and to go to bed with you every night and pleasure you."

"Every night?" she asked, needing to laugh with how much joy was filling her heart.

"And twice on Saturdays," he added with a wink.

"Twice on any day would be fine." But she wouldn't risk him feeling deceived. She must tell him everything. "I have no dowry," she confessed. "I didn't mention that before, but I am firmly of the belief it is why I have been left upon the shelf."

"It is ridiculous you should have felt inferior for even the space of a second," he said. "On the other hand, those short-sighted men did me a good turn. *You* are your own dowry, and worth every penny, too. From now on, instead of a shelf, you shall be upon a pedestal, Lady Hargrove."

She shook her head, unable to take in that she had love and security, both at the same time. And all she had to do was be herself.

"Is it Saturday?" she asked, turning on her side and reaching out for her fiancé.

EPILOGUE

Later That Night . . .

Glynnis gave such a large sigh that James turned over in bed and eyed her in the moonlight. He still could not believe how lucky he'd been to encounter her on the road, nor forget the irony of her being in the wagon of priceless art, with her not realizing she was more valuable than any of it.

If he hadn't taken a chance on the emotions of his heart, he would have stayed in London, visited his mistress that night, and been deservedly miserable for the rest of his life. Instead, as soon as he'd stepped into his home, he'd been filled with the urge to return to his Welsh-born lady, to knock aside his competition, and declare his love for her.

In the end, James had trusted what he'd seen with his own eyes and what he'd experienced when their mouths fused—that she cared for him above anyone else.

His future viscountess was staring at the ceiling, her beautiful brown eyes open.

"What are you thinking?" James asked her.

"I believed I was so clever with my plan to snag a husband. Yet once I had achieved my goal and knew I would have the security I craved so desperately, the victory was hollow. Even knowing I would be taken care of for the rest of my days, I couldn't live with another man after falling in love with you."

She turned her face to him. "In the end, I didn't need to get myself compromised at all."

He offered an expression of mock outrage. "Why, Miss Talbot, I thought I had compromised you quite well over the past few hours."

Smiling at him, she agreed, running her fingers down his bare arm. "You have. I'm awfully glad of it, too. I'm also most thankful my trap in London did not work."

"Why?" he asked. "You would have become my viscountess months ago." He touched his finger to the tip of her breast, and she shivered.

"I now know what an awful start that would have made to our marriage." Glynnis recalled James's anger that night in the library. "You might never have forgiven me, and resentment would have made for a terrible bedfellow."

He considered for a moment. "I agree. Falling in love was much better."

She clicked her tongue. "If anyone knew a rake such as you could say such a thing." And she laughed, a sound that touched his heart and aroused his cock, too.

"Despite my declaring this instant that I am forsaking my raffish ways and all other women for you alone, you shall *not* tell anyone that I spoke of love and such," he warned, his eyebrows coming close to meeting as he scowled at her.

"Perhaps I will," she teased.

"You won't." He rolled on top of her and pinned her to the sheets.

"Or what?" his fiancée asked, wrapping her arms around his neck.

"Or I shall refuse to compromise you ever again."

Her eyes widened in mock horror.

"In that case, it will be entirely our secret," Glynnis vowed.

James lowered his head and kissed her. A few minutes later, when they were both inflamed, he showed her once again that she owned his heart—completely, utterly, and forever.

Thus from the golden dawn to silent night,
Each passing hour presents some new delight.
The charms of nature that adorn the place,
The martial melody, the sportful race,
The crowded Steyne, the libraries, the play,
Or merry dance, concludes the festal day.

– *Brighton. A Poem* by Mary Lloyd, 1809

Finis

ABOUT THE AUTHOR

USA Today bestselling author Sydney Jane Baily writes historical romance set in Victorian England, late 19th-century America, the Middle Ages, the Georgian era, and the Regency period. She believes in happily-ever-after stories with engaging characters and attention to period detail.

Born and raised in California, she has traveled the world, spending a lot of exceedingly happy time in the U.K. where her extended family resides, eating fish and chips, drinking shandies, and snacking on Maltesers and Cadbury bars. Sydney currently lives in New England with her family—human, canine, and feline.

You can learn more about her books, read her blog, sign up for her newsletter (and get a free book), and contact her via her website at SydneyJaneBaily.com. She loves to hear from her readers.

Printed in Great Britain
by Amazon

58434330R00179